PRAISE FOR LIS

"Lisa Gray explodes onto the literary stage with this taut, edge-of-the-seat thriller, and her headstrong protagonist Jessica Shaw, reminiscent of Lee Child's Jack Reacher, delivers a serious punch."
　　　　　—Robert Dugoni, *New York Times* bestselling author

"Atmospheric and beautifully written. Lisa Gray is becoming a firm favourite in this house."
　—Ian Rankin, bestselling author of the Inspector Rebus series

"*Thin Air* is an exciting whodunit that kept me guessing until the end. PI Jessica Shaw is so capable and strong, I couldn't get enough of her!"
　—T. R. Ragan, bestselling author of the Lizzy Gardner series

"One of this year's best new thrillers."
　　　　　　　　　　　　　　　　　　　—Evening Standard

"You'll find this one hard to put down."
　　　　　　　　　　　　　　　　　　　　—Daily Record

"Sets off at a fantastic pace, with plenty of twists and turns."
　　　—Claire McGowan, bestselling author of *What You Did*

"A fast-paced, perfectly plotted killer of a thriller with a fantastic female lead and a cracking premise."
　　　　　　　　—Susi Holliday, author of *The Hike*

TO
DIE
FOR

ALSO BY LISA GRAY

THE JESSICA SHAW THRILLER SERIES

STAND-ALONE BOOKS

TO
DIE
FOR

LISA GRAY

THOMAS & MERCER

Published by Thomas & Mercer, Seattle

www.apub.com

Amazon, the Amazon logo, and Thomas & Mercer are trademarks of Amazon.com, Inc., or its affiliates.

ISBN-13: 9781542035316
eISBN: 9781542035323

Cover design by Dominic Forbes
Cover image: ©tony ranger / Shutterstock; ©ganjalex / Shutterstock; ©AMA / Shutterstock; ©Ildiko Neer / ArcAngel

Printed in the United States of America

For my book buddy Danny Stewart

PROLOGUE
MALIBU BEACH DRIVE

The house was to die for.

A custom-built, brand-new construction right on the beach. And not just any old beach—one of the most exclusive in the world. Concrete stilts thicker than tree trunks held the five-bed, five-and-a-half-bath property aloft above golden sands and foaming waves, like a sparkling trophy under the blazing Malibu sun.

Floor-to-ceiling pocket doors offered indoor-outdoor living and framed views of the Pacific Ocean and a cerulean sky so blue it looked like it was straight out of a Lori Mills landscape. Speaking of local artists, a dozen original works hung on the crisp white walls, adding little explosions of color everywhere.

The finishes throughout the house were porcelain and walnut and marble. The furniture was beautifully staged and eye-wateringly expensive. An entertainer's kitchen boasted state-of-the-art appliances that had never been used and likely never would be. Anyone rich enough to live in this house didn't cook—they ate out or ordered in. There was a temperature-controlled wine cellar, a triple-bay garage large enough for three Ferraris, and not one but two walk-in closets that even Carrie Bradshaw would be impressed by.

The house on Malibu Beach Drive was, in short, an oceanfront masterpiece.

The party was for Realtors and big-time buyers and was invite only, as opposed to a regular open house. Which meant the cream of the Southern California real estate industry and those with enough cash in the bank to write a check for $50 million. No nosy neighbors or lookie-loos or curious tourists walking in off the street.

The top Malibu agents, still pissed at losing the listing to a relatively small Hollywood brokerage, showed up to see for themselves exactly what they'd missed out on.

Even they agreed the house was to die for.

The vintage Dom Pérignon flowed, and seafood canapés from Nobu were delicately nibbled.

There had been some unexpected entertainment earlier in the form of raised voices, a drink being thrown, and a couple of attendees being escorted from the premises. Now that order had been restored, there was only the low hum of polite conversation.

Then someone mentioned the pool.

"A place like this has to have a pool, right?" asked one of the guests as a waiter topped off her champagne.

"Who needs a pool when you have the ocean right on your doorstep?" another replied, gesturing to a view of the afternoon rays bouncing off the waves.

"I'm sure they mentioned a pool," the first woman said. She grabbed someone as they walked past. "You're with the listing agency, aren't you? Be a sweetheart and show us where the pool is?"

"Of course," said the agent. "It's around the side of the house. It's custom tiled and really quite stunning. Follow me."

Louboutin and Manolo heels click-clacked on the tiled floor as the trio made their way through the open pocket doors onto the balcony and turned the corner onto the pool deck.

The wind whipped at their hair. The sun momentarily blinded their eyes. A faint smell of salt and seaweed carried on the breeze. The three women walked toward the pool.

First, they noticed the blood.

Then they saw the body floating facedown in the water.

That's when the screaming began.

1

ANDI
BEFORE

It's not running away. It's moving on. Big difference.

That's what Andi Hart told herself for the hundredth time as she scanned both sides of the street for a parking spot on a busy stretch of Santa Monica Boulevard between La Cienega and Crescent Heights. It was almost noon, and the day was sunglasses bright and warm enough for short sleeves. The early-lunch crowd had already filled nearby sidewalk cafés, and the foot traffic consisted mostly of hipster types and moms pushing strollers.

She found a space, parked, and made her way toward a shop front at the end of the block with a "For Lease" sign in the dusty window. The vacant unit was gray and drab and nondescript and looked smaller than it had in the photo on the website.

Andi pushed open the door and stepped into soupy heat. Either the old AC unit was busted, or no one had bothered to switch it on for the showing. The space was long and narrow like a shoebox. A shotgun corner unit. One thousand square feet and small enough to have "½" tacked onto the end of the street number, as if it were an afterthought. Andi used to sell little shotgun houses all the time back home when she was just starting out as a real estate agent.

Today, she would be the one doing the buying rather than the selling. At least, that was the plan anyway.

The Realtor was in his early forties, with black curly hair cropped short and glistening with too much product. He wore an open-necked white shirt under a charcoal suit and smelled like a cologne counter at Macy's.

"Nick Flores," he said, extending his hand. "Good to meet you."

"Andi Hart."

They shook, and it was more of a limp finger shake, the way some men do with women. Flores squinted at her. "Actually, I think we've met already. You're a Realtor too, right?"

Shit.

"Right."

"I'm sure I was at one of your open houses. Remind me who you're with again . . . ?"

"Saint Realty."

"The place on Sunset?"

Andi nodded. "That's the one."

"Seems like a cool agency. Great location too."

"It sure is."

Flores was right. It was a cool agency. Andi wouldn't even be thinking about leaving if she didn't have to.

Flores clapped his hands together, indicating it was time to get down to business. "So you wanted to have a look around this great little unit today. Are you moving on from Saint? Looking for a space of your own? This would make a terrific base for a small up-and-coming business."

"It's not for me." The lie came easily. "It's for a client."

"Fantastic. Will your client be joining us? Should we wait for them before starting the tour?"

Andi gazed around, taking in the entirety of the empty room. Figured the tour wouldn't take a whole lot of time.

"No, it's just me. I'm viewing on their behalf."

"Okay, no problem. And this client of yours . . . what are they planning on using the space for?"

A woman in denim cutoffs and a white tank top walked past on the street outside with a panting pug on a pink leash.

"A dog-grooming business," Andi said. "Lots of celebrity clients."

"Perfect!"

Andi's cell phone buzzed in the back pocket of her jeans. She pulled it out and glanced at the screen. It was an incoming call from Diana.

Shit.

David and Diana Saint were her bosses at the brokerage where Andi had worked for the last three years. David was the broker-owner and his wife, Diana, took care of the admin side of the business. Neither of them knew Andi was planning on quitting and effectively setting up a rival company. They didn't even know she'd gotten her own broker's license.

A lot had changed in the last six months.

Andi sent the call to voice mail. She hated keeping secrets, especially from Diana. Though Diana was her employer, Andi thought of the woman as a friend. She felt like a cheating spouse who'd been caught with his pants around his ankles, as if her boss knew exactly what she was up to right now.

Flores showed Andi around. As expected, it didn't take long and there wasn't much to see. Dirty white walls begging for a lick of paint. An ugly navy carpet worn thin by thousands of shoe soles over the years. Despite the full-length windows at the front of the building, the interior still managed to feel dark and dingy. There was enough room for a few desks, four at most, for the team she planned to assemble over time. Maybe a meeting area too if she was really smart with the floor plan.

It was a lot smaller than the office suites Andi had already checked out on Sunset. The kinds of places where agents from Keller Williams and Rodeo Realty and the Lux Group were based in glass-and-concrete tower blocks with gleaming elevators and marble flooring and oak desks and enviable views of the Sunset Strip. She'd had showings at 8560 Sunset—that had once been the Playboy Building—and the 9000 block and the 9200 block. They were all way, way out of her reach. The Strip was where Andi wanted to be, but her bank balance said otherwise.

So here she was on Santa Monica instead. It was still a good address, in a vibrant neighborhood. Lots of foot traffic. Great restaurants and boutiques and coffee shops on the doorstep. She could already picture herself grabbing lunch at Hugo's or picking up some groceries from Gelson's on her way home from work.

Andi knew she could make the location work for her. But the frontage lacked curb appeal, and there was a takeout place right next door. It was also at the very top end of her budget. The unit would need to be completely fitted out, not to mention the addition of plenty of air freshener plug-ins to cover up the stink of greasy fries and charred meat. Then there were the utilities, building services, and other property expenses to consider too.

Her cell buzzed against her butt again. Andi ignored it.

She was moving on.

Definitely not running away.

God knows she'd done enough of that already. This time it was different. She wasn't relocating to another state. She wasn't even changing cities. She'd barely be a couple of streets south of Saint Realty if she did set up shop here on Santa Monica.

If.

"The rate is thirty-one dollars per square foot a year, right?" Andi asked with a frown.

"That's right." Flores smiled. His teeth were very white and were, by far, the brightest thing in the dreary room.

"It's a little overpriced."

The smile faltered. "Not really."

"Okay, it's a lot overpriced."

Flores laughed nervously. "Come on, it's a steal. You know it is."

"Not according to the comps in the neighborhood. I checked already. A unit twice this size leased for fifty-one dollars per square foot just down the block."

Now it was Flores's turn to frown. "That was six months ago. The market has changed."

"I'll pay twenty-six dollars. I think that's a fair price."

"You? I thought you said you were representing a client."

Dammit.

"I meant that's what my client is willing to pay."

"No can do. I don't have authorization to negotiate the rate."

"There's always room for negotiation. I'm a Realtor too, remember? That's what we do. Negotiate."

"Not this time. Sorry."

"Seriously?" Andi said, exasperated. "The place has lain empty for two months. Clearly no one else is willing to pay thirty-one dollars per square foot either."

"We have two other interested parties."

Andi stared at him. "Is that so?"

Flores's face reddened under his tan. "No rate reduction. Sorry."

Andi sighed. Her cell vibrated again. Shorter this time. A text. She took the phone from her pocket. It was a message from Diana. Curt and straight to the point.

Call me back asap. It's urgent.

"Shit," Andi said. "I have to go."

"Speak to your client," Flores called after her as she made her way to the door. "I'll follow up with you later this afternoon."

"Don't bother unless you're willing to negotiate. Twenty-six dollars!"

Andi headed outside onto the street and returned the call. Diana answered immediately.

"Andi, finally!"

The Saints had moved from London to Los Angeles twenty-five years ago, but both still sounded like they were straight out of a Richard Curtis movie.

"Sorry, I was . . . in the middle of something. What's up?"

"Look, I know you booked a personal day for today, but I need you to swing by the office."

"Uh, now?"

"Yes, Andi. Now. It's important."

"Is everything okay?"

"Everything is fine. But there's something we need to discuss. Immediately."

Diana didn't sound fine. Her voice was strained and higher pitched than usual. Andi thought she could hear David in the background. Her throat tightened.

"And it can't wait until tomorrow?"

"No, Andi. It can't."

She didn't want Diana to know she was just a few streets away, scoping out potential premises for her own agency.

"Okay, I'm at home right now. Give me fifteen minutes. Twenty max."

"Fabulous. Make it ten."

Diana ended the call.

Andi's palms were sweating. Her fingers left damp prints on the cell phone. Her heart pounded.

She knows.

Diana must have found out about her plans to ditch Saint and set up on her own.

Andi's heart beat faster.

But did Diana also know the reason why?

2

ANDI
BEFORE

Andi walked through the front door of Saint Realty twelve minutes later, her belly fizzing with nerves and her brain buzzing with questions.

Had she been spotted going into one of the tower blocks along the street?

Had a rival agent in those offices ratted her out?

Had Nick Flores mentioned today's viewing to one of her coworkers?

Like the unit on Santa Monica, Saint Realty's office was a shop front straight off the street, but that's where the similarities ended. Deceptively small from the outside, the interior was a huge industrial-style space with exposed brick walls, wood-and-chrome desks, plush velvet sofas in jewel tones, and big modern light fixtures. It felt very New York to Andi, even though it was in the heart of Sunset Strip.

She expected Diana to pull her aside and guide her upstairs to the mezzanine where David's office was located. It was rarely used, other than for private meetings with potential clients or a quiet word with an agent who wasn't meeting their targets. David and Diana both preferred to spend their time at their respective desks in the large open-plan area along with everyone else.

Andi wondered if David would be participating in this urgent chat with Diana too. Her gut cramped at the thought. That would be bad. Really bad.

Instead, Andi saw that both of her bosses, as well as Saint's four other agents, were gathered around the conference table in the rear of the room.

Hunter Brooks stabbed at his cell phone, a look of intense concentration on his face. Fair haired, tan, and classically handsome, he'd been at the brokerage the longest out of the agents, joining as an ambitious twentysomething more than a decade ago. He was fiercely competitive and had been Saint's top-ranking agent until Andi joined.

Rich kid Myles Goldman—a former student of Beverly Hills High School and currently an ambitious twentysomething—drummed his fingers impatiently against the tabletop. He wore a tailored blazer, a smart shirt, and a huge platinum Rolex encrusted with tiny diamonds. Andi couldn't see what was going on beneath the table, but she guessed very tight jeans and designer leather loafers with no socks. Myles' signature style.

Krystal Taylor flicked her long blond hair over her shoulder and watched Andi with narrowed eyes, no doubt disapproving of her off-duty outfit of T-shirt, jeans, and sneakers. Krystal wouldn't be seen dead in flats, let alone sneakers. Her footwear of choice always had red soles and heels high enough to give an exotic dancer vertigo.

Verona King stared off into the distance, as though lost in thought. Late forties and a happily married mom of two, she hustled harder than anyone Andi had ever met in order to support her family.

Diana spotted Andi, got up, and strode over to where she was still standing in the doorway. As she got closer, Diana broke into a smile, and Andi could see her eyes were shining. Excitement, rather than tension. So that's why she'd sounded so weird on the phone. Andi's shoulders dropped an inch with relief.

"Thanks for getting here so quickly," Diana said, taking Andi by the arm and steering her toward the others. "David has some news—*big* news—and he wanted you to hear it too."

Andi slipped into a vacant seat, and Myles muttered something that sounded like "finally" under his breath.

David said, "Thank you for coming in, Andi. I'm sure you had some stuff to attend to on your day off. I really do appreciate it."

"I was at home doing some chores. No big deal." Andi avoided making eye contact. Again, she had that feeling of being caught red-handed.

"Didn't I just see your car parked on Santa Monica Boulevard, like, twenty minutes ago?" Krystal asked. "I passed it on the way back from my listing appointment on Melrose."

Andi felt Diana's eyes on her. "Nope. I was at home. Like I said."

"I'm sure it was your car. You're still driving that old blue Beemer, right?" Krystal said it like it was Columbo's battered Peugeot she was talking about. Myles snorted. Andi had treated herself to the pre-owned 2018 BMW coupe with her savings after a great first year in Los Angeles.

Andi squeezed the words out through gritted teeth. "It wasn't my car."

Krystal was about to say something else, to no doubt argue the point about the car, but she didn't get the chance.

"Okay, guys," David said. "Let's get started. If that's okay with you, Hunter?"

"Huh?" Hunter looked up from what appeared to be some frantic texting. "Uh, sure thing. Sorry." He placed his phone face-down on the table.

David held up some official-looking papers. "This here is a listing agreement. Looks like every other listing agreement you've ever seen at Saint, right?"

He peered at them over his horn-rimmed glasses.

There were nods all around. Diana smiled knowingly, like she already knew the punch line to a joke. Verona and Myles seemed intrigued, Krystal looked bored, Hunter still appeared distracted.

"Wrong!" David said triumphantly. "This is a listing agreement for a fifty-million-dollar beachfront house in Malibu."

That got everyone's attention.

"Fifty million dollars?" Krystal's pale blue eyes widened.

"Seriously?" Verona, who had appeared tired and drawn for days, was suddenly alert.

"Wait—this is *our* listing?" asked Myles.

David grinned. "The deal was signed off on with the developer this morning. I don't have to tell you that this is, by far, Saint's biggest-ever listing. If we can sell this house, it'll propel us into the big time. A game changer. Obviously, I'll be the selling agent on this one. But what I would really love is for one of you to bring me a buyer."

Krystal nodded vigorously. "Double-end it." If she were a cartoon character, she'd have dollar signs popping out of her eyes right now.

In real estate deals, *double-ending* was when the same brokerage acted on behalf of both the seller and the buyer. If one of David's five agents had a client willing to write an offer on the Malibu house, Saint Realty would be set to make a hell of a lot of money from the listing.

"That's right," David said. "Although, to be clear, the property *will* go on the market once it's been staged and photographed, and there will also be a brokers' open this Friday. Top brokers and buyers only. Diana is taking care of everything."

"Will it be our usual commission rate?" Hunter asked, his cell phone now completely forgotten.

"Yep."

Everyone quickly did the math in their heads. Five percent of the sale price split fifty-fifty between the selling agent and the buyer's agent, with the brokerage then taking a 20 percent cut of the buyer's agent's fee.

"But that means . . . ," Myles started.

David cut him off. "One million dollars for whoever finds a buyer for the house."

"Holy shit," said Verona. "This all sounds great. But I have to ask—if the property is in Malibu, why didn't the developer go with a local brokerage who knows the comps and the area? Why us?"

Good point, Andi thought.

David appeared put out by the question. He ran a hand through his floppy hair and huffed out an impatient sigh. "You know what my old mum used to say? 'Never look a gift horse in the mouth.' Sometimes, when an opportunity like this one lands in your lap, you just have to grab it with both hands. No questions asked. Simple as that."

He went on. "You have less than a week before the property officially hits the market. Make the most of it. Start talking to your clients—now." He turned to Andi. "Can you get started right away? Diana will reschedule another personal day for you. I'm thinking this house could be perfect for one of your clients out east."

"Sure," Andi said. "No problem to reschedule."

Krystal said, "Um, hello! You do know you have four other agents all perfectly capable of finding a buyer too, don't you?"

"Yes, but Andi has been Saint's top-ranking agent for over a year now."

"Only because she's given all the best listings," Hunter muttered.

David said, "Listen, guys. Any one of you could have a client willing to write an offer. That's why we're *all* heading out to Malibu first thing tomorrow for a tour of the property."

There was a hum of excitement around the room.

One million dollars.

Enough for Andi to set up her own brokerage. To pay for decent premises. Take on an assistant. A life-changing sum of money. David was right—she *was* Saint's best agent, and it had nothing to do with favoritism. It was because Andi was damn good at what she did.

One million dollars.

As Andi looked around the table, she saw her own excitement and determination reflected on the faces of Krystal, Myles, Verona, and Hunter.

Her fellow agents. Her coworkers. Her competitors.

Andi was sure she saw desperation there too. Like they all had their own reasons for needing the cash. For some reason it was a thought that unnerved her. Goose bumps prickled her skin, and she shivered in the warm room.

3

ARIBO
AFTER

The call came between the main course and dessert.

Detective Jimmy Aribo was having lunch in one of the best restaurants in Calabasas with his wife. It was one of Denise's favorite places to eat, but it had been months since their last visit because Aribo didn't take her out nearly as much as he should. They were seated at an intimate table for two out on the terrace. The tiled courtyard, trees, sunshine, and soft music made it feel as if they were dining in Tuscany rather than on their own doorstep.

It was a late lunch, rather than dinner, because they had tickets for Howard Jones at the Ace Hotel that evening. Aribo had booked the meal and the tickets as a surprise for their twentieth wedding anniversary. He'd also splurged on the most expensive wine on the menu. He was feeling pretty confident about his chances of getting laid tonight.

Aribo and Denise had been married for almost as long as he'd been on the job. Twenty-three years at the Los Angeles County Sheriff's Department. When he retired, he'd get a nice pension and maybe a gold watch. Denise deserved a medal. Right now, though, she'd have to settle for some good gnocchi and '80s music instead.

"You're buzzing," Denise said.

"What?"

"Your cell phone. It's buzzing."

"It is?" Aribo patted the pockets of his pants.

"Jacket pocket."

Aribo found the phone in the blazer he'd slung over the back of his chair.

"It's Tim."

"You'd better answer it," Denise said resignedly.

Aribo hesitated. "I took a personal day especially. That's why the ringer is off."

"Just answer it."

Tim Lombardi was Aribo's partner at the LASD and had been given strict instructions not to call today. And yet here he was, calling anyway. They'd worked together for more than a decade, and sometimes it felt like a marriage too, but with fewer benefits.

"Tim. You know I'm not on duty today. This had better be good."

"I know, I know. It's your anniversary. Twenty years, huh? Tell Denise I said hi. The thing is, we have a situation. A suspicious death. I'm sorry, Jimmy, but we need you down here."

"Why didn't the captain call me?"

"Garcia is a chickenshit. He's scared of Denise. So I got the short straw."

Aribo smiled despite himself. "She's not so bad. A pussycat, really."

Denise raised an eyebrow and topped off her wineglass. She didn't refill his glass.

Lombardi said, "Uh-huh."

Aribo said, "Okay, what do we have?"

"A body in the pool at a property on Malibu Beach Drive."

Malibu Beach Drive meant very rich people, which meant media interest, which meant a lot of scrutiny from the top brass.

"Shit. Why suspicious?"

"We have blood at the scene. Possible head trauma. Some disturbed outdoor furniture. Our floater wasn't exactly dressed for swimming either."

"What're you thinking? Some kind of domestic gone bad?"

"Uh-uh. Not a domestic. A brokers' open was happening at the property when the call came in."

"What?"

"It's a kind of party for real estate agents."

"Yeah, I know what a brokers' open is. What you're saying is, we have a floater at a party full of people?"

"That's what I'm saying."

A waiter brought over a plate with two chocolate soufflés and scoops of vanilla ice cream. Sparklers were jammed into the soufflés, the words "Happy Anniversary" written around the edge of the plate in a fancy chocolate-sauce scrawl. Talk about timing.

Aribo said, "I can be there in half an hour."

Denise pulled the dessert plate toward her, stony faced. The sparklers had fizzled out. She cut off a chunk of soufflé with a fork and stuffed it in her mouth. Aribo knew he had no chance of getting laid tonight. Not now.

Lombardi said, "Here's the thing, Jimmy. We've got fifty witnesses here. But no one saw anything, and no one heard anything."

4

HUNTER
BEFORE

Hunter Brooks eased his sleek black Rolls-Royce Ghost into the driveway of his Spanish colonial revival home in Brentwood and shut off the engine. He was feeling both pumped and pissed.

Pumped at the prospect of a cool million landing in his checking account and the difference it could make to his life. Especially right now.

Pissed because David, his longtime boss and onetime mentor, obviously didn't think he was up to the job. Had made it clear to everyone in the whole damn office that he thought Andi Hart had the best chance of securing a buyer for the Malibu property.

Hunter didn't like Andi—and not just because she was selling more real estate than he was.

The whole laid-back New Yorker thing really bugged him. It was as if she thought she didn't have to make an effort like everyone else. Seriously, what was going on with the scuffed boots and battered leather jacket and messy hair? Andi didn't dress like other women he knew. But there were plenty who seemed to love her style, especially Hollywood's young creatives, the up-and-coming actors and musicians and artists, who all wanted to work with her. Add those to the clientele she already had on the East Coast and Hunter had to grudgingly admit that her client list was dynamite.

Naturally, he had done his homework when Andi Hart first joined Saint. An old buddy of his was in the real estate game in Brooklyn and had discreetly asked around about her. But there was no dirt to be had, nothing that stood out as being unusual or interesting—other than the fact that she appeared to have left Manhattan in a hurry. Quit her job and her apartment and her boyfriend within the space of a week and then pulled up stakes and moved out here to La-La Land.

Hunter found his phone in the car's side pocket and realized it was still off. After David's big announcement, he'd wanted to make some calls from the desk phone without any distractions, without his cell constantly blowing up with unwanted texts. He turned it on now as he got out of the Rolls and made his way to the front door. The phone sparked to life and pinged several times with message alerts. Hunter paused to read them.

Charlie Vance: I'm not messing around, Hunter. I need more money.

Charlie Vance: Hunter?? You'd better answer me . . .

Melissa: Hey sweetie, how's your day going? I was thinking of making roast chicken for dinner tonight? Love you xx

Betsy Bowers: I have a client interested in your listing on Homedale. Can we arrange a showing asap?

Melissa: Just tried to call. Why is your cell phone off? I got the chicken. Dinner should be ready around seven xx

Charlie Vance: DO NOT IGNORE ME. You know what will happen if you do.

Hunter fired out a quick response to Betsy Bowers, setting up an appointment with her client for the following afternoon.

As he went to open the door, he noticed for the first time that there were no lights on in any of the windows. It was almost seven p.m. Hunter frowned.

He went inside. Usually, by early evening Melissa had lamps blazing in every room. Tonight, the entire downstairs was in darkness. There was no aroma of chicken or anything else cooking either. No pots clanging or dishes clinking in the kitchen. No television blaring in the lounge. None of the usual sounds and smells that greeted him when he got home from work.

"Melissa?" he called. "You home, sweetheart?"

No answer.

Her car had been in the driveway. Hunter had parked his own right next to it. He went into the lounge and found it empty. He went through to the kitchen. The vintage O'Keefe & Merritt stove and oven were both off. The large island, where Melissa prepared their meals, was spotlessly clean. Then he noticed his wife's phone on the counter and her purse sitting next to it. Hunter touched the screen and saw several unread and unanswered texts from a couple of her girlfriends.

That wasn't like Melissa at all. A bad feeling settled in his gut. Something was wrong. Very wrong.

"Melissa!"

The word came out strangled.

Silence.

Then . . . something. A cry or a yelp. Coming from upstairs.

Hunter took the stairs two at a time. There was a slash of light beneath the door of the family bathroom. As he got closer, he heard weeping coming from inside. He tried the handle. The door was unlocked.

Melissa was slumped on the floor, her hair covering her face. There was blood on her hands and bare legs. Broken glass everywhere. The bathtub and floor tiles were also smeared with blood.

"Oh, God. Melissa." Hunter dropped to his knees next to her. Something wet soaked into his dress pants. His heart thrummed in his ears. "What the hell happened? Are you okay?"

"Oh, Hunter," she cried, throwing her arms tightly around his neck and burying her face in his shoulder. She was breathing hard and sobbing and hiccupping all at the same time.

Hunter tried to swallow down the fear and panic that was bubbling up inside him. "Did someone do this to you? Was someone in the house? Did they hurt you?"

Melissa sat back and looked up at him blankly. Her face was a mess of snot and tears and mascara streaks. Her eyes were puffy red pillows. She shook her head. "No one was in the house."

Hunter became aware of a strong, pungent odor catching in his throat and stinging his eyes. He realized the source of the broken glass was a couple of his expensive cologne bottles that were usually on top of the vanity.

"Tell me what happened, Mel."

"The clinic called." Melissa's tears started again. "It didn't work. I'm not pregnant."

Hunter felt his stomach drop like an anchor from a boat.

"Oh, baby." He pulled her to him and stroked her long dark hair. "I'm so sorry."

He let her cry softly for a while, the fear and panic replaced by despair and guilt.

"I really thought it had worked this time," she said. "It just felt different from before. I was so *sure*. Then Dr. Kessler's secretary called with the results, and I got so mad. I smashed some stuff. Cut myself trying to pick up the glass. It's so fucking unfair!"

"I know, I know," he soothed.

Hunter examined the cuts on Melissa's hands and legs and was relieved to see they were superficial. He found a first aid kit in the vanity, then cleaned up the blood with antiseptic wipes and applied some Band-Aids to the wounds.

"I think you'll live." He smiled. "I can't say the same about my bottles of cologne, though."

Melissa returned the smile, then her expression grew serious again. "We'll keep trying, right? Another round of IVF. More tests. Whatever it takes. We can afford it, can't we? You sold that house on Doheny just last month. We can use the commission from that."

Hunter hesitated. "Why don't we talk about it later?"

"You're not giving up, are you?" Melissa grabbed his shirt violently and balled her fists. "Tell me you still want to be a dad. Tell me you haven't given up on our baby. Tell me you haven't given up on *me*."

"Of course I haven't." He sighed. "All I want is for you to be happy, Mel. More than anything in the world. We'll make another appointment with Dr. Kessler, see what she has to say. Okay?"

His wife nodded. "Okay."

"Why don't you go lie down while I clean up in here and then make dinner? I'll wake you when it's ready. How does that sound?"

"Sounds great." Melissa kissed him gently. "What did I do to deserve you, huh?"

Once he was done in the bathroom, Hunter went downstairs and found the chicken in the fridge. He put it in the oven and set about preparing a salad. He opened a bottle of Châteauneuf-du-Pape for himself. Melissa had given up the booze a few years ago in the hopes of improving her chances of getting pregnant. He drank down the glass of red wine fast. Poured himself another.

His cell phone shrilled, startling him. The name that flashed on the screen was Charlie Vance.

He rejected the call. The phone rang again immediately. Again he sent it to voice mail. Hunter was about to shut it off for the night, just as he'd done earlier, when a text came through.

I'm outside. If you won't answer my calls, maybe you'll answer your door.

Hunter darted into the lounge and peered through the window. It was fully dark now. A car was parked under a streetlight. The headlights were on. They flashed twice in quick succession.

Fuck.

Hunter called the number for Charlie Vance.

"What the hell do you think you're playing at?" he hissed.

"You left me no choice, Hunter."

"So, what? You think it's okay to just show up at my home? Are you fucking crazy? That wasn't part of the deal."

"Neither was you ghosting me. Now, do I have to get out of the car or what? I'm not alone, in case you were wondering."

The timer on the oven buzzed noisily in the kitchen. Hunter glanced at the ceiling, wondering if Melissa was awake. He cussed under his breath. "Okay. What do you want?"

"I want to talk. Face to face. We need to discuss some changes to our financial arrangement."

"When?"

"Tomorrow."

"It'll have to be late afternoon. I have work appointments I can't get out of. Important listings."

"Good. You're going to need the money. Four p.m. Usual place. Don't be late."

5

KRYSTAL
BEFORE

On the other side of the 405, in the foothills of the Santa Monica Mountains, Krystal Taylor's house was also cloaked in darkness. Her chest tightened and so did her grip on the steering wheel of her lipstick-red Porsche 911.

But unlike Hunter Brooks, she was not alarmed—or even surprised—by the sight of the black windows and empty driveway as she approached the Trousdale Estates property. These days, it was hardly an unusual occurrence to discover no one was home.

It didn't mean she wasn't mad as all hell about it, though.

Krystal couldn't remember the last time she and her husband had sat down to dinner together. Had it been last month? Longer? It didn't really matter. The point was they were spending less and less time in each other's company. Sure, she had her own hectic schedule, but Micah was out a *lot* recently.

Once inside, Krystal deactivated the alarm and slipped out of her Louboutins. She left the heels lying by the front door. Micah hated messes, but so what? He wasn't here to have a say in the matter. She padded barefoot through the house, flicking on light switches as she went. Krystal didn't bother calling out to ask if anyone was home. She already knew the answer.

The note was on the kitchen table. The page had been ripped from a legal pad and folded twice. Micah's familiar loopy handwriting in blue ink on cheap yellow lined paper.

Work dinner with Al. Potential new gig. Don't wait up.

There was no "Hi, honey" at the beginning or kiss at the end. The purpose was to impart the most basic information. Nothing else. Just like all the other little notes he'd left for her when he had a so-called work engagement that would keep him out until past midnight.

Work.

Krystal laughed bitterly, the sound loud in the silent kitchen.

Micah Taylor didn't even have a job. Not really, not anymore.

He was a former NFL wide receiver who'd spent his entire career with the Los Angeles Rams, before retiring the day after they lost Super Bowl LIII.

These days, his "work" involved appearing at celebrity charity events (for a fee, of course) or cutting the ribbon at the opening of a new pizza joint or a slot on *Dancing with the Stars* (despite having two left feet) or anything else his longtime agent, Al Toledo, lined up to keep the postfootball cash rolling in.

Krystal balled up the scrap of paper and dropped it into the trash. Some women found handwritten notes from their husbands romantic or cute. Krystal didn't.

She fished in her Louis Vuitton tote for her phone and called her husband, even though she already knew his own phone would be off. It was as though she got some kind of grim satisfaction from being proved right. It went straight to voice mail. Krystal disconnected without leaving a message.

Micah's explanation for being unreachable so often was that unnecessary interruptions during important meetings—such as silly calls and texts from his wife or buddies—were unprofessional.

"But what if there's an accident and I can't get hold of you?" she'd asked him once.

Micah had shrugged. "I'm pretty careful. Why would I have an accident?"

"I meant what if *I* have an accident?"

There had been another shrug. "Then I guess you could call a girlfriend or one of those people you work with or 911 if it's really bad?"

It didn't take Krystal too long to figure out the real reason for Micah going dark was that she might be able to track his whereabouts with one of those "find my phone" apps that he didn't fully understand. That she'd discover he wasn't where he claimed to be or—more specifically—wasn't with whom he claimed to be with.

Micah thought he was so clever, but Krystal sure as hell hadn't married him for his brains. To be fair, it wasn't her academic prowess that had attracted him to her either, but she was way smarter than he—and most other people—gave her credit for.

A while back, she'd logged on to Amazon and purchased a GPS tracker for $150. A small black device that fit in the palm of her hand and was easily installed and easily concealed. Krystal figured its official purpose was locating lost or stolen vehicles, but it worked just as well for keeping tabs on lying husbands.

It was magnetic and could be attached to any flat metal surface, but she'd decided against the underside of his car. For one, there was no way Krystal was getting down on her hands and knees to reach under the super-low suspension of his Aston Martin. Secondly, that was too obvious—Micah had no doubt seen the same movies she had. Instead, she'd hidden it in a far corner of the trunk behind the set of expensive golf clubs he'd used only once.

Krystal pulled up the GPS's tracking app now and studied the map. It offered real-time information, and the stationary little red pin indicated the car wasn't moving. It appeared to be parked in the vicinity of Grandmaster Recorders, a restaurant and bar in West Hollywood.

"Huh," Krystal said out loud.

It wasn't the information she'd been expecting to see. Maybe Micah was telling the truth for once. Maybe he *was* having dinner with Al Toledo and a client. There was only one way to know for sure. Krystal picked up her purse, made her way down the hallway, and slid the Louboutins back onto her feet.

As she cruised down Loma Vista Drive, flanked on either side by towering trees, luxurious homes, and construction sites where even more multimillion-dollar properties were being built, Krystal's thoughts raced every bit as fast as the Porsche.

Who is Micah with? What is he doing?

Krystal had a horrible feeling she already knew the answer to those questions. She headed east onto Doheny before joining Sunset, where neon lights fizzed and popped and billboards tried to seduce. She continued past the sleek glass modernism of the Pendry, and the faded glamor of the Chateau Marmont perched high on its hilltop, and the minimalistic sharp lines of the trendy Moment Hotel.

Each one of them a stop on a road map of infidelity.

Once on Cahuenga, Krystal found a space behind a large SUV about fifty yards from the restaurant so that she had a view of the entrance without her brightly colored ride being too conspicuous.

Grandmaster Recorders had once been an old silent movie theater before being transformed into a recording studio in the early '70s and counting the likes of Stevie Wonder, David Bowie, and Bonnie Raitt among the stars who'd recorded there. It was now a place to eat and drink, rather than make music, but it still attracted the A-list. It was one of Micah's favorite haunts.

Krystal sat and waited and watched and thought about all the other occasions she'd spied on her husband.

The first time she'd tailed him using the tracker, it had led her to the Sunset Tower Hotel. She'd walked right in and scoped out the lobby, bar, restaurant, and other public areas. There had been no sign of Micah. She'd returned to her car and made a point of mentally noting every vehicle that left the premises around the same time as his Aston Martin. She'd then gone through the same process at the Pendry, and the Chateau Marmont, and the Moment.

A pattern began to emerge. A silver Mercedes roadster with the top down, driven by a redhead who always wore large sunglasses so that her face was partly obscured. Krystal couldn't tell how old, or attractive, the woman was. Two things she was pretty sure about, though: the bitch had money, and she was screwing Krystal's husband.

A little over an hour later, Micah emerged from Grandmaster Recorders. He was hard to miss: six foot one, 190 pounds, skin as dark as the night sky, sneakers as white as the moon, and wearing a lurid sports jacket that cost more than most people made in a month. Still as fit, solid, and handsome at forty-four as he had been at the height of his playing career.

His companion was definitely not Al Toledo.

She was slim and petite, almost a foot shorter than Micah, with thick red hair brushing narrow shoulders. No sunglasses this time. She was probably late thirties. Krystal punched the steering wheel and swore. The woman wasn't even younger or prettier than she was. It was the ultimate insult.

Micah handed a ticket to the valet and waited for his car while Krystal's world crashed down around her. He was now flaunting his infidelity for the whole damn world to see. Either Micah was even dumber than she'd thought, or he no longer cared who saw him stepping out with someone who wasn't his wife.

He was really going to do it, Krystal thought. Her chest heaved, and she thought she might throw up all over the leather upholstery. He was really going to leave her. Worse than that, he was going to leave her with nothing.

She had signed a prenup. Al—the brains behind the Toledo-Taylor partnership—had made sure of it. Krystal had had some misgivings at the time, but Micah had always been so generous with his money. He'd showered her with expensive gifts when they were dating and had promised her a bountiful monthly allowance and her own platinum Amex card once they were married.

Krystal had convinced herself she would never have to worry about a divorce.

Then she found out about the affair, and everything had changed.

She already had her own checking account for her "pocket money" from her "little job," as Micah put it. Four months ago, she'd quit squandering her commission payments on shoes and purses and had started saving the cash, along with whatever was left over from her monthly allowance. Figured she might need the money one day.

Now things were escalating, moving quicker than she'd anticipated. The rainy day was fast approaching, and Krystal had nowhere near enough savings. She was not prepared to give up the standard of living she'd become accustomed to. She would not go back to being penniless Kasey Franks from Grapevine, Texas.

Krystal Taylor didn't do poor anymore.

As she watched her husband hold open the passenger door of his car for the redhead, her thoughts drifted to David Saint's announcement—the $50 million Malibu beach house and the potential commission up for grabs.

One million dollars.

It was a good start.

Krystal Taylor was going to get her hands on the money—and no one was going to stand in her way.

6

ANDI
BEFORE

Andi woke before the alarm and watched from bed as the sky outside the window bled from navy and violet to orange and gold.

She pulled up the emails on her phone and saw she had a couple of "keep me posted" responses from clients in Manhattan regarding the Malibu property. She'd done as David had asked, put out some early feelers, but she'd be in a much better position to share information after seeing the place for herself this morning.

There were also two messages from Nick Flores that she'd yet to respond to.

The first was an email that had landed in her inbox just before five yesterday evening, informing Andi his client was willing to come down to thirty dollars per square foot for the unit on Santa Monica Boulevard. He'd then followed up with a voice message a little over two hours later, sounding huffy and harried over the racket of little kids bickering.

"Okay, you win," he'd said. "Twenty-eight dollars. That's our best and final. Let me know if you want to proceed."

Andi smiled to herself. So much for no negotiation on the rate.

She knew twenty-eight dollars was not Flores's best and final, that she had a decent shot at convincing him to drop even further to twenty-six. Plus, it was fun to let him sweat a little. In any case, everything would change if she found a buyer for Malibu Beach Drive.

Andi was excited about the day ahead and what it might mean for her career.

She kicked off the sheets, showered, and had a breakfast of bacon, eggs, and black coffee out on the patio. Evergreen shrubs and bursts of showy cerise bougainvillea made the spot feel like her own personal paradise despite being only fifteen minutes away from the craziness of the Strip.

Andi occupied the upper floor of a modest single-family dwelling with wood siding the color of raw cookie dough. Built sometime in the '40s or '50s, it had more recently been converted into two tiny apartments. Her own entrance was accessed via a tight staircase straight off the street. Located just off Laurel Canyon Boulevard, it was within spitting distance of Jim Morrison's onetime home that had been the inspiration for the song "Love Street." After enjoying the sun for a while, Andi went back inside and dumped the dirty dishes in the sink.

She went to the closet and picked out a cute Marc Jacobs dress she'd found on the discount rack at Century 21 a few years back. It was still one of her favorites, and she always felt good wearing it. Then she paused.

David had told them the developer would be showing them around the Malibu home. Would she be dressy enough? Or would she come across as someone who hadn't bothered to make any effort? Especially compared to her fellow agents?

Verona always nailed the business-chic look. Her bright, figure-hugging dresses complemented her dark skin, and her mid-height heels managed to be sexy yet professional. Krystal's style was similar, only, the dresses were shorter, the heels were higher, and there was an extra zero on the end of the price tag.

Andi had a more laid-back approach to fashion, but today, she would be meeting a developer—one who already had a $50 million property as part of his portfolio. What other inventory might he have in the works that he'd be looking to list? If Andi was serious about branching out on her own, she'd have to impress the right people.

You have to look pretty if you want to sell pretty houses, sweetie.

Andi could hear her mom's voice so clearly just then, she could have been standing right there in the room next to her. Patti Hart had also been a Realtor and was the reason behind Andi's choice of career.

She blinked back unexpected tears, slipped on a pair of sandals, and applied a slick of mascara and lip gloss. She gave her reflection the once-over and decided she'd have to do. Andi found her phone and gasped when she saw the time.

Shit.

She was going to be late unless she hit the gas hard. She grabbed her purse and car keys and prayed the traffic wouldn't be the usual bumper-to-bumper nightmare.

As she rushed down the stairs onto the street, Andi almost collided with her downstairs neighbor. Jeremy Rundle was tall and thin, with a bland face and receding hairline, though he wasn't even thirty. He worked from home—something to do with computers—which could mean anything from YouTube gamer to professional hacker.

"Whoa. Sorry, Jeremy. Didn't see you there."

He flushed pink, grunted, and held up a quart of red-top milk. "I was just at the Country Store, picking up some milk."

"So I see."

"I always have Cheerios in the morning. But I was all outta milk. Can't have Cheerios without the milk, huh?"

He stared at her intently, like he was challenging her to disagree.

"Uh, I guess not," Andi said. "Enjoy your breakfast, Jeremy. I gotta run."

The guy was a little weird, no doubt about it, but one of the benefits of having him as a neighbor was that he didn't drive. He rode a bicycle that he kept chained to the railing of her staircase, so there was never any dispute over who got to use the patch of baked dirt that just about passed for a driveway.

The drive to Malibu would take around an hour, and Andi decided to go the more scenic Pacific Coast Highway route rather than the 101. It would be good to roll down the windows and feel the breeze on her face and smell the ocean.

The journey was barely underway when Andi realized there was something wrong with the car. The steering felt hinky, like it was pulling to the side, and the knotted leather vibrated under her grip. It was a struggle to build up any speed. She'd filled the tank the night before, so she wasn't running low on gas. Then Andi noticed a loud, flapping sound, as though the vehicle was unleashing machine-gun farts. The Country Store was just up ahead, so she eased into the lot and shut off the engine, then climbed out into the dry heat and got down on her haunches and immediately saw what the problem was. A flat tire.

"Fuck."

There was a spare in the trunk, but Andi had no idea how to replace a flat. She found her AAA card in the glove compartment and called for roadside assistance. She was told to expect a wait of at least thirty minutes.

"Fuck."

So much for a good day for her career.

Andi pulled up Diana's number.

"Andi . . . hi . . . what . . . ?"

The words were lost to a gust of wind and a burst of static. Andi guessed Diana was already on the road and had the windows down.

"Diana?" she yelled, pacing the parking lot, a finger jammed in her free ear. "I can't hear you!"

There was sudden silence as though the windows had been buzzed shut, then Diana's voice again, clearer this time.

"Any better?"

"Much."

"We're in the car. I've got you on speaker. David's here too. What's up?"

"I have a problem. A flat tire. I'm still in Laurel Canyon."

"Bloody hell, Andi," David cut in before Diana had a chance to respond. "The appointment's in less than an hour. How long will it take you to change the tire?"

"Seriously? You actually think I'm going to get out a jack and lug wrench and change it myself? AAA will be half an hour, maybe longer."

David said, "For fuck's sake." There was another hiss of static, but Andi caught the cussing loud and clear.

Diana said, "We're already on the PCH, Andi. There's no way we can turn around and pick you up. I expect the others will be the same."

"You could try and get an Uber?" David suggested.

"I should probably wait for AAA. I can't be without a car."

"I don't believe this," he snapped.

David sounded very pissed, almost irrationally so. Andi was pissed too—she'd been hoping to impress the developer, and now she was going to look like an unreliable flake instead—but there was nothing she could do about a flat tire. It was bad luck, but it was hardly the end of the world. She'd still take a drive out to Malibu and check out the house. It just wouldn't be today.

Diana said, "I'll email you the property details to look over. We can catch up in the office later."

Then the line went dead.

Andi sighed and headed toward the store for some sustenance. She could be waiting a while.

Forty minutes, two Dr Peppers, and a family-size bag of chips later, an AAA truck pulled into the lot next to her Beemer. A guy with wraparound shades and navy coveralls jumped out, the fluorescent strips on his uniform flashing in the sun. The name "Mike" was stitched in white above his right breast.

Andi read through her emails while Mike got to work. There was another follow-up from Flores, chasing her on his so-called best and final offer. He was getting desperate. She responded to some correspondence relating to other listings. The email Diana had mentioned arrived with the Malibu Beach Drive details on an attachment, and Andi saved it to read later once she was at her desk.

"I didn't even realize the tire had blown out," she told the AAA guy when he was done. "I'm just glad it didn't happen on the freeway, or I could've been in big trouble."

Mike peered over the shades. "This wasn't a blowout."

"It wasn't? What happened? Did I hit a nail or something?"

"Screwdriver."

"Huh?"

"The puncture was in the sidewall, not the tread. Nice and neat." He shrugged and wiped greasy hands on his coveralls. "Maybe a knife, but my guess is a screwdriver."

"A screwdriver? I don't understand. What are you saying?"

"I'm saying this was no accident. You ask me, someone messed with your car on purpose."

7

VERONA
BEFORE

Verona King flipped the sun visor, pressed down on the gas, and tried to focus on the drive to Malibu.

Tried very hard not to think about dying.

Her own mortality had been on her mind a lot these past few days, her thoughts waging a war inside her brain like a scene from a bad soap opera.

Everything's going to be just fine. Nothing to worry about!

How the hell can it be fine with your family history?

The urban sprawl of the 101 through Woodland Hills gave way to the soft rolling hills of Calabasas.

It'll be a false alarm, it usually is in these situations.

Yeah, but what about Aunt Mimi?

Verona navigated the winding road through the Santa Monica Mountains, barely even noticing the picturesque surroundings.

Be optimistic! Assume it'll be good news.

But what if it's the worst possible news?

She continued along Malibu Canyon Road, past one of the newer "Malibu—21 Miles of Scenic Beauty" signs, and caught glimpses of blue as towering palm trees shivered in a light wind. Then it was onto the PCH and a proper view of the ocean in all its sparkling glory.

Richard knew something was wrong. Of course he did. She'd been distracted, and she wasn't sleeping. She'd taken to going for dawn walks and midnight drives. It was something Verona did when she was stressed. Her husband would be assuming it was a work issue weighing heavily on her mind. If only it were that simple. Richard wouldn't pressure her; he would wait for her to talk it over when she was good and ready.

She should probably tell him. Then again, why share the worry? Surely it was better to wait until there was something to tell.

Cars belonging to Krystal, Hunter, and Myles were lined up on the street outside the house. David and Diana's Maserati was on the dusty shoulder on the other side of the two-lane road, where the bluffs loomed overhead. Verona parked behind it. She checked her makeup in the sun visor's little mirror. She looked tired, and she felt it too. She'd had, what, maybe two hours' sleep? Even so, it was time to put on her best game face.

David had collected a set of keys when signing the listing, so the others were gathered inside in the vast air-conditioned living area. There was no sign of Andi or the developer. They stood around making small talk until Marty Stein finally showed up fifteen minutes later, sweating and flushed and apologetic. He was short and squat with a cantaloupe belly under a cheap navy T-shirt and creases around the crotch of his cargo shorts from the drive.

Krystal looked aghast. To be fair, Marty Stein looked like a man who didn't have fifty dollars in his wallet, never mind the cash to build a $50 million dream home. Then again, plenty of millionaires, even billionaires, chose to dress like regular guys in low-key jeans and tees.

David did the introductions. Stein's eyes were on Krystal the whole time. Not in a hungry or sexual way, Verona thought. More like he was intrigued by her.

"You must be Andi," he said, pumping Krystal's hand enthusiastically. No doubt she would have frowned if her Botoxed face would have allowed her to, but Krystal settled for pursed lips instead to demonstrate her displeasure at the mistaken identity.

"No, I'm Krystal Taylor," she said, her voice colder than the AC.

Verona noticed Hunter's jaw working when the developer mentioned Andi's name. Myles rolled his eyes. Hunter wasn't a fan of Andi's and didn't try to hide the fact. He was clearly threatened by her success. Myles, well, he didn't really like anyone. Verona preferred to be friendly and courteous. She'd worked with Andi—and the others—more than once on a listing and didn't feel the need to wear her rivalry like a badge the way the men did.

That didn't mean Verona wasn't competitive, though. She was. Tough too. As a woman, she'd had to work her ass off to get to where she was now, to be taken as seriously as her male coworkers. As a Black woman, even more so. She'd had to tolerate the pats on the butt, the dinner-and-drinks invitations, the blatant requests for sex. On more than one occasion, she'd had the door slammed in her face at a listing appointment or a showing because of the color of her skin. And she had never let it grind her down. If anything, it had made her all the more determined.

Yes, Verona King was tough all right. But was she tough enough for what might lie ahead?

Stein was speaking again. "So we're just waiting on one more?" He smiled expectantly.

"Actually, no," David said. "Andi isn't going to make it this morning."

David seemed very stressed.

Verona's heart lurched. "Is she okay?"

42

"Car trouble."

"She's not hurt, is she?"

"She's fine." David's lips were thin and colorless. "Just . . . not where she's supposed to be."

"That's a real shame," said Stein, and Verona noticed a look passed between him and David. Had David been singing Andi's praises to the developer? Otherwise why was her absence such a big deal?

"I guess we'd better get started, then," Stein went on, with noticeably less enthusiasm now.

Interesting.

The house was gorgeous, no doubt about it. Everyone nodded their appreciation as Stein showed them the custom-designed kitchen with stainless-steel appliances, the rooftop terrace with fire-pit and Jacuzzi, and the primary en suite with rainfall shower and walnut soaking tub. The games room and media room and home office meant the property was perfect for both work and play, the developer pointed out to more nods of approval.

Verona couldn't imagine being rich enough to live in a house like this. If she was being really honest, she wouldn't want to. Even when it was expertly staged with furniture and artwork and soft furnishings, she thought it would still be a house rather than a home. That didn't mean she wasn't hellbent on finding a buyer for it, though.

Her patch was the Valley, where most of the properties she sold were in the $1 million to $5 million range. It was also where she lived on a quiet, treelined street in Encino that was a home as well as a house.

Verona didn't think Malibu Beach Drive would sell at full ask, but mid to high forties seemed realistic. Still a hell of a lot of commission. Money for her boys so they would not have to struggle through life like she had. She swallowed past a sudden lump in her throat. Verona's sons would be taken care of whether she was around or not. She'd make damn sure of it.

The tour ended on the pool deck, which was tucked around the side of the main level and boasted views of the Pacific and a stretch of golden sandy beach. The money shot. The reason why people were willing to pay the big bucks.

"Just imagine watching the sunset from this spot," said Stein. "The Queen's Necklace all lit up along the coastline at night. I've seen it, and let me tell you, it's quite something."

He was saying all the right words, but Verona couldn't help but think the developer's heart wasn't in it, that he was simply going through the motions.

When the tour was over, Verona sat awhile in her Mercedes SUV. She saw David and Diana emerge from the house along with Stein, and then Diana made her way to the car while the two men talked. Stein had his hands on his hips and didn't look happy, and David combed his fingers through his hair nervously and nodded a lot.

After they'd left, grim thoughts returned like an unwelcome, persistent visitor. Verona pushed them aside to try to focus on the job at hand and compile a mental list of clients with enough cash to write an offer for Malibu Beach Drive. Only one sprung to mind. A Silicon Valley venture capitalist, who was looking for a base in Southern California. Somewhere he could entertain friends and business associates, as well as a place to unwind during his frequent trips to Los Angeles.

She spoke to his secretary and was pleased to discover he was in town and available to meet for lunch the following afternoon. It seemed like a good sign. Next, Verona made a reservation at one of his favorite restaurants.

Finally, she made the call she'd been putting off for days. Her heart pounded so loudly, she could barely hear the ringing on the other end of the line.

"Medical center. How may I help you?"

Verona was forty-nine years old. She'd spent the last couple of years worrying about turning fifty. The big five-oh. Wrinkles and hot flashes and pee escaping when she laughed. She'd laugh right now at how silly and vain she'd been if she weren't so scared.

If she weren't so terrified of *not* being fifty.

"It's Verona King," she said. "I'd like to make an appointment with Dr. Fazli. It's important that I see him as soon as possible."

8

ANDI
BEFORE

Andi was hardly ever in the office on her own.

Even though the agents spent a lot of time showing luxury homes and schmoozing with clients, a staff of seven meant the workspace was never empty. There was always noise and activity and conversation. Fingers tapping on keypads, phones ringing, emails pinging, deals being done or falling through, gossip being shared.

Now there was only the steady drone of traffic outside on the Strip. The occasional impromptu splutter from the coffee machine. The quiet should have been a welcome change, an opportunity for Andi to catch up on some work without interruptions, but she didn't welcome the solitude.

It felt weird and creepy.

The knowledge that someone had deliberately tampered with her car wasn't helping. The AAA guy had tried to reassure her. Told her it was probably bored kids with nothing better to do, claimed he saw this kind of thing all the time. She tried to tell herself that Mike was right. Just kids being assholes. But it wasn't the kind of neighborhood where the local youth ran wild with screwdrivers busting folks' tires for shits and giggles. And her street was tucked away off the main drag, so it wasn't exactly an obvious choice for opportunistic criminals either.

But if not kids, then who?

The coffee machine rumbled and spurted again, and Andi started. A shudder rippled through her body. What was that old saying?

Someone walking over my grave.

She turned her attention back to the laptop and tried to focus on what was on the screen. Andi had an email offer on a midcentury modern in the Hollywood Hills at the full asking price of just under $2 million. A nice little earner. She should have been buzzing. Instead, she was antsy. She couldn't shake the feeling of being watched. She felt like the tropical fish she'd kept in a tank as a kid that kept dying on her.

Andi shook her head. She was being ridiculous. The vandalized tire was freaking her out.

Probably just kids.

Andi picked up her branded "Saint Realty" mug that David insisted everyone use—no "World's Best Mom" or "LA Dodgers" mugs allowed in this office—and made her way to the coffee machine. A caffeine hit would probably make her even more jittery, but what the hell. Hopefully the others would be back from Malibu soon.

As she loaded a caramel latte pod into the machine, her eyes were drawn to the window. An unfamiliar gold car was on the street outside. It was a big boxy vintage thing with a long hood and trunk and a hard top. Its side windows were tinted. Not black, more of a sepia tone that complemented the color of the paint, but still too dark to see inside. Andi couldn't tell if the vehicle was occupied or not.

Maybe the driver had ducked into a nearby store to pick up a sandwich or a smoothie. Or maybe someone was behind the wheel. Again, she had the strange feeling of being watched. It was as though she could physically feel the weight of unknown eyes on her. The baby hairs on her forearms stood to attention. Andi stared hard at the car. Suddenly there was a burst of dirty smoke from the exhaust, and then it was gone.

She frowned and took the caramel latte back to her desk, then blew on the hot drink as she opened the email Diana had sent her with the Malibu Beach Drive details. She was still pissed at missing this morning's tour and coming across as unreliable. The developer might even think she'd overslept or forgotten about the appointment and had used the flat as an excuse.

Even if Andi had a client willing to write an offer, she knew she could still lose out on the commission if another agent—either at Saint or a different brokerage—also found a buyer and the developer opted to work with them instead. Maybe he'd already decided she was too unprofessional to close the deal.

Diana had included a couple of exterior shots of the property and a handful of interior ones. There would be further photography once the house was staged with furniture and decorative accessories. Those were the ones that would be included on the MLS listing and sent to prospective buyers.

The place was stunning, even without the staging. All glass and concrete and gorgeous beach views. Andi opened the attachment and read through the basic info she'd need to learn for any showings—number of bedrooms, baths, dimensions, finishes, and so on. Her eyes traveled down the page and snagged on the name of the developer's company.

Petronia Property Group.

Andi stared at the words, her heart punching harder than a boxer with a grudge.

A petronia was a type of bird, namely a rock sparrow. It was probably also the name of a few unfortunate babies too. Definitely the kind of thing businesses would take inspiration from when deciding upon a moniker. No doubt there were thousands of companies all over the world with *petronia* as part of their name.

Just a coincidence.

Then Andi thought of the gold car that had been parked outside the office just now. It wasn't the same one as back then. Different color, different style. But similar. Always those old muscle cars from the '50s and '60s.

She was about to google Petronia Property Group when David and Diana walked in. David headed straight for the stairs to his office without glancing in her direction. Diana watched him thoughtfully, then turned to Andi.

"Everything okay with the car?" she asked.

"All taken care of," Andi said, making an instant decision not to share Mike's theory about the screwdriver sabotage. "Sorry I missed the tour. I'll head out there in a day or two."

"Don't worry about it." Diana smiled. "These things happen."

"David seemed pissed."

"He'll be fine. You get that stuff I sent you?"

Andi nodded. "Just reading through it now."

"Good, good. I'll be upstairs if you need me."

Diana followed David's steps up to the mezzanine level. The front door swung open again, the street noise momentarily louder, as Verona arrived.

"Hi, Andi. Did you get your car fixed okay?"

"Yup, just a flat. How was the tour?"

"Oh, it was fine. It's a beautiful home, all right. Top-of-the-range appliances, full-length pocket doors, high-end finishes, pool deck, and so on. Everything you'd expect from a house in that price range." She glanced upstairs to where David and Diana were deep in conversation in the glass-walled office and lowered her voice. "It's just a little soulless for my taste, you know what I mean?"

"Sure, I know what you mean."

"Even so, I could happily wake up to that view of the ocean every morning," Verona said, unpacking a salad box she'd picked up on the way back. "Totally to die for. I have no doubt it will sell. Maybe not at full ask, but it will sell for sure. Someone is going to make a hell of a lot of money on that house. Mostly David."

"Uh-huh. Did you meet the developer? What was he like?"

Before Verona could answer, Krystal entered the office carrying a bubblegum-pink Birkin bag in one hand and a giant to-go coffee in the other. No sign of food. Andi had never seen the woman eat.

"Hey, ladies," Krystal said. "What's happening?"

"Andi was just asking about Malibu Beach Drive," Verona said.

"Yeah, David wasn't happy you weren't there," Krystal said. "What's with you two?"

"The developer?" Andi prompted Verona, ignoring Krystal.

Sweat pooled beneath her armpits, and she realized her fists were clenched.

"Guy by the name of Marty Stein." Verona shrugged. "Never met him before. Not someone I'm familiar with. Then again, fifty-million-dollar Malibu homes aren't usually on my radar."

Marty Stein.

Andi was pretty sure she didn't know him either.

"I'm surprised fifty-million-dollar Malibu homes are on Stein's radar." Krystal wrinkled her nose as though someone had spritzed drugstore perfume. "The man looked like a vagrant."

"He did not!" Verona said disapprovingly.

"Honestly, I thought he was a tradesman or the janitor or something."

"Okay, so his style was more Target than Tommy Hilfiger, but so what? Don't be such a snob, Krystal."

"And he was short and fat." Krystal shook her head mournfully, as though personally offended by the man's appearance.

Andi was relieved. She was pretty sure she didn't know Marty Stein.

She thought about the gold car and Petronia Property Group.

Coincidences.

That was all.

9

ARIBO
AFTER

Aribo got on the 101, then took the exit for Las Virgenes Road.

The gas stations and fast food chains gave way to luxury-housing communities, and then it was nothing but parched grass and sun-dried hills for a while, the Santa Monica Mountains looming large in the distance.

He got caught behind two slow-moving cyclists in the middle of the road and leaned on the horn until they got out of the way. Aribo stamped on the gas again. Cotton-ball clouds floated across a cornflower-blue sky as he continued onto Malibu Canyon Road, then it was a short hop along the PCH before turning onto Malibu Beach Drive just before four p.m.

He didn't need the street number to identify the death house. Yellow crime-scene tape cut off the road on either side of the property. There were marked and unmarked cop cars zigzagged outside, along with vehicles from the crime scene unit and the county medical examiner's office. A media truck was already setting up farther down the street.

A patrol officer jotted down Aribo's name on a clipboard and lifted the tape for him to duck under. He entered the house straight into a vast air-conditioned living space that contained around a dozen people, a mix of cops and witnesses who were still being interviewed. Then he was through the open balcony doors and back outside in the blistering heat.

The pool deck had been sectioned off with more yellow tape. CSU techs worked the scene while the deputy medical examiner waited for them to finish so she could work on the body.

"Nice threads," Lombardi said, his mouth twitching. "Not sure you would have blended in with the crowd at an '80s New Wave gig, though. Isn't it all big hair and eyeliner and lipstick?"

"That was the New Romantics."

The two men couldn't have been any more different in appearance. Lombardi was over six feet tall and all lanky, awkward limbs. His pale skin was already turning pink in the sun. Aribo was Black, five foot nine, and had an athletic build from regular workouts. Right now, he was wearing a short-sleeved navy-and-pink Hawaiian shirt with tan slacks and slip-on deck shoes.

"I was dressed for the restaurant," he said, pulling on latex gloves and a pair of paper booties. "It was supposed to be a special occasion, remember?"

"Yeah, sorry about that." Lombardi grinned. "I guess you're not getting laid tonight, huh?"

"What do you think?"

One of the CSU techs had already taken preliminary photos and video of the scene. Lombardi had made some sketches in his notepad too. Aribo didn't have a notepad with him because he hadn't been planning on writing a review of the restaurant or the concert.

He surveyed the pool deck. There were two outdoor lounge chairs at the foot of the pool on either side of a low table. In this multimillion-dollar pad, where everything appeared to be perfectly positioned, the lounge chairs were noticeably askew.

A kidney-shaped blood stain was on one side of the pool, and the body was on the other. There were drops of blood right on the edge of the pool. Some more on the other side of the larger stain. The blood was telling a story, but Aribo wasn't sure what it was yet. He considered entry and exit points and noticed a tall wooden gate at the far end of the deck.

"What do we have so far?" he asked.

Lombardi said, "One of the guests called 911 with a report of a body facedown in the pool and a request to send help immediately, even though she thought the person was dead already. While this was happening, another guest jumped in and dragged the floater out and attempted CPR. That's why the stiff is on the other side of the pool from the blood. The responding officers got here right after the EMTs, who didn't need too long to confirm the floater was deader than a dinosaur. Man, it's hot today."

Sweat beaded Aribo's own brow and snaked down his back. "Yeah, and I should be sipping an ice-cold Corona in the shade right about now. What else?"

"Did you see Dwayne Johnson's twin inside? He's the hired muscle."

"They have security at brokers' opens?"

"They do at fancy ones like this. Couple of billionaires on the guest list, as well as that actress from the new Spielberg movie. The good news is that all the guests were given a QR code that had to be scanned on the way in. You know, to prevent lookie-loos and poor people from getting a peek inside. So we have a list of everyone who entered through the front door. Most of them arrived around noon."

"And the bad news?"

"The Rock wannabe didn't do exit scans. Forty-eight people scanned in, but we only had forty-four witnesses at the scene.

Which means some folks had left the party by the time it all kicked off at the pool. We're still trying to track them down and establish when exactly they split. Plus, we still need to ID our floater, who is, presumably, one of the missing four."

Aribo was quiet for a moment.

"What are you thinking?" Lombardi asked.

"Forty-eight? Does that not strike you as a weird number? Not forty-five or fifty. Forty-eight. It feels . . . uneven."

"I'll check it out. Find out if there were a couple of no-shows and, if so, why."

Aribo went over to the blood stain and got down on his haunches for a better look. It had dried into the concrete. He touched it with a gloved finger, and the latex came away clean. The sun was beating down hard, but he thought the blood had been there a while.

He got up and went over to the furniture. "What do you think happened here with the lounge chairs? The positioning is all screwed up."

Lombardi said, "I think rich people call them *chaises*."

"Okay, what happened with the chaises? Some kind of struggle?"

"Looks that way."

Aribo noticed two ring marks on the surface of the table, like the kind found in bars made by drinks in sticky tumblers. He bent down and searched around the . . . what had Lombardi called them? *Chaises.* There was a bottle cork tucked behind the leg of one. He got closer, so he could read the lettering stamped on it.

"Cristal."

Aribo signaled to the CSU tech with the camera and told him to take some pictures of the cork in situ before it was bagged for evidence.

He said, "There were a lot of champagne bottles on the kitchen island when I got here. Are they all Cristal?"

Lombardi went to the yellow tape and got the attention of one of the deputies and told him to go check what kind of champagne was being served to the guests. The uniform came back less than a minute later.

"Only vintage Dom Pérignon at the party," he said. "No Cristal."

Aribo said, "So we have two people out here drinking a different brand of champagne from what was being served up to the guests but no bottle and no flutes. Just a big blood stain and a dead body."

He turned his attention back to the gate at the far end of the pool deck, and his partner saw him looking.

"It provides direct access to the beach below," Lombardi explained. "We've got a section of sand taped off too and a search going on down there. Seems like the most likely escape route. That or our perp smashed someone's skull in and then walked back into a room full of people."

"Is the gate locked?" Aribo asked.

"It has a security panel on the outside, so you need the four-digit code to access the pool deck from the beach. No panel on the pool side, so anyone can open the door from here. It locks automatically when closed."

"Which means the killer could have accessed the property from the beach and made their escape the same way. We need the door handles and security panel dusted for prints and the names of everyone who knew that code."

"Already done," Lombardi said. "The developer, the staff from the listing agency, and the decorator all had access to keys and the code."

"Are there security cameras inside or outside the property?"

Lombardi shook his head. "There's an alarm system but no cameras. I guess it'd be up to whoever bought the place to install their own."

"Anybody knock on any doors yet? A neighborhood like this has to be full of those doorbell-camera things."

"Not yet. We've been trying to corral the witnesses and interview them separately. But it's like I said on the phone—no one saw anything, and no one heard anything. Most of them didn't even go out onto the balcony. Nobody went near the pool deck until the body was discovered. We'll move onto the street canvass next."

"Who found the body?" Aribo asked.

"Three women." Lombardi consulted his notes. "Marcia Stringer and Betsy Bowers from the Bowers Group, and Andi Hart from Saint Realty. Saint is the agency that's supposed to be selling this place. Good luck with that now."

"And the hero who jumped in the pool?"

"Another Realtor. Guy by the name of Nick Flores. He gave a preliminary interview to the responding officers, who kept him here. He's waiting inside for us to speak to him."

Aribo nodded. "Good. What about the 911 caller?"

"Andi Hart was the one who called it in."

"Is she still here?"

Lombardi shook his head. "She was already gone when I got here. She gave a statement to a deputy and then split."

"What did she tell the deputy?"

"That she didn't see anything other than someone in the pool. No suspicious behavior beforehand, no one hanging around near the pool deck. She stepped away to make the call when Flores did his *Baywatch* thing. Claims she didn't even see the body after it was out of the water."

Aribo said, "We need her to come into the station ASAP. I want to speak to her—and I want to hear that 911 call too. You said she worked for the listing agency? That means she had the code for the beach gate, and she was one of the first on the scene."

Lombardi nodded. They were both thinking the same thing. They'd seen it enough times in other cases.

That the person who called in the crime often turned out to be the killer.

10

HUNTER
BEFORE

Hunter parked on the street to the north of Echo Park Lake. It was a glorious day. Families and dog walkers and skateboarders and joggers were all making the most of the late-afternoon sunshine.

The lake had been a reservoir for drinking water over a hundred and fifty years ago, and more recently, its shores had been occupied by a homeless encampment, before the tents—and their inhabitants—had been unceremoniously cleared out. An oasis in the middle of the city, it was bordered by Silver Lake to the west and Chinatown to the east and boasted lotus-flower beds, wild geese and swans, and sumptuous foliage.

Hunter took off his jacket, hooked it on a finger, and slung it over his shoulder. As he walked through the park, he thought about the showing on Homedale earlier. It had gone well. Better than well. The buyer's agent, Betsy Bowers, had tried to play it cool, but her client, not so much. The client might as well have had hearts for eyes, like that little emoji Melissa was always texting him. The woman was gone. Hook, line, and sinker. Hunter fully expected an offer to land in his inbox within the next twenty-four hours.

Bowers was a ball-breaker and would come in with some bullshit lowball offer, but he knew he'd get her up. He was confident he would close the deal.

Hunter Brooks was a closer. That's what he did.

He wandered past a cluster of picnic benches and did the math in his head. He should bank somewhere between fifty and sixty grand in commission. A tidy amount that would hopefully put an end to the threatening texts for a while. Naturally, he wouldn't tell Melissa about the sale.

Right on cue, his cell phone pinged with a message.

Charlie Vance: You're late.

It was ten past four. Hunter swore, under his breath so the other people on the walking path wouldn't hear.

Hunter wasn't meeting Charlie Vance, and the reason he wasn't meeting Charlie Vance was because Charlie Vance was dead.

The man had been a very good client before all the juicy sirloins and bottles of red wine he favored finally caught up with him and his heart gave out two years ago. Hunter had sent flowers to Mrs. Vance expressing sadness at the passing of her husband. He was sad all right, sad at the loss of business Vance had brought his way. He'd deleted the man's details from his cell phone and forgotten all about him.

Then Hunter had been hit with bombshell news that meant awkward calls and texts at all hours of the day and night. Calls and texts he had no option but to acknowledge. Melissa had been suspicious, of course.

His wife was vaguely aware of the name Charlie Vance from those "How was your day?" chats at the dinner table but wouldn't have paid enough attention to remember the old boy had since shuffled off to that big old steak house in the sky.

So Vance had been resurrected, at least as far as Hunter's cell phone contacts were concerned. A demanding—but very important client—who had no respect for Hunter's office hours was how he'd sold it. Thankfully, Melissa had bought it.

Hunter came to a small playground where little kids were running amok, screaming and giggling and clambering onto slides and climbing frames. A dark-haired woman sat on a bench watching them, a stroller parked next to her. The other moms were in groups of two or three, chatting and keeping a watchful eye on their little ones. Other than the baby, the dark-haired woman was alone. Hunter took a seat next to her.

"Sorry I'm late," he said. "Work."

Carmen Vega turned her big brown eyes on him, and he felt his breath catch, like it always did when she looked at him. Even wearing leggings and sneakers and a T-shirt with spit-up all over it, she was absolutely gorgeous.

"You're here now," she said. "I guess I should be grateful you even showed up."

He smiled wryly. "You didn't exactly give me a whole lot of choice. What the hell were you thinking, coming to my house like that?"

His tone was gentler now, the anger from last night gone.

"You didn't give me a whole lot of choice either," she said. "You know you can't ignore my calls. And you definitely can't turn your cell phone off like that. That's not okay, Hunter. What if something happened? How was I supposed to reach you?"

"You're right. I'm an asshole and it won't happen again." He shifted on the wooden bench. "Look, about the money—"

Carmen Vega cut him off. "We'll come to the money in a moment. Aren't you going to say hello to Scout first?"

"Oh. Sure."

Hunter leaned over the stroller and pushed back the canopy that had been shading the baby from the warm afternoon sun. The little boy stopped playing with his toes long enough to stare up at him suspiciously. Hunter reached out a finger and stroked a velvety cheek.

"Hey, Scout," he said softly.

Carmen said, "You do know you're allowed to hold him, right?"

Hunter turned to her. "Yeah?"

He reached into the stroller and picked up the baby, whose face immediately turned beet red with fury. He unleashed a loud wail, fat tears dampened his cheeks, and his chubby legs bicycled as he wriggled in Hunter's arms. The other moms stared in their direction. Hunter turned to Carmen, panicked. "Is he okay?"

She laughed. "He's fine. Just not used to strangers."

"I guess I deserved that."

Hunter held Scout close to him, inhaling his baby smell. He stroked his hair and shushed him gently as the baby continued to squirm and whimper. Eventually—amazingly—the baby quieted and seemed almost content.

After a while, Carmen took Scout from him and laid him back in the stroller. "Let's take a walk," she said.

They strolled past the Lady of the Lake statue and the spouting geyser fountains with the bold outline of Downtown in the background. A bunch of people were out on the water on the swan paddle boats.

"I want to go back to work," Carmen said.

"Really?" Hunter couldn't hide his surprise. "But Scout is only seven months old."

"Yes, and I love spending time with him, but I can't be a stay-at-home mom forever. I'll lose my business and all of my clients. I'm already taking on some work, a few commissions here and there."

"You are? When did this happen?"

"Five or six weeks ago."

"You didn't tell me."

"I haven't seen you to tell you. The thing is, I need to go back full time. As soon as possible. My mom has been a star, taking care of Scout whenever I ask, but I can't expect her to babysit five days a week. It just wouldn't be fair to her no matter how much she adores him."

"So what're you saying?"

Carmen stopped walking and turned to face him. "I'm saying I need proper childcare—and childcare is expensive. More than I can afford. I need more money, Hunter. A lot more."

Hunter puffed out a heavy sigh. "I'm already paying plenty. More than I *have* to pay."

"I know, but it's not enough." Carmen glanced down at Scout, who was sleeping now. "He's not some problem that's going to go away, you know. This is just the start of it. There will be birthdays and Christmases and school fees and college tuition. Having a kid is a lifelong commitment. And I want the best for my son. For *our* son."

Hunter Brooks loved his wife. He really did. More than anything in the world.

When he and Melissa first got married, everything was great. They were soulmates and best friends, as well as lovers. Babies were always going to be a part of the plan, so a year after the wedding, Mel threw away her birth control—and all her inhibitions. They had sex everywhere: in the back of the car, on the beach under the moonlight, even in the bathroom of a restaurant between the starters and the mains.

Then, as their second anniversary approached, it dawned on Melissa that they'd been trying for a baby for almost a year—and nothing. It just wasn't happening for them. First came the supplements and the apps charting her menstrual cycle and highlighting the days when she would be most fertile. When that didn't work, the hospital appointments followed, then the tests, and then the expensive fertility treatments.

Hunter's test results had come back clear. His sperm count was absolutely fine. A problem with Melissa's fallopian tubes was the reason why getting pregnant was proving such a challenge. Even so, he'd felt like a failure. Hunter Brooks was a closer, it was what he did. But no matter how hard they tried, how much they wanted it, giving Melissa the baby she so desperately craved was a deal he just couldn't close.

By then, their sex life was run to a schedule. They only made love when the charts and apps said it was the right time. And when they did, it was like they were going through the motions, a means to an end. There was no spontaneity, no joy, no excitement. There wasn't even any real intimacy anymore. Just the inevitable, agonizing wait to find out if this time it would work.

Then Carmen Vega walked into Hunter's life, and it was like experiencing one of those big tremors that occasionally shook the city. She was undoubtedly beautiful, but it wasn't just her appearance that knocked him for a loop. It was the way she spoke, the way she held herself, the way she looked at him. Everything about her turned him to mush. He was like a teenager with a first crush.

Carmen was an interior decorator who'd been hired by Saint Realty to stage one of Hunter's properties. The first time they met to go over the plans, it was electric, the chemistry flowing between them undeniable. The second time, when Carmen provided a tour of the house to show him her work, they'd gotten as far as the bed in the primary suite before giving in to their desire.

They'd hooked up another handful of times before Hunter's conscience got the better of him and he ended it. He was infatuated with Carmen, but he loved Melissa. Then his former lover completely blew up his life with two words: *I'm pregnant.*

They'd been careful, had used protection, except for that first time. Carmen didn't expect Hunter to leave his wife, but she did expect him to pull his weight financially.

He was racked with guilt and terror and fear. But another part of him was proud.

Hunter Brooks was still a closer after all.

Seven months ago, Scout Brooks Vega was born, and it had been both the best and worst day of Hunter's life.

"How much for childcare?" he asked Carmen now.

She told him.

"Seriously? *Shit.*" Hunter massaged his temples, felt a vein pulsing. He'd come here expecting to throw a few grand her way from the Homedale sale, but what she was asking for was insane. "Honestly, I don't see why you can't just work a couple days a week until Scout is old enough for preschool."

Carmen burned him with a hard stare. "You'd be happy to put up the cash for childcare if your wife had a baby, though, wouldn't you? I bet you wouldn't stop her from going back to work if that's what she wanted."

He didn't answer.

"That's what I thought," she said, misunderstanding his silence. "Just figure out the money, okay? Or next time I might have to ring the doorbell and introduce Scout to Melissa."

Hunter gaped at her. The threat had always been implied but had never actually been spoken out loud until now. The words hung between them like morning smog.

"You wouldn't."

"Try me."

"Okay, okay. But I need time to get the cash together."

"How long?"

"I've got a listing in Brentwood that I'm expecting an offer on. Melissa doesn't know about it. Just give me a week or two, okay?"

"Commission?"

He hesitated. "Thirty grand."

Carmen nodded. "It's a start. Two weeks."

As Hunter walked away, Carmen's words came back to him. *Having a kid is a lifelong commitment.*

She was right. The financial demands were never going to end. Scout was a lifelong commitment—and a lifelong secret. One that Melissa could never, ever find out about.

No matter what.

The surface of the lake sparkled, and Hunter thought about Malibu Beach Drive and a million bucks and how much he needed that money.

11
KRYSTAL
BEFORE

"Hey, what's for dinner?" Micah asked, leaning down to brush Krystal's cheek with a kiss, his big hand resting lightly on her shoulder.

It was the first time in weeks they'd both been in the house together with no other plans for the evening. She tried not to flinch at his touch. If Micah thought a passionless peck was going to soften her up and compel her to prepare a meal for him—especially after what he'd been up to last night—he could forget it.

"Dinner is whatever you decide to order for yourself," she said. "I'm not hungry."

"You're not cooking?"

Krystal gestured to the laptop that was open in front of her where she sat at the kitchen island. "Does it look like it? I'm working."

"I thought it'd be nice for us to sit down and eat together, is all. I feel like I've hardly seen you recently. I miss you, baby."

And whose fault is that?

Krystal gave him a smile sweet enough to rot teeth. "Sorry, not tonight. I really am busy. But if you want to make something for yourself, feel free. I can go work in the study instead."

Krystal wasn't sure what exactly Micah used his study for, or why he even had one, but what she did know was that he didn't like her going in there.

"No, that's okay. Stay here. I'll order in some pizza."

"You do that, honey. None for me."

She watched him wander off, cell phone in hand, then heard the sound of the television blaring in the den. Gunfire and bad music. One of those awful video games, but at least it would keep him occupied for a while. Krystal rummaged in her purse and found the business card she'd stashed in there the night before.

When Micah had left Grandmaster Recorders with the redhead, Krystal had gone straight home. She'd known from the GPS tracker that he'd headed to the Studio City neighborhood. Google Street View confirmed it was a residential dwelling—and a swanky one at that. Presumably, the redhead's home.

A memory from months earlier had come back to Krystal as she'd stared at the woman's house on her phone. She'd walked into Micah's study without knocking one day, and he'd been reading an official-looking document. When he'd spotted her standing in the doorway, he'd been like a kid caught with his hand in the cookie jar. He'd quickly shoved the paperwork into a desk drawer.

Krystal had forgotten all about the official-looking document— until last night. As she'd steered the Porsche through the after-dark streets, she'd started wondering if what she'd seen that day had been divorce papers. Papers Micah planned on serving her with when the time was right.

So while her husband was busy entertaining his lover in Studio City, Krystal had gotten busy in his study. She'd tried to pick the desk drawer's lock with a bobby pin. Then she'd tried to jimmy the drawer open with a knife. Then another couple of attempts with the bobby pin. Just when she'd been about to give up, Krystal had found the key taped to the underside of the desk.

Typical Micah.

When she'd opened the drawer, the document was gone. Krystal guessed it had been given to Al Toledo for safekeeping.

Maybe Micah wasn't so stupid after all.

The drawer contained a stack of business cards from the various events Micah attended, where he pressed the flesh and tried to convince people with money to pay him to endorse their products or make a guest appearance on their TV shows. Krystal had riffled through the cards and found one that got her thinking.

She looked at the card now. It was for the founder of a Japanese tech brand who'd paid Micah a lot of money to be one of their ambassadors for a year after his Super Bowl appearance. Krystal had met the founder—a terrifying woman by the name of Ryoko Yamada—at a glitzy party to launch the new collection of headphones Micah would be modeling. Ryoko Yamada was so rich she made Mark Zuckerberg look poor. She was based in Tokyo but spent a lot of time in the States, and Krystal wondered if she might be in the market for a $50 million beach house in Malibu.

A mere drop in the Pacific Ocean for someone like Ryoko Yamada.

Krystal opened a new email and typed out a message introducing herself as Micah Taylor's wife and providing a reminder of their brief meeting at the headphone launch in Hollywood. She explained she was now working in the luxury Los Angeles real estate market and had a tip about a superhot property that Ryoko Yamada might be interested in. Krystal attached the details of Malibu Beach Drive and hit "Send."

Then she turned her attention to Marty Stein.

When Krystal met him this morning, she'd been almost as disappointed as when she'd discovered Chanel's New York Red lipstick had been discontinued.

The feeling apparently wasn't mutual. Stein had clearly been attracted to her because he'd been unable to keep his grubby little eyes off her, although he had become weirdly uninterested in the tour—and all the agents—when he'd discovered Andi Hart wouldn't be there.

He wasn't wearing a wedding ring, and she'd asked some subtle questions to confirm there was no Mrs. Stein on the scene and therefore no one to stop them from getting to know each other better. Not that a wife would have been a barrier anyway. A hobbit like Marty Stein was hardly going to turn down Krystal Taylor.

The issue was whether Krystal would be willing to "go there" in order to gain an advantage, to get the inside track on Malibu Beach Drive, and to make sure she was given preferential treatment if there were multiple offers.

When she'd first arrived in LA as a wannabe actress straight off the bus from Texas, Kasey Franks—as she'd been back then—had had to quickly become acquainted with the Hollywood casting couch. Her acting career didn't amount to much more than a pet-food commercial and a small part in a pilot for a dreadful comedy-drama, which thankfully never saw the light of day, before she finally called it quits, accepted she was not going to be the next Jennifer Aniston, and turned to modeling instead.

But yes, Krystal had done things back then that she wasn't proud of, and yes, she'd do them all over again with Marty Stein if she had to. She just wasn't convinced the guy was the rich and powerful developer that everyone thought he was. If there was one thing Krystal could smell a mile off, it was money. And all she'd gotten from Stein was a whiff of cheap cologne and a hint of halitosis.

Krystal found the email Diana had sent to all the agents with the details of Malibu Beach Drive and noticed the property was actually owned by a company called Petronia Property Group.

The doorbell rang just then, and the video-game racket stopped. Muffled voices came from the front door that went on for way longer than the handover of a stuffed-crust meat feast should take. She rolled her eyes. The Postmates guy was probably a Rams fan who was thrilled to discover the Micah Taylor who'd placed the food order was *the* Micah Taylor, and they were no doubt now discussing his career highlights and posing for selfies together. Finally, the door closed, and the gunfire and bad music resumed, and Krystal turned her attention back to the screen and finding out as much as possible about Petronia Property Group.

Which was enough to establish that Marty Stein wasn't much more than a glorified tour guide. A minor partner in the business.

Krystal smiled. She'd been right.

Someone else was calling the shots. Someone who wasn't at the Malibu house this morning and whose name, as far as she was aware, was not known to the other agents at Saint Realty. Krystal looked at the photograph on the screen and reread the credentials. This man was the complete opposite of Marty Stein. This man had looks *and* money.

Her smile got bigger.

He was just her type.

12

ARIBO
AFTER

While the deputy medical examiner carried out the on-the-scene examination, Aribo and Lombardi went inside to interview Nick Flores. It was a chance to get out of the heat and into the blissful chill of an AC system so good it made a meat locker feel like a sauna.

Flores was sitting on a large cream L-shaped couch next to one of the deputies, who'd been tasked with babysitting him until the senior investigators spoke to him.

He wore dark blue jeans and a white dress shirt. His shoes were drying off on the floor next to him. His hair and clothing were still damp, and a wet patch tinged with blue dye had spread around him where he sat on the couch. The stain was seriously going to piss someone off, although maybe not as much as the reduction in sale price the death was going to cause.

Then again, Malibu wasn't so far from Hollywood, so maybe some ghoul would snap the place up at full ask and use it as the on-location set for a movie about the murder.

If it even was a murder.

Aribo still wasn't sure what exactly they had here. Just that something wasn't right. Hopefully the DME would come up with some answers.

Someone had found a towel for Flores, and he had it wrapped around his shoulders like a boxer. He was shivering. Probably a combination of the shock and taking an unexpected dip in a cold pool.

The two detectives pulled over some chairs from the dining table so they were facing him. They introduced themselves, and the "babysitter" took the hint and left. They offered Flores a drink before starting, although, looking around, expensive champagne seemed to be the only thing available. That or tap water. Flores shook his head.

Aribo took the lead, while Lombardi took the notes.

"Why don't you talk us through what happened, Mr. Flores?" Aribo said. "In your own words."

Flores nodded. "I was chatting with Marcia and Betsy over by the pocket doors, and one of them—I don't remember who—wanted to know if the house had a pool. They asked one of the agents from the listing agency, and she offered to show them the pool deck."

"This agent was Andi Hart?" Aribo asked.

"That's right. Andi. The three of them went out onto the balcony and headed off in the direction of the pool deck."

"You didn't want to see the pool?"

"Nah. The bubbly was going straight through me, and I was waiting for the downstairs toilet to be free so I could go take a leak. The en suite bathrooms upstairs were all off limits."

"Right. Then what happened?"

Flores twisted the wedding band on his ring finger. "I heard all this screaming, so I ran out to the deck and saw someone was in the pool. They were facedown and fully clothed, and my first thought was to get them out of there. So that's what I did. I jumped in and got them out."

"And you attempted CPR?"

"Yeah, hands only. You know, chest compressions."

"Not mouth to mouth?"

Flores shook his head. He swallowed hard, his Adam's apple bobbing up and down like a nodding dog ornament in the back of a car. "There was all this white foam stuff around the mouth. I could tell, even as I was doing the chest compressions, that it was too late. Way, way too late."

Flores's eyes filled with tears, and he looked away.

"You did what you could, son," Lombardi said.

"Let's just back up a few steps," Aribo said. "When you entered the pool deck, what were the three women doing?"

Flores thought about this. "Marcia and Betsy were screaming their heads off and clinging to each other. I remember I had to push them out of the way to get to the pool. Betsy's gonna give me hell for that."

"And Andi Hart? What was she doing?"

Flores frowned. "Uh, I'm not sure. Everything happened so fast. It's all kind of a blur."

"I understand," Aribo said. "Take your time. Was she trying to help the person in the pool? Was she blocking the way like Marcia and Betsy? Was she screaming too?"

Flores scrunched up his face again, like he was thinking hard. He closed his eyes as though trying to watch a replay of the events at the pool. He opened them and said, "I think she was moving away from the pool deck back toward the balcony. She wasn't screaming."

"So not particularly panicked or upset?"

"Dazed, maybe? I'm honestly not sure. I wasn't paying a whole lot of attention to her."

"Did you know the deceased?"

"No, I don't think so."

"So not a guest at the party?"

Flores shrugged. "It's possible, I guess. It was pretty busy, lots of people milling around. I didn't speak to everyone. I didn't know all the guests."

Aribo said, "Did you notice anything unusual during the party? Anyone acting suspiciously? Any arguments or tension? Anything like that?"

"Oh, sure. There was tension all right. A full-blown argument too."

The detectives exchanged glances.

Aribo said, "Tell us about the argument."

Flores said, "Two women and a guy had a serious dustup over there by the big canvas of the ocean. I've seen the guy around, but I didn't recognize the women. One of the women threw a drink in the other one's face. Then she started attacking the guy. I was over here, too far away to hear what was being said. All three of them left soon after. I think the guy on the door got involved. That's when Marcia and Betsy came over to talk to me. They were pretty excited about all the drama."

"You also mentioned some other tension?"

Flores looked uncomfortable. He twisted the wedding ring again. "Yeah, I think I might have had something to do with that, said something I shouldn't have. Just blundered right in there with my size tens and got Andi in trouble with her boss."

Aribo and Lombardi shared another look.

"What did you say?" Aribo asked.

"I told the guy she was leaving to set up her own brokerage. I didn't realize he was her boss. I guess he didn't know. They went into the theater room to talk it over, and Andi seemed upset when she came back out."

"What about her boss?"

"I don't remember seeing him again. Maybe he left."

Lombardi said, "Okay, son. I think we've got everything we need for now, but we will need you to come into the Lost Hills station to make a formal statement." He handed over a card. "Call the front desk number to arrange a time that suits. And call my cell if you remember anything else that might be useful."

Flores nodded and turned the card over in his hands. Then he looked at them. "Actually, there was something else."

"What's that?" Lombardi said.

"A bunch of people seemed to be looking for someone. I guess the guy was supposed to be at the brokers' open and didn't show up. Andi's boss said he wasn't answering his cell phone."

One of the no-shows?

"You remember the guy's name?" Aribo asked.

"Just the first name. It was Myles. Everybody was looking for Myles."

13

MYLES
BEFORE

"Steak and cocktails on a school night?" Jack Dunne said. "What's the occasion?"

Myles Goldman smiled mysteriously. "We're celebrating."

They were in Dan Tana's, an Italian restaurant housed in a yellow bungalow on Santa Monica Boulevard. The low lighting, checkered tablecloths, and Chianti bottles hanging from the ceiling reminded Myles of those old mobster movies his father liked to watch. The place was a little old-fashioned for Myles's taste, but he had been coming here for as long as he could remember with his folks. It was also still a popular haunt with the Hollywood A-list, and that was good enough for him. In this town, it was all about keeping up appearances. Plus, the chicken parmigiana was to die for.

"Yeah?" Jack raised an eyebrow. "What are we celebrating?"

"Oh, just the small matter of me making a million dollars in commission."

Jack almost choked on his martini. "Seriously? When did this happen?"

Myles held up his hands. "Okay, so I haven't found a buyer yet. But I will."

They ate, and Myles told Jack about Saint Realty landing the $50 million listing for Malibu Beach Drive and this morning's tour—the house, the beach, the view.

The competition.

"So what's the plan?" Jack asked when Myles was done.

"The plan?"

"For selling the house. Making sure you're the one who gets the money."

Myles said, "You mean other than my excellent contacts, first-rate salesmanship, and money-can't-buy charm?"

Jack grinned. "Yeah, other than all of those."

Myles leaned across the table, placed a hand on his boyfriend's, and held his gaze. "I want that money, Jack. And you know I always get what I want."

"I sure do." Jack winked. "It was either take out a restraining order against you or agree to go on a date with you." He tossed his napkin on the table and slid out of the burgundy leather booth. "Why don't you come up with an unbeatable strategy while I visit the little boys' room?"

Myles knew Jack was joking, but the remark got him thinking all the same.

David Saint clearly thought Andi had the best chance of bringing a buyer to the table, but Myles disagreed. David's judgment was clouded by the fact that he was clearly hot for her, same as he had been for Andi's predecessor, Shea Snyder.

True, Andi was the brokerage's highest-ranking agent, but he did not think she had a suitable client list for Malibu Beach Drive. She mostly represented fledgling starlets looking to blow their first big paycheck on trendy pads in the Hollywood Hills. Not the kind of people willing—or able—to write an offer even close to $50 million.

Likewise, Verona. The woman had experience on her side, but she was small time. Almost exclusively the Valley and almost always inventory priced under $5 million. Krystal was ambitious and keen to shed her trophy-wife image, but ironically, she largely relied on her husband's old football buddies for business. Sure, she'd had a few nice sales, but again, Myles did not believe many ex-ballplayers were about to drop fifty big ones on a house.

Which left Hunter Brooks.

Myles figured he was the real competition, at least as far as the agents at Saint were concerned. Brooks's top territory was Brentwood, but recently he'd been trying to muscle in on the Platinum Triangle—Beverly Hills, Bel Air, and Holmby Hills—which Myles firmly considered to be his own patch. He'd grown up in the 90210 zip code and had always been more than happy to utilize his father's rich and powerful connections when selling real estate in that exclusive triumvirate.

In the last six months or so, Brooks had secured three lucrative listings in the Beverly Hills Flats, much to Myles's displeasure. It was his own fault, he'd been distracted, had dropped the ball, and Brooks had swept in on his turf.

Yes, Hunter Brooks was the one to watch all right.

Which is why Myles had decided to watch him earlier this afternoon.

He'd heard Brooks tell David and Diana that he had a showing in Brentwood after Malibu so he would be late getting back to the office. That's why Myles had been surprised—and intrigued—when he'd spotted the distinctive black Rolls-Royce Ghost parked all the way across town next to the entrance to Echo Park Lake. Myles might have assumed it was someone else's wheels if it weren't for the vanity plates identifying its owner.

Brooks hadn't mentioned anything about another appointment in Downtown, so Myles had suspected he might be meeting a client. Someone top secret that he didn't want anyone else at the brokerage to know about. A potential buyer for the Malibu house.

Myles had left his own car on a nearby side street, headed into the park, and strolled along the walking path that bordered the lake until he'd spotted Hunter Brooks.

He was with a dark-haired woman, who was dressed casually in leisurewear. Myles had been disappointed. He assumed the brunette was Brooks's wife, whom Myles had met a couple of times and, he remembered, was slim with dark hair.

A stroller was next to the woman, which confused Myles because he was pretty sure Brooks didn't have any kids. He was definitely the type who would boast about their achievements and force coworkers to look at boring photos of them if he did. Verona kept framed photos of her two sons on her desk at the office (Myles couldn't remember their names), whereas Brooks had none.

The dark-haired woman had then turned momentarily in his direction, and Myles had realized she was not Brooks's wife after all. There was something familiar about her, but he couldn't place where he knew her from. Then he'd watched as Brooks reached into the stroller and picked up the baby, cradling it in his arms.

Myles had been convinced in that moment that the woman *was* a client, that Brooks was doing that baby-kissing thing politicians do when they're trying to garner votes, that the man really was willing to resort to anything to secure a sale. Myles had held up his cell phone and started filming, even though he didn't really know what exactly he was filming.

Myles pulled out the phone now and dismissed the Instagram notifications, online poker offers, and software update alerts. He opened his videos and hit play on the one he'd recorded earlier. He watched it again with a frown. There was something kind of tender in the way Brooks held the baby, who was clearly not happy about being that close to Hunter Brooks. Myles didn't blame the kid.

Jack returned from the restroom, and Myles tucked the phone back into his pocket. They had dessert and another cocktail and chatted a while. Myles asked for the check. An elderly waiter fetched the card machine, swiped the plastic, knotted his brow, and swiped again. He looked at Myles, embarrassment etched on his face along with the deep wrinkles.

"I'm so sorry, Mr. Goldman, but your card has been declined."

Myles felt the chicken parmigiana churn in his gut.

"Um . . . I should have some cash." Myles opened his wallet again, hoping Jack and the waiter wouldn't notice that his hands were shaking. The section for bills was empty. He swallowed hard.

Before Myles could say anything, Jack handed over his own card. "Don't worry, honey. I'll get it."

Myles just nodded.

Once the waiter had left with the payment and a generous tip, Jack said, "Wow, I'm surprised—and a little impressed—by this new mild-mannered Myles Goldman."

"Huh?"

"I thought you'd be mad, insist the waiter keep on trying the card machine. Threaten to have him fired if he couldn't get it to work."

Myles attempted a chuckle that sounded more like a croak. "My father would not be happy if I made a scene in his favorite restaurant. And I just remembered I was sent a new card and forgot to put it in my wallet. This one has expired. I'll repay you for dinner."

Jack dismissed the offer with the wave of a hand. "Hey, I don't mind paying my own way. I'm not with you because of your money and visits to fancy restaurants, you know?"

"I know, you're with me because my ass looks great in tight jeans."

Jack grinned. "Guilty as charged. Although, obviously, you'll be paying for dinner all the time once you get that million dollars."

They made their way outside and waited for the valet to bring Myles's car.

"Your place or mine?" Jack asked.

Myles hesitated. He'd had other plans for the rest of the evening that didn't include Jack. He could already feel the restlessness kicking in, the tension in his muscles, the quickening of his pulse.

Jack picked up on the hesitation. "Look, I don't have to stay over," he said quickly. "It *is* the middle of the week, and we both have work tomorrow. I just thought . . ."

Get a grip, Goldman, Myles thought. *You're really choosing a laptop over your hot boyfriend?*

Myles leaned over and kissed him hard on the lips. "Of course I want you to spend the night. I have to get up early for the gym before the office, but I'll sneak out real quiet so I don't wake you."

When Myles had first met Jack Dunne almost a year ago, he'd fallen hard and fast. Jack was six years older and made it clear from the start that he was looking for a relationship. Myles hadn't been after anything serious, was content to play the field, keep his options open. That all changed with Jack. Now with their one-year anniversary approaching, Myles knew what they had was the real deal. He'd deleted all the dating apps from his phone within a week of their first date and had never looked back. Had never once been tempted to reinstall them and see who else was out there.

The bad feeling in his belly returned now. If only Myles could bring himself to delete the other apps too. If only there were no secrets to sour this otherwise perfect relationship.

The Lambo smoothly navigated the curves and bends of Sunset Plaza Drive, making the steep climb up into the Bird Streets, so called because the streets had names like Thrasher Avenue and Warbler Way and Skylark Lane.

Myles had purchased a three-bed, three-bath midcentury modern on Blue Jay Way three years ago with money from his trust fund when he turned twenty-five. His father had been impressed by his choice of home because of the George Harrison song and less impressed when Myles had asked who George Harrison was.

He parked his yellow Lamborghini Huracán in the garage, went into the house, and spotted the pile of mail he'd dumped on the sideboard in the hallway earlier.

Myles quickly swept the letters into a drawer before Jack could see them.

14

ANDI
BEFORE

Andi picked up takeout from her favorite Italian restaurant and a bottle of wine from the Country Store on the way home from work. She wouldn't usually indulge in either unless it was the weekend, but it had been an unexpectedly stressful and shitty day.

And it wasn't like there was anyone around to disapprove of her life choices.

There was no sign of Jeremy's bike when she parked in the drive and no lights on in his apartment. Dusk had fallen over the tight, narrow street. A soft breeze rustled nearby shrubs and the leaves on the trees. There was no one else around. A coyote screamed somewhere up in the hills. The night air was warm on her bare arms.

She went inside and dumped the food and wine on the kitchen counter. The pinot grigio was still cool from the store's refrigerator. Andi poured herself a large glass and got a plate out of the cupboard for the pennette arrabbiata.

She watched an old rerun of *Magnum, P.I.* while she ate. TV dinners for one sucked. Tom Selleck wiggled his eyebrows at some woman, and Andi's thoughts wandered to getting back in the dating game again. She'd gone on a few dates when she'd first arrived in LA but had still been too hung up on Justin to really give any of those guys a chance.

She'd thrown herself into work instead. It had paid off in terms of making money and contacts, but her downtime had suffered as a result. She had no real friends here, and her sex life was as barren as a ghost town in the desert. Andi received the occasional dinner invitation from a client but figured it was best to keep business and pleasure completely separate. That's why what happened six months ago had really shaken her.

Andi rinsed off the plate and fork and refilled the wineglass, opened the dating app she had not used for almost a year. After ten minutes of swiping left, she gave up. Definitely no Thomas Magnums lurking in there looking for a life partner.

Her finger hovered over the Instagram icon. She muttered, "Fuck it"—which was almost always a prelude to a bad decision—and tapped it. Then typed Justin's name into the little search box against her better judgment. The booze and nostalgia were both hitting her hard tonight.

The most recent photo was of her ex with a redhead called Janie. Justin and Janie. It was sickeningly cute. Andi knew from her social media stalking that they'd been together for over a year now. Justin seemed happy, and Andi knew she should be happy for him. She had treated him like trash. They'd been talking about getting a place together, a little apartment in the East Village, when everything had changed in a heartbeat.

She'd been walking down the street and happened to glance in the window of a diner and saw someone she recognized sitting there, eating a sandwich. *Him.* Brazenly eating a fucking sandwich just a few blocks from where she worked. Andi had told herself he would only be in town for a day or two for business or vacation. Then she'd discovered that wasn't the case. She'd made a few calls and found out he was renting office space in the city. He was going nowhere.

When the past gate-crashed the present, it had a bad habit of fucking up the future.

Instead of moving in with Justin, Andi had ended the relationship. She didn't give him an explanation or a reason why. She just left him and her job and her apartment and New York. All the things she loved most in the world. Just like that.

Andi had picked LA because it was literally on the other side of the country and about as far away as she could get.

She shut down Instagram, and the smiling photo of Justin and Janie, and checked her emails. Nick Flores's message was still sitting in her inbox, unanswered. There was an unread email from a Gretchen Davis that had been sent about an hour earlier.

> Dear Ms. Hart,
>
> I hope this message finds you well. I'm writing on behalf of Walker Young, who is seeking to increase his property portfolio on the West Coast. Mr. Young would like to arrange a call to discuss working with you. Please let me know your availability at your earliest convenience.
>
> All best,
>
> Gretchen Davis
> (Personal assistant to Walker Young, CEO)
> Young Global Management

Andi ran Young's name through Google and let out a low whistle. He was a New York investment firm owner, and his company's headquarters occupied a floor of the Solow Building on West Fifty-Seventh Street. Young was also, apparently, worth more than $3 billion. That was *billion* with a *B*. She fired off a response to Gretchen Davis with times she'd be free to get on a call or a Zoom with Walker Young.

Maybe today wouldn't be such a washout after all.

She took her wineglass into the bathroom and turned on the bathtub faucet. Dumped some fancy bubble bath into the water, undressed, and climbed in. Between the booze and the bubbles and the warmth of the water, Andi felt her muscles begin to relax as she settled back in the tub. Her eyelids grew heavy, and she told herself she'd close her eyes just for a moment.

She opened the front door and stepped inside the house. Dropped her bag at her feet.

She knew immediately, and instinctively, that something was very wrong.

The shattered pieces of a glass vase lay on the hallway floor, along with scattered flowers and a puddle of water. A lamp had been knocked off the side table too.

The living room was warm and stuffy and silent apart from the whoomph of the ceiling fan. Despite the movement of the blades slicing vainly through stagnant air, there was a stillness that unnerved her. It was the kind of stillness that followed an explosion of violence. She knew this all too well. The wooden window blinds were partially closed, preventing prying eyes from witnessing what went on beyond the white picket fence and immaculately kept lawn and cheerful yellow door.

She went back into the hall, past the broken vase, spilled water, flowers, and lamp. Continued to the kitchen. Her shoulders were tight with tension, her heartbeat loud in her ears. She was scared of what she might discover. Scared of being discovered. But she thought that whatever had happened here was over now. She was alone.

An empty vodka bottle was on the kitchen table. A chair had been upended.

Then she noticed the back door was ajar.

She didn't want to see what lay beyond the door. She knew it couldn't be good.

The door caught in the breeze and banged against the wooden frame. Over and over and over again . . .

◆　◆　◆

Andi woke with a start, sloshing water over the side of the tub. It took a beat or two for her to remember where she was. The bath water was cold, and her skin had pruned. A loud banging was coming from the hallway. The banging wasn't part of the dream. Someone was at her front door.

She climbed out of the tub and pulled on a terry-cloth bathrobe. Her cell phone was in the other room, so she had no idea what time it was or how long she'd been dozing, but she guessed it was late. Andi wasn't expecting any visitors. She made her way slowly into the hallway, flipping on the light. Instead of heading for the front door, she turned and made a detour to the kitchen.

Her phone was on the counter. She touched the screen. It was almost ten thirty. Her eyes went to the wooden knife block. Andi told herself she was being stupid. Then she figured it was better to be stupid than murdered. She picked up the biggest knife and returned to the hallway.

The banging had stopped now.

A folded sheet of paper had been slipped under the door. Andi hooked the security chain in place, tightened her grip on the handle of the knife, and cracked the door open. The top of the staircase was empty. She unhooked the chain and opened the door all the way, then stepped outside. There was no one there.

Andi went back inside, locked up tight, and picked up the note. Her name was on the front and had been spelled wrong.

Andy

Not even Andie, like MacDowell. Andy, like Andrew.

It was written in big, jagged letters, like a serial killer's writing. She laughed. As if serial killers had a particular style of handwriting. Then she thought of the slit tire, and the laugh died in her throat. She unfolded the sheet of paper, half expecting to see cutout letters from a magazine, like in the movies, but there was just more of the same weird scrawl.

Andy,

I tried knocking but you didn't answer. There's something you should see.

Jeremy

The TV was still on, an old movie she didn't recognize now blaring. The lights were on too, and her car was parked right outside.

You didn't answer.

She felt bad for a moment, thinking the guy must've known she was home and assumed she'd refused to open the door to him. Then again, it was pretty late to call on a neighbor, especially one whom you weren't exactly friends with.

There's something you should see.

Andi couldn't imagine Jeremy Rundle having anything she'd be remotely interested in seeing—but a part of her was intrigued all the same. He'd never come to her door before. But she wasn't intrigued enough to get dressed and head down to his apartment at such a late hour. Whatever it was, it could wait until morning. She was beat. It was time to call it a night.

Andi replaced the knife in the block and turned off the TV and the lights. As she climbed into bed, she thought about the dream in the bathtub. She hadn't had the dream since moving to Los Angeles.

She hoped sleep would come quickly tonight and that it wouldn't be haunted by ghosts from the past.

15

HUNTER
BEFORE

Hunter and Melissa were having breakfast when he asked if she'd mind doing "a little favor" for him.

"Sure," she replied absentmindedly, pushing scrambled eggs around the plate. "You want me to pick up your dry cleaning?"

Melissa was still very down about the latest round of fertility treatments not being successful and having to wait a couple of weeks for another appointment with Dr. Kessler to discuss their options going forward. Hunter thought she looked tired and like she'd lost more weight.

"No, not the dry cleaning," he said. "Although if you're going to be nearby the dry cleaner's later, you may as well pick it up, thanks."

He told her what he wanted her to do, and Melissa stared at him, a forkful of food paused halfway to her mouth.

"Wait," she said, dropping the fork back onto the plate. "Let me see if I've got this right. You want me to call one of your coworkers, at your office, and pretend to be someone else?"

"That's right."

"Why on earth would I do that?"

"To help me. To help us. Just trust me, okay?"

That was the thing about Melissa, she did always trust him. It didn't always make him feel good about himself, but it did make life a whole lot easier sometimes.

Melissa sighed wearily as though she didn't have the energy to disagree with him. Hunter knew she hadn't slept much the night before, had been aware of her tossing and turning in the bed next to him.

"Okay," she said. "What exactly is it you want me to do?"

They went over the script a few times, and Hunter asked her to make the call around ten a.m. He'd be at his desk and in a prime position to see how it was playing out and if his plan was going to work.

Hunter had no shortage of confidence in his own abilities when it came to most things in life, and that included selling real estate. He was a closer. He was the best agent at Saint Realty, and he didn't give a rat's ass if David's stupid ranking system said otherwise. Everyone knew David had the hots for Andi and that's why she got all the best listings. It'd been the same with Shea Snyder—and look how that had turned out.

Hunter already had Brentwood sewn up, and he was making good progress in Beverly Hills too, now that Myles was more interested in online casino games than he was in hustling for business.

But Malibu Beach Drive was the big prize. And Hunter didn't mind playing dirty and taking the competition out of the game to get what he wanted.

He'd been working late at the office yesterday, after the rendez-vous with Carmen Vega in the park, so he'd agreed to lock up when David and Diana left for the evening. Diana liked to keep tabs on the agents' movements, so Hunter had taken the opportunity to have a peek at her desk planner and had noticed an entry for the following day.

Verona King had a lunch appointment at one of LA's best restaurants at noon to discuss Malibu Beach Drive. There was no mention of whom she was planning on entertaining, but Hunter had a pretty good idea. Verona only had one client with anywhere near enough funds to buy the beach house. A Silicon Valley asshole by the name of Don Garland—who should have been Hunter's client and top of *his* list of potential buyers.

◆ ◆ ◆

At just past ten the following morning, Hunter heard Verona's desk phone ring, and his heart did a little kick. He leaned back in his chair to better listen to what she had to say. Would she fall for it? Even if she did guess something was off, there was nothing to pin the ruse on him. Not yet anyway. By the time she did realize she'd been duped, it would hopefully be too late.

Verona greeted the caller, and after a short pause, said, "Oh, that's a real shame."

The disappointment in her voice was unmistakable. There was no hint of suspicion either. Melissa was clearly smashing it. Then Verona was talking again, sounding much perkier now.

"Two p.m.? Yes, yes. Uh-huh. No, that's absolutely fine. No problem at all. Thanks for letting me know."

Hunter grinned to himself. He couldn't help it.

"What are you smiling at?" Krystal asked with narrowed eyes.

"Just thinking of something funny I said to the barista when picking up my coffee this morning. I can be pretty hilarious sometimes."

"Weirdo," she muttered.

At a quarter to noon, Hunter picked himself up from his desk, told Diana he had a last-minute showing at Homedale, and made the short drive along Santa Monica Boulevard to Century City.

The restaurant was a fancy farm-to-table dining experience in a sleek modern building within spitting distance of Avenue of the Stars. When he arrived, Hunter spotted Don Garland seated in one of the plush velvet booths, perusing a menu.

The maître d' asked if he had a reservation, and Hunter gestured in Garland's direction. "I'm meeting someone," he said. "He's already here." He strode across the dining room before she could say anything else.

"Mr. Garland," he said.

The man looked up at him blankly. "Do I know you?"

Garland was a big man with fleshy features, a telltale booze-hound's purple nose, and gray eyebrows that didn't match his suspiciously black hair.

"I'm a real estate agent with Saint Realty," Hunter said.

Recognition slowly dawned on Garland's face. "Oh, I remember you. Harrison, right?"

"Hunter. Hunter Brooks."

"Right. Well, I'm actually meeting a coworker of yours for lunch, so . . ."

Garland let the unfinished sentence hang in the air, a clear signal for Hunter to get lost.

"I'm afraid Verona isn't coming. Something came up."

"What do you mean she's not coming?" Garland snapped. He slammed the menu on the table with a loud thud. Other diners glanced up from their duck salads and Alaskan halibut to stare at them.

"May I?" Hunter gestured to the vacant seat facing Garland.

"No, you may not."

"Okay."

Hunter continued to stand, feeling as though the eyes of the whole restaurant were on him.

"Explain," Garland barked. "Why the hell hasn't my office called to let me know the meeting's been canceled?"

"It was all very last minute, sir. An important client of Verona's is in town for one day only, and he insisted on meeting with her."

"More important than me? Is that what you're telling me?"

Hunter shrugged and smiled apologetically. "I offered to come meet you instead. Didn't want you to have a wasted trip."

"Is that so?" Garland eyed him skeptically, like he wasn't buying any of his spiel for a minute. "You know, I never did like you, Harrison. Too cocky for my liking. I much preferred the woman."

A couple of years ago, Garland had approached Saint to find a property for him in Los Angeles. David had decided Hunter and Verona were the best fit for his needs because Garland was almost sixty and had made it clear he didn't want anyone too young and "green" looking after his interests. Hunter was actually not that much older than Andi or Krystal but vastly more experienced at buying and selling LA real estate.

They'd both met with the man separately, and he had chosen to work with Verona. As far as Hunter knew, she still hadn't closed a deal for him. She'd shown him a bunch of places, and he had lost out on at least one of them to a higher bidder. Garland might be smart when investing in promising start-ups, but he hadn't been too clever when it came to picking the right agent.

Hunter cleared his throat. "That may well be the case, Mr. Garland. But I'm here and Verona isn't."

A waiter came to take the drinks order, and Garland asked for a glass of pinot noir. The waiter looked expectantly at Hunter, probably wondering why he was standing, and Hunter looked expectantly at Garland.

"Do you know what Ms. King wanted to discuss with me today?" Garland asked.

"I do," Hunter said. "A very exciting property that isn't even on the market yet." He held up a leather portfolio with his initials stamped in gold on the front. "I have all the details right here."

Garland considered this information, while Hunter and the waiter both stood there waiting.

Finally, he nodded. "Sit."

Hunter sat.

"A drink, sir?" the waiter asked.

"I'll have the wine too."

"I'm assuming you'll be taking care of the check?" Garland said. Like the guy didn't have a hundred million in the bank.

"Of course."

"Make it a bottle of pinot noir," Garland told the waiter, before shooing him away. Then he turned his attention to Hunter. "Well, get on with it, son. I don't have all goddamn day."

Garland's florid face was unreadable as Hunter went through the details of Malibu Beach Drive, showing him the photography and outlining all the high-end specs. Garland ordered the baby kale to start and the sea bass for the main, which were both the most expensive options on the lunch menu. He drank the wine quickly. The man reminded Hunter of Charlie Vance, with his love of booze and good food. And that story hadn't exactly had a happy ending.

When Hunter was done talking, Garland said, "I tasked Ms. King with finding me a property in Los Angeles. Malibu isn't Los Angeles. Tell me why I'd want the hassle of an hour's drive after a day of meetings in the city?"

"It's a beautiful drive. Gorgeous scenery and—"

Garland cut him off. "I don't care how good the scenery is, it's going to get old fast if I'm driving the same route every time."

"You'll also have the ocean right on your doorstep," Hunter pointed out. "Like, literally. Step outside and you're on the beach, with the sand between your toes."

"Why do I need the ocean on my doorstep or the sand between my toes? I'm not a goddamn surfer or swimmer or beach volleyball player. Fifty mil to spend all my time hauling my ass back and forth between here and Malibu?" Garland shook his head. "I don't know about that."

"Trust me, when you see the house, you'll be totally blown away." Hunter gestured to his folio. "These photos don't do it justice. And you might not think being so close to the ocean is a big deal, but just wait until you step out onto that private deck—"

"Let me guess, I'll be 'totally blown away,' right?"

Hunter grinned. "Right. It's a great house for both relaxing and entertaining. You'd be in good company too. It's a *very* exclusive neighborhood."

Garland riffled through the photos again as he chewed on his fish. Eventually, he said, "Okay, I'll go take a look at the house. It'd better be worth it."

"Fantastic." Hunter smiled broadly. "How long are you in town for?"

"I leave first thing Friday morning."

Friday was the day of the brokers' open. Hunter was glad Garland would be back in San Francisco by then. The last thing he wanted was Verona accosting the man at the event and trying to win him back as a client.

Hunter said, "Okay, let me see if I can arrange a private viewing for Thursday evening once it's been staged. How does that sound?"

"It sounds fine." Garland drained his wineglass and stood up. "Call my office with the details."

Then he was gone. Hunter asked for the check and tried not to wince when he saw the damage. Unlike Verona, he didn't have Diana's approval to expense the lunch, and he very much doubted she'd be willing to cover the cost when she found out he'd poached a coworker's client.

He didn't care. He'd take the hit. It'd be worth it if Garland came through with an offer.

Hunter leaned back and smiled to himself as he considered a job well done. He finished his own wine. He'd only had the one glass, partly because Garland had guzzled the rest of the ninety-dollar bottle and partly because there was more work to be done today. He consulted his wristwatch and saw it was a quarter to two. He'd better get out of there fast before Verona showed up for her "rescheduled" lunch date.

She was now firmly out of the equation as far as Hunter was concerned.

He'd have to figure out how to deal with Andi and Krystal.

But he already had something in mind for Myles Goldman.

16

VERONA
BEFORE

Verona felt bone tired despite the two cups of strong coffee she'd already had today.

It had been another night of tangled bedsheets and ceiling gazing. Maybe what she needed was some hard liquor instead of caffeine. To crawl into a bottle and drink until she passed out. But that wasn't an option right now. She needed to be on her A game. Don Garland was no pushover.

She'd learned every detail about Malibu Beach Drive and practiced her pitch a dozen times, and she'd made sure she looked the part too. Verona knew Hunter Brooks thought Garland had chosen to work with her because Verona had fluttered her eyelashes at him or flashed a bit of leg. That wasn't true. Garland was an asshole, but he'd never once been inappropriate or stepped over a line. He'd told her he liked her no-bullshit style, whereas he thought Hunter could host his own TED Talk on bullshit. Still, it didn't hurt to look good.

She climbed out of the car and smoothed down her electric-blue skirt suit. As she made her way to the restaurant's entrance, she thought again of yesterday's tour of the house and Marty Stein's odd reaction to Andi's absence. The animated exchange between Stein and David afterward. But there'd been zero recognition on Andi's face at the mention of Stein's name back at the office, so presumably, there was no history between the two of them. And hadn't he mistaken Krystal for Andi in any case?

Verona pushed at the door of the restaurant—and nothing happened. The place was all shut up. She checked her watch. It was five to two. She fished in her purse for her cell phone and called them.

It rang and rang and then a cheerful-sounding woman eventually answered. Verona explained she was outside and unable to access the premises.

"I'm sorry, but we're closed now. We reopen at five for dinner."

"But you can't be closed," Verona said. "I have a lunch reservation for two p.m."

"I'm so sorry, but there must be some kind of mistake. Our lunch hours are eleven thirty to one thirty. Did you make the reservation yourself?"

"I did." Verona tried not to sound as impatient as she felt. "Well, I actually booked a table for noon for a very important business meeting. My client's office then called this morning to say the reservation had been moved to two p.m. due to a mix-up with his calendar. They assured me they'd spoken to the restaurant, who'd confirmed the change of time."

"I really don't know what to say. I guess there was another mix-up at their end?"

A thought occurred to Verona just then. "My original reservation was under the name of King. Noon, like I said. Could you please check if the reservation was marked on your system as a no-show?"

"Of course. One moment, please."

The upbeat hold music didn't match Verona's mood. She was starting to sweat in the afternoon sun, and her shoes were pinching her toes. Where was Garland? Why wasn't he also here trying to get into the restaurant? Something was starting to stink about this whole situation. After a few minutes, the cheerful woman came back on the line.

"The noon reservation was fulfilled. I just spoke to the waiter who attended to the table. He said the patrons were two gentlemen."

"Did he remember what these gentlemen looked like?"

"Are you okay to hold the line again?"

"Sure."

Another minute passed. More annoyingly upbeat music. Then the woman came back on and said, "One was an older man with very black hair. The other was fair and tan and in his late thirties."

Hunter Brooks.

Rage descended so fast Verona could barely speak. Somehow, she managed a shaky "Thank you" before going back to her car. She took some deep gulps of air and waited until her heart rate returned to something like normal. Then she pulled up the number for Don Garland's office. The same woman she'd spoken to yesterday answered.

"Hi there, this is Verona King. I'm calling about—"

"Let me stop you right there, Ms. King," the woman interjected coldly. "I have a message here from Mr. Garland to pass on to you if you called. He wanted me to let you know that he's now working with another agent, and your services are no longer required."

Verona gripped the cell phone tightly. "I think there's been some kind of misunderstanding. If I could just speak to Mr. Garland for one minute and explain?"

"I'm afraid that won't be possible. Mr. Garland is in meetings all afternoon. I'm sure you can appreciate that he's a very busy man. Or maybe you can't. Have a good day, Ms. King."

The line went dead, and Verona felt sick to her stomach. Not only had she just lost her best shot—her *only* real shot—at a huge payday, she'd also delayed her appointment with Dr. Fazli for nothing.

The first opening the medical center had clashed with the lunch date with Don Garland, so she'd had no choice but to wait an extra day for the next available consultation. She could have been sitting here with her fears already eased by her doctor. Instead, she still had nothing but worry on her mind. The comfortable life she and Richard had built for Eli and Lucas would come crashing down if she were too sick to work and the medical bills started to pile up. And it would be even worse if her boys were to lose their mom, just like she'd lost Aunt Mimi.

She put the car into drive and made her way back to the office. Told herself not to make a scene when she got there. She was Verona King, and Verona King was the ultimate professional. Verona King did not lose her shit in the workplace.

Fifteen minutes later, she stepped through the front door of Saint Realty and spotted Hunter reclining in his chair, phone to his ear, laughing like he didn't have a care in the world.

Verona King lost her shit.

She stormed over to him and screamed, "You fucking asshole!"

Hunter raised his eyebrows at her, then spoke into the phone. "No, not you, Betsy. You're not a fucking asshole. Let me call you right back."

He calmly replaced the receiver in the cradle. "Some kind of problem, Verona?"

"Damn straight there is." She got right in his face and pointed a finger at him. "And the problem is you."

Hunter scooted his chair back, putting some distance between them.

The office was suddenly quieter than a library. Andi looked concerned, Myles seemed intrigued, David and Diana wore identical alarmed expressions, and Krystal smiled as though she was enjoying the show.

Diana said, "Verona, please calm down and tell me what's wrong."

Verona jerked a thumb at Hunter. "He sabotaged my lunch date with Don Garland, that's what's wrong. Switched the times so that he could meet with my client instead. I've just been fired."

Diana frowned. "Is this true, Hunter?"

He shrugged. "I have no idea what she's talking about."

"So you weren't just having lunch with Don Garland?" demanded Verona. "With *my* client?"

"It's none of your business who I had lunch with."

Diana said, "Just answer the question, Hunter."

"Yeah, I had lunch with Don Garland. So what?"

Diana said, "Oh, Hunter . . ."

Krystal said, "Oh, wow."

Verona yelled, "You stole my client!"

Hunter said, "Ladies, if I could get a word in edgewise here, then I could explain what happened. I was at the restaurant having lunch by myself, going over some paperwork, when I spotted Don Garland and went over to say hello. It only seemed polite. Turns out, he was real pissed because Verona hadn't turned up for a meeting. By this point, she was almost a half hour late. So I stepped in to try to salvage the situation. Really, you guys should be thanking me. If it wasn't for me, it'd be the whole brokerage getting fired, not just Verona."

"You're a lying piece of shit, Brooks." Verona was yelling again, ignoring Diana's advice to calm down. "I got a call this morning from someone claiming to be from Garland's office saying the lunch reservation had been rescheduled. That's why I wasn't there. You were behind that call."

Hunter shook his head with a fake incredulous smile. "So now you're accusing me of impersonating Garland's secretary to trick you? And how did I do that exactly? With one of those voice distorter things that murderers use on TV shows?"

Krystal snorted a laugh.

"Shut it," Verona snapped at her. Then she said to Hunter, "You got someone to make that call for you. I know you did."

"You do realize how crazy you sound, don't you?" Hunter said. "Look, if you can't handle the play, maybe it's time to get out of the game."

Verona put her hands on her hips and glared at him. "What the hell is that supposed to mean?"

"It means you've been off your game for days. You look like you're not sleeping. Your mind is somewhere else most of the time. You fucked up, got the times wrong. It happens. But don't go making accusations against other people to cover up your own mistakes."

"This isn't high school, Hunter. It's not a game. This is people's lives you're messing with. And it's damn unprofessional too."

"Unprofessional?" Hunter said. "You want to know what's unprofessional? Screaming obscenities like a crazy person when a coworker is on a call discussing an offer on a house. Betsy Bowers was with her client and had the call on speakerphone. Now I have to go try to repair the damage you've likely caused with that potential buyer too, same as I had to do with Don Garland."

A heat spread across Verona's chest that was so intense she could have been standing over a boiling pot on a stove. Burning with anger and humiliation, she turned and headed for the door. She could hear Andi asking if she was okay as she passed by her coworker's desk, but Verona wasn't okay. She had to get out of there.

Verona was not a violent woman. She'd never once lifted a hand to her kids. Had brought them up to be respectful and had taught them that violence was never the answer.

But in that moment, Verona wanted nothing more than to hurt Hunter Brooks and make him pay for what he'd done.

17

ARIBO
AFTER

By the time Aribo and Lombardi were done with Flores, the deputy medical examiner had finished up with the body. The detectives returned to the poolside for an update on her findings.

"Nice outfit, Jimmy," Isabel Delgado said. "I'm really digging the palm trees."

"It's supposed to be my day off."

"It's his wedding anniversary," Lombardi chimed in. "Twenty years."

"Oh dear." Delgado shook her head and tutted. "I guess you're not getting laid tonight, huh?"

"What do you think?"

The trio crouched down next to the body. "What have we got, Doc?" Aribo asked.

"See the foam at the mouth and nostrils?" Delgado said, pointing to the face. "That's hemorrhagic edema fluid. The cause of death was drowning, as opposed to the blows to the head. I'll come to those in a moment. I expect once the decedent is on the table, we'll find fluid in the lungs and water in the stomach. That's the easy part. Establishing whether the death was accident or homicide—not so easy."

She signaled for her assistant to help turn the body over onto its front.

"The decedent suffered head trauma prior to entering the pool, namely two deep lesions to the back of the skull. Those injuries are antemortem."

Delgado pulled aside the deceased's hair with gloved fingers so that the detectives could see the wounds. They were about the size of a quarter and around an inch apart. One appeared to be deeper than the other.

"You think someone struck our vic on the back of the head twice with a blunt instrument?" Aribo asked.

Delgado pursed her lips. "The shape of the wounds would indicate so, yes. But . . ."

"But?"

"I'm ruling nothing in or out until I've performed the autopsy and established whether cardiac arrest or seizure or brain aneurysm or any other naturally occurring event resulted in loss of consciousness that led to a fall causing the head trauma."

"But the head trauma appears to have been caused by blows, rather than a fall?"

"*Appears* to be, yes . . ."

"If you had to lay your cards on the table right now?" Aribo pushed.

Delgado shook her head with a smile. "You know me better than that, Jimmy."

"And you know I'm like a dog with a bone. Come on, Doc. Give us something to work with here."

Delgado sighed. "Okay, my opinion is that some sort of blunt instrument was used to inflict two blows. The victim fell to the ground and bled heavily from the wounds, before falling or being pushed into the water. Death then occurred as a result of drowning."

"What kind of blunt instrument?"

She spread her hands out in a "Who knows?" gesture. "Hammer, base of a bottle, heavy ornament, hefty flashlight . . . Take your pick. But this is all off the record until after the autopsy. No official cause of death until then."

"When is the cut likely to happen?" Aribo asked.

"Tomorrow lunchtime. So much for my weekend neighborhood cookout, huh?"

"You could always go after?" Lombardi suggested.

"I don't know about that, Tim. That's the funny thing about cutting open a body, it really puts you off the sight of cooked meat right after."

"Yeah, I guess it would," he mumbled, embarrassed. Lombardi was divorced and had a crush on the deputy medical examiner that was like something out of a Hallmark movie, but he'd never had the guts to ask her out on a date.

The three of them stood.

Aribo said, "I noticed the vic is wearing a watch and that the face is smashed. Please tell me it's stopped and can give us a time of death?"

Delgado smiled. "Yes, it's stopped. It probably stopped working the moment it hit the concrete and the mechanism was damaged. So the time on the watch is probably indicative of when the victim was struck but not necessarily the exact time of death."

"What time is it showing?"

"Just after 8:40."

"Huh?" Aribo asked, confused. "That can't be right."

"It fits with my own estimation. The condition of the body—in conjunction with the temperature of the water—indicates death occurred sometime between seven p.m. and eleven p.m. That's your window, Detectives."

"What?"

Aribo and Lombardi stared at each other, then looked at the DME.

"Are you saying our vic died last night?" Aribo said. "Not today, during the brokers' open?"

"That's what I'm saying."

Lombardi said, "So a houseful of people have been shooting the shit and throwing expensive bubbly down their necks, and the whole time there was a dead body right outside just a few yards away?"

"That's right," Delgado said.

She indicated to her assistant to pass her some evidence bags.

"We recovered these items from the body." She handed the bags to Aribo. They contained a sodden wallet, a cell phone, and two house keys on a chain. "There's a DL in the wallet that'll provide a preliminary ID, as well as some credit cards, an unidentified key card, and almost two hundred in cash."

"Is the cell phone working?" Aribo asked hopefully.

"Nope. It's as dead as, well, its owner."

"We'll see if the tech guys can work a miracle with it."

Lombardi said, "I guess the expensive watch—even with the smashed face—and the credit cards and the cash mean we can rule out robbery as a motive?"

Aribo nodded. "Looks like it. We'll need to extend the time frame of the neighborhood canvass to cover the last twenty-four hours. I want the footage from those doorbell cameras, and I want to speak to everyone who had access to a key to this house and the beach-gate code. I want to know exactly where each and every one of them was last night. And I want to know if any of them were here drinking champagne with our victim."

18
ANDI
BEFORE

Andi had been planning on using the conference table in the rear of the office for the Zoom call with Walker Young.

She'd be out of earshot of everyone else and figured that would be enough privacy. But after witnessing the showdown between Verona and Hunter, it seemed like the smart move would be to go someplace else for the conversation with the Manhattan billionaire.

David and Diana didn't know about the email from Young's office. Andi had wanted to see how the call would play out first, find out if he wanted to hire her, before bringing them news of a wealthy new client. Now she was glad she'd kept it to herself.

Andi no longer knew whom she could—and could not—trust at Saint Realty.

She packed up her laptop, notepad, and phone, and strolled over to Diana's desk. "I'm going to go grab a late lunch, if that's okay?"

"Sure, no problem." Diana smiled, but it appeared strained after the argument.

Verona hadn't returned to the office, but tension still hung in the air like smoke after a fireworks display.

Andi hitched her backpack onto her shoulder and was about to walk away when David cleared his throat. "Actually, Andi. Could I have a word before you go?"

"Sure. What's up?"

He jerked his head in the direction of the mezzanine. "In my office?"

Andi thought Diana stiffened slightly, although her eyes never moved from the laptop screen.

"Okay."

Andi followed David upstairs. It was the first time she'd been in his office alone with him in six months.

"Close the door," he said.

Andi hesitated and then did as he asked. The others were downstairs. The office had glass walls. Nothing was going to happen in here that shouldn't. Not this time.

David perched on the edge of his desk, like a college professor trying to be relatable to his students. He was aiming for casual, but the way he kept pushing his hair back off his face betrayed his agitation. He gestured to a chair, an invitation for her to sit down.

Andi shook her head. "I don't really have time to get comfortable. What did you want to discuss?"

"I thought you were only going out for lunch? Are you meeting someone?"

"No, but it's after three, and I'm starved, so . . ."

"Okay, got it. You want to eat. I'll get straight to the point. Where are we with Malibu Beach Drive? Any interest so far? Potential offers?"

Andi stared at him. "That's what you wanted to talk to me about? In private? Why not just hold a roundtable meeting with all the agents together to provide progress reports like we usually do?"

David blinked rapidly behind his glasses, another one of his nervous tells. Andi used to find it quite endearing in a Hugh Grant kind of way. Now it just irritated the hell out of her.

He said, "Because this property is a big deal and you're my best agent. I'm really relying on you to find me a buyer."

"The house isn't even on the market yet. Any number of agents could bring you a buyer from any number of brokerages. I get that you'd like it to be someone here at Saint, so you get a cut of the buyer's agent's fee too, but I don't see why it has to be me. If anything, Hunter and Myles are more likely to have clients able to offer that sum of money."

"So you don't want one million dollars?" David snapped. "You're not even going to try? You're just going to let Hunter or Myles swoop on in and take the cash?"

Andi folded her arms across her chest. "That's not what I said at all. I've been speaking to clients, trying to drum up interest. It just feels like you're putting a lot of pressure on me where Malibu Beach Drive is concerned, and I'm not sure why. First, the overreaction to me missing the tour. Now the private pep talks. What's going on?"

David was quiet for a moment. Then he said, "You're talented, Andi. This deal could take you to the next level, that's all. I'm sorry if you feel like I'm putting pressure on you."

Andi nodded curtly. "Okay. Apology accepted. Anything else?"

"Um, yes." He did the hair-pushing and eye-blinking thing again. "I think we need to talk about what happened. You know, six months ago . . ."

Andi moved toward the door. "No way. I am not doing this."

"Andi, wait. Please." He worried at his hair again. "I think Diana has started to notice something is wrong."

"I told you I wouldn't say anything, and I haven't."

Andi opened the door and jogged down the stairs before he could say anything else.

She got into her Beemer and headed west along Sunset, before dropping onto Sweetzer. The sooner she had her own brokerage, the better. As she turned onto Fountain, she thought she caught a glimpse of a gold car behind her. When she looked again, it was gone. Maybe she was losing her mind. Andi headed south onto Fairfax at the Village Synagogue and tried to put David Saint out of her mind.

With a bit of luck, Walker Young would be her ticket out of there.

◆ ◆ ◆

Andi's favorite deli in LA had been an old Yiddish movie theater in a previous life. The marquee was still there, advertising their "Open All Night" hours, although the neon was off until after dark when it would be a beacon for the late-night party crowd.

With its art deco styling and trademark ornate-leaves ceiling, Canter's hadn't changed since moving into the neighborhood in the '50s. Andi found a table for two that would only be accommodating one. The menu, like the decor, was old school, and Andi ordered what she always did: pastrami on rye, washed down with a Dr Pepper from the fountain.

She sat back in the leather seat and savored the sandwich and the chatter of the other customers around her. Whenever she ate here, she could almost fool herself into believing she was back home. By "back home," she meant New York. Home wasn't necessarily where you were born; it was where you felt you most belonged.

When she was done eating, Andi checked her reflection in the napkin dispenser for any trace of slaw or meat stuck between her teeth. She was all good. Once the laptop was fired up, she plugged in her earbuds and waited for the Zoom call to connect. She was uncharacteristically nervous.

Walker Young's face appeared on the screen. He looked exactly how she expected a rich businessman to look: clean shaven, expensive haircut, starched white collar, and silver satin tie. Behind him was a view of Manhattan—the real deal, not one of those fake Zoom backdrops—and Andi's heart hurt with longing. He noticed her own surroundings.

"Canter's, huh?"

Andi grinned. "Best pastrami sandwich outside of New York."

"Can't argue with that. I always pay a visit whenever I'm in town. You spotted any celebs in there yet?"

"Just that British guy from *The Late Late Show*. You?"

"Jim Carrey."

"Okay, you win."

Young laughed, and Andi felt herself start to relax.

He said, "Speaking of being in town, I'm going to have a fair amount of business out there in the coming months, and I can't abide staying in hotels, so I'll be needing some sort of semipermanent base. That's where you come in."

"Are you looking for a rental or to buy?"

"To buy. The plan is to lease it when I'm here in New York."

"I'm sure I'll be able to find what you're looking for. But I'm curious—how did you hear about me?"

"You were recommended by some acquaintances of mine."

"You mind me asking who?"

"Jocelyn Rowe and Patricia Howard." He didn't elaborate any further.

Andi nodded. She'd found an apartment for Rowe in the Upper East Side and a vacation home for Howard in the Hamptons but hadn't been in touch with either woman since relocating to LA, so she was surprised that they'd mentioned her to Young. She guessed word had gotten around about her move.

Walker went through his requirements, while Andi jotted some notes.

He wanted views of the hills or the ocean because he was tired of staring out windows and seeing nothing but buildings. He'd need a minimum of four bedrooms. A private pool was a must as he liked to keep in shape by swimming twenty lengths each day. A theater room would be a bonus because he was a big TV and movie buff. ("Did you know scenes from *Mad Men* were filmed where you're sitting right now?")

Malibu Beach Drive checked almost every box. Almost. The only sticking point was the asking price. Young's budget was $40 million, but she was hoping he'd be willing to go higher for the right property. Thankfully, he was. Andi told him about the beach house, and he seemed to like what she had to say. He seemed to like her too.

Work commitments in New York meant Young would be unable to fly out to LA for showings, so any purchase would have to be sight unseen, which was never ideal, but Walker was trusting Andi's judgment. She told him she'd head out to Malibu the next day and shoot some video on her cell phone to send to him.

They disconnected, and Andi celebrated landing a billionaire client with another Dr Pepper.

When she returned to the office, David and Diana had already left for the day. There was still no sign of Verona. Only Krystal, Hunter, and Myles were at their desks. She knew all three were desperate to know what the confab in David's office had been about. Krystal was the one who asked.

"Your little chat with David earlier seemed kind of intense," she said.

"Not really," Andi said. "Just work stuff."

"Malibu Beach Drive?"

"Among other things."

"He never gets that wound up about my work. Just saying."

Andi ignored her. She was buzzing. The call with Walker Young had gone better than she could have hoped for, and she wasn't going to let anyone ruin her good mood.

As she pulled into her driveway after work, Andi remembered the note Jeremy had left for her.

There's something you should see.

His bike wasn't chained to its usual spot, so Andi didn't think he'd be at home, but she rapped a knuckle on his front door anyway and waited. As expected, there was no answer. Whatever it was, it would have to wait.

She trudged up the staircase, still thinking about Walker Young and having enough cash to be her own boss one day very soon.

Lost in thought, she didn't notice the tiny red light blinking between the leaves of a hanging planter outside her door.

19

MYLES
BEFORE

A sparkling diamond dropped into place with an audible flourish. Then another. Myles held his breath. The world around him disappeared. It was just him and that final, spinning reel. That was all that mattered.

After what felt like forever, it finally juddered to a stop. A third pale blue diamond. A winning set. Triumphant trumpet toots exploded from the laptop, jarringly loud in the enclosed space of the car.

Myles breathed out slowly. Silently fist-pumped the air.

The numbers in his account balance rapidly updated—bolstered by the newly won $1,000—bringing the grand total to $5,000 and more noisy fanfare.

Two boxes flashed up on the screen. CASH OUT and PLAY AGAIN.

Myles had won two games in a row now. Up two grand in the space of a few adrenaline-soaked minutes. A smart player would stop while they were ahead. His finger moved across the trackpad until the cursor hovered over the CASH OUT option.

Then again, when you were on a winning streak, it seemed crazy not to ride the wave. And Lady Luck wasn't just smiling on Myles, she was practically insisting he keep on going. Another rapid swipe of the finger and the cursor now hung seductively above the PLAY AGAIN box. He clicked on it quickly, heart punching in his chest.

A new box appeared, pulsing in garish pink and blue. A single question this time:

STAKE?

A grand seemed like a good amount. Enough to give the pot another nice boost if he won but not a catastrophe if he didn't.

Myles paused a beat, then typed $5,000 and clicked SPIN! before he could change his mind.

The jangly music started up again, and the reels whirred loudly as they began to spin. Most nights, when he lay in bed and closed his eyes, Myles could see the lucky sevens and gold bars and glittering bunches of grapes as though they were tattooed on the underside of his eyelids. He could hear the incessant electronic soundtrack of beeps and chimes and jingles, even though his bedroom was silent.

The first reel stopped. Cherries. Myles drummed his fingers on the laptop. The middle reel ground to a halt too. Cherries again. The sound of his rapid breathing almost drowned out the gaudy tunes.

"Come on. Come on."

The final reel stopped spinning.

A golden bell.

Shit.

Myles hated the cherries. He never won with the goddamn cherries.

There was no triumphant music this time. Only the BETTER LUCK NEXT TIME! message that he was all too familiar with, followed by the soul-sucking sound of the virtual cash draining from his account. A big, fat zero where $5,000 had been just seconds earlier.

A sharp rat-a-tat-tat on the window next to him made him jump. "Holy shit!"

Myles instinctively snapped the lid of the laptop shut.

Hunter Brooks was outside the car. He made a winding motion with his hand, even though the Lambo had electric windows. Myles buzzed the driver's side down. He hadn't noticed the Rolls entering the parking lot.

Hunter leaned on the door. The sleeves of his shirt were rolled to the elbows, his top button was undone, and his tie was pulled askew. His summer tan was coming along nicely, and he smelled good. But whenever Myles started to think of him as attractive, Hunter opened his mouth, and Myles remembered what a prick he was. Like now.

"Ouch," Hunter said. "That looked painful."

"What?"

He nodded at the laptop. "The slots. Bad loss, huh?"

"Not really. Just passing the time until you decided to show up."

"Well, I'm here now, bud." Hunter grinned. "You ready to lose again?"

Myles had been surprised—and more than a little wary—when Hunter had invited him for an after-work game of squash. They'd never played sports together before or worked out together or even socialized with each other unless it was at one of David's dinner parties, which were not Myles's idea of a good time.

"You play, right?" Hunter had asked earlier when they were both in the office.

"A little. I'm more of a tennis guy, truth be told."

"Buddy of mine has let me down, and I have the court already booked and paid for. Six thirty. You up for it?"

Myles wasn't up for it. He and Hunter had never been buddies, and he had no interest in striking up a friendship now. Myles didn't like him, and he sure as hell didn't trust him. Verona was right. Hunter was a jock who'd never grown up, who thought real life was like high school. And Myles certainly hadn't fraternized with letter jacket–wearing assholes like Hunter Brooks in high school.

"I don't have my gym bag with me," he'd lied. Myles worked out every morning. He always had his athletic gear in the trunk of his car.

"You can swing by your place and pick it up. I'll meet you at the sports club. It's the one on Sepulveda."

"I'm not a member. I'm with the Los Angeles Athletic Club."

"Not a problem. I already have a day pass."

Myles went silent. The last thing he wanted was to spend any downtime with the guy, especially after the way he'd treated Verona. Myles couldn't care less about the woman—although the spectacular way in which she'd lost it had been a sight to behold—but he cared even less for Hunter and his dirty tactics.

Then Hunter had said, "You worried I'm going to whup your ass? Is that it? I don't believe it—Myles Goldman is a chickenshit!"

Myles Goldman was not a chickenshit when it came to sports or anything else.

"What time did you say the court was booked for?"

Once they were outfitted in tees, shorts, and gleaming white sneakers, they both went through some warm-up exercises, Myles wondering how long it'd take for Hunter to get to the point of this charade.

He didn't have too long to wait.

"Any interest in the beach house yet?" Hunter asked nonchalantly while pretending to concentrate on stretching his hamstrings and quads.

As though Malibu Beach Drive wasn't the whole reason for him challenging Myles to a game.

Myles sprinted the length of the court and back again before answering. "Why? You want to treat my clients to lunch too?"

Hunter laughed, all white teeth and cold eyes. He did a set of arm circles, followed by leg swings. "Right place, right time, my friend. That's all."

"You really expect me to believe you didn't sabotage Verona's meeting on purpose?" Myles gestured around the four walls of the court. "It's just us boys here. You can tell me."

"Uh-huh. You want to know what I think, Goldman?"

"The suspense is killing me."

They both hit some on-court warm-up rallies.

Hunter said, "It doesn't matter whether I set her up or not. It's completely irrelevant."

"Yeah? I'm not sure Verona would see it that way."

"Real estate is a cutthroat business. You have to be strong—ruthless even—if you want to survive. And you have to be good. Verona isn't good enough—it's as simple as that. If she was halfway decent at her job, she'd have closed on a thirty-million-dollar property for Garland long before Malibu Beach Drive came up."

"So you did set her up," Myles stated.

"Let's spin the racket. If it's 'up,' I'll serve first."

"You didn't answer the question."

"Neither did you."

"What question?"

"Have you had any interest in Malibu Beach Drive?"

Myles spun the racket, and it landed with the Dunlop logo facing up. "You're serving first. Let's go."

They played hard and fast, sneakers squeaking on the wooden floor, both of them striking the ball against the front wall at lightning speed. Hunter was bigger and stronger and had a fifty-pound advantage that was all muscle, but Myles was quicker. Myles took the first point.

Hunter leaned over to catch his breath. "More of a tennis guy, huh? Not too bad at all, Goldman."

"It's like you said, Brooks. You want to win, you have to be ruthless. Ready to have your ass whupped again?"

Forty minutes later, they'd won two games apiece. Both men were panting and sweating. Hunter had barged into Myles twice, knocking him off his feet both times. He was either a clumsy player or a dirty one. Myles could take a wild guess.

"You think you'll convince Garland to write an offer on Malibu?" he asked when they stopped for a water break.

Hunter leaned against the wall, breathing hard. His heather-gray T-shirt was dark with perspiration at the neck and underarms.

"I think so," he said. "What about you? Daddy lined up any buyers yet?"

"Maybe. I guess you'll have to wait and see."

Myles thought of the woman Hunter had met in the park. He still couldn't figure out what was going on there.

He said, "It's always the rich old white guys, isn't it?"

"What is?"

"The ones with the money. The big hitters. The millionaires and billionaires. It's never young women who buy places like Malibu Beach Drive. You ever wonder why that is?"

If the brunette at Echo Park Lake was a client, Hunter wasn't biting.

He shrugged. "Not really. Men are better at business, so they make more money. It's that simple. That's why Andi, Verona, and Krystal will be selling real estate forever, and I'll be retired by the time I'm fifty. I don't know who's going to buy Malibu Beach Drive. Probably an old rich white dude like you said. But I do know who's going to find the buyer—and that's me."

"Don't bet on it."

"I'm not the betting man, Goldman. You are. And that's the difference between you and me. You rely on luck when playing the slots, whereas I never leave anything to chance. That's why I always win. As you're about to find out."

"We'll see about that. Next game's the winner?"

Hunter nodded grimly and pushed himself off the wall. He jumped up and down, sliced the racket through the air a couple of times, and let out a whoop. He had a wild look about him all of a sudden, like he was all keyed up. His eyes shone under the strip lights, and he eyeballed Myles like he was a coyote cornering a puppy.

"Let's do this!" he screamed.

Myles rolled his eyes.

Jock asshole.

Hunter served. Myles hit a smart return volley. They played a fierce and competitive game that seemed to go on forever. Myles's legs began to ache, and his muscles burned, but he told himself to push through it. He would not lose to Hunter Brooks, who was now grunting louder than Sharapova and the Williams sisters combined. Myles smashed another ferocious shot, and Hunter swiped wildly for the ball, missing it completely.

What happened next unfolded faster than the blink of an eye, yet seemed to play out in agonizing slow motion at the same time.

The racket slipped from Hunter's grasp and bounced on the wooden floor. He stumbled—once, twice—arms windmilling as he lost his footing. His hands reached out, grabbing at air before clamping onto Myles's right wrist. The joint bent forward painfully, and Myles dropped his own racket. Then he was on the floor, his wrist caught under his body at an unnatural angle. Hunter landed heavily on top of him. All one hundred and seventy-five pounds of him.

The wind was knocked clean out of Myles. There was a sickening crack that echoed around the small room like gunfire. Then nothing but unbearable, white-hot pain.

20

HUNTER
BEFORE

It was almost ten p.m. when Hunter finally got home.

A couple of lamps were on, but the house was silent. He'd called Melissa earlier to let her know he'd be home later than planned because he was at the emergency room with a coworker who'd had an accident during their squash game. She'd told him she was going to take a sleeping pill and have an early night. He opened the bedroom door a crack now. His wife was snoring softly, her dark hair fanned across the pillow.

Hunter moved quietly down the hallway to the family bathroom, so he wouldn't wake her by using the en suite. He peeled off his shorts and T-shirt, the sweat long since dried, and dumped them in the laundry basket. He got in the shower and washed the stink of the game and the hospital from his skin.

Once he'd dried off, Hunter headed downstairs to the kitchen and opened a bottle of California blush he'd bought in bulk from a local vineyard. He was too wired to sleep. He poured a glass and took it outside to the back garden, along with his laptop.

The day had surrendered to the night some time ago, but it was still warm out. The only sounds were the chirping of crickets hiding in the lush foliage and the tinkle of the waterfall feature. Twinkly outdoor lights that Melissa had wanted installed for parties and barbeques and the glow of the underwater pool lights provided the only illumination.

He got settled into a chair next to the pool and sipped the wine, reflecting on what had been a good, productive day.

The wait at the emergency room to confirm the fracture had been longer than Hunter would have liked, but it was a small price to pay for what had been a perfectly executed plan. He'd gone over it in his head a number of times beforehand but hadn't been sure if he'd be able to pull it off. The timing and positioning had to be just so. What if Myles only suffered a sprain? Or no injury at all? What if he only winded himself?

Hunter wanted to put the guy out of commission awhile, but he didn't want to cause any serious damage—nothing that could result in an assault charge or litigation action. Myles's father owned a law firm and probably had those kinds of lawyers on speed dial. A squash game, a stumble, a broken wrist, and no witnesses to say Myles wasn't entirely responsible seemed like a good plan.

And it had worked like a charm.

Hunter had already done his homework. It wasn't advisable to drive with a cast, and if Myles couldn't drive, he couldn't take potential buyers all the way out to Malibu for showings. Based on the amount of screaming the guy had done in the ambulance, Hunter figured the doctors would be pumping him full of the good drugs for a few days too. Hopefully, Malibu Beach Drive would be the last thing on Myles's mind right now.

Verona King was no longer a threat.

Myles Goldman was out of contention too.

And Melissa had remembered to pick up his dry cleaning.

All in all, it had been a very good day.

There was just one thing putting a damper on his good mood. Andi Hart.

There had been undeniable tension between her and David during their meeting in his office earlier. The glass walls meant their every move could be seen from the desks downstairs, and it didn't take a body-language expert to work out they were having a very heated discussion about more than just property listings.

Then Andi had returned from lunch an hour or so later a changed woman. She could barely keep the grin off her face and had been practically thrumming with excitement. Hunter knew she liked to frequent Canter's Deli, and he also knew from personal experience that their sandwiches were pretty good—but not that good. No one got that excited about a fucking sandwich. Something was up. Either Andi had used lunch as an excuse for a little afternoon delight with a secret lover, or she was meeting someone for a different reason. Someone she didn't want anyone else at Saint to know about.

Hunter opened the laptop. It was time to do some digging where Andi Hart was concerned.

His buddy in Brooklyn had failed to come up with any dirt when he'd asked him to poke around a few years back, but the guy was a Realtor, not Jim Rockford. Dan Spindel's digging wouldn't have amounted to much more than work and social-circle gossip.

Hunter decided to start in the obvious place—social media. He quickly drew a blank with Facebook and Twitter. He didn't even bother trawling through TikTok because Andi was mid to late thirties like himself, and he couldn't imagine her posting lip-syncing or dance-routine videos for the purpose of entertaining complete strangers.

She did have an Instagram account, but it was set to private, and she did not appear to have posted any photos. Maybe she only had an account so she could see other people's feeds. All five of the agents had login access to the Saint Realty account, where they posted about their own listings. Some—like Krystal and Myles—had personal profiles too, where they uploaded photos of their glamorous lifestyles for the whole world to see. Where it was a competition for likes and follows.

But not Andi. Set to private. No photos. No followers.

Hunter dug out the emails from Dan Spindel to remind himself of the information his Brooklyn source had provided at the time. Back then, it hadn't seemed like much. Now, Hunter figured, there might just be some useful nuggets amid all the superfluous fluff.

Spindel had met Andi's boyfriend once at a brokers' open. He'd seemed like a "good dude," and they'd chatted a while because the boyfriend—his name was Jason or Justin, Spindel couldn't remember which—was a senior lecturer in art history at Columbia, and Spindel took a semester as a freshman there before dropping out.

Hunter found the university's website, quickly found Andi Hart's ex on the faculty list, and established that Justin Wittman was a lot more active on social media than his former girlfriend was.

Several photos on his Instagram feed showed Wittman with an attractive redhead who was, presumably, Andi's replacement. Hunter gave the redhead a final appraising glance before scrolling through the rest of the photos. It took a hell of a lot of scrolling—three years' worth of dinners, sports events, and nights out at the theater—to find what he was looking for. A handful of photos of Wittman with Andi Hart.

The most recent—and the last one of them together—was taken in a restaurant. Wittman was holding up a fat, juicy burger. Andi looked happier than Hunter had ever seen her. The caption read: A burger to die for!! #eastvillageeats #burgerheaven #davidscafe

The next was a posed shot in Central Park on a sunny day. Both of them were wearing sunglasses and holding ice creams (If you don't like mint choc chip, we can't be friends! #centralpark #parklife).

Then Wittman and Andi at Madison Square Garden with matching goofy grins (Game night! Hope me and my girl are still talking later! #goknicks).

And finally, another dinner outing, this time with two other couples (Good food! Good friends! #nyceats #friends #goodtimes).

Four photos. That was all.

Hunter got the impression from Spindel that Andi and Wittman had dated for a while, and four photos wasn't much to show for a long-term relationship. He guessed Andi was the one who was camera shy, because Wittman sure as hell wasn't. The guy annoyed Hunter with all his dumb posts and even dumber hashtags.

He stared at the images of Andi again. It felt kind of weird having a glimpse into the life of someone who was so resolutely private—like peeking through the curtains of their bedroom window or something—but Hunter didn't think Wittman's Instagram account was particularly useful.

With social media a bust, he decided to switch his focus to Andi's employment background.

All real estate agents had to be licensed, and all were searchable under the licensees' section of each state's regulatory-body website. He tried California first and was surprised to get a hit for "Andi Hart," as he'd assumed Andi would be short for Andrea. Apparently not.

The entry checked out in terms of place of employment (Saint Realty on Sunset Boulevard) and the date she moved to LA (three years ago). Next, Hunter pulled up the website for the state of New York. That entry was null and void now, which wasn't a surprise as she'd since moved states, but something didn't add up about the dates of when it had been active. The licensure date was just ten years ago. That didn't sound right.

Hunter opened Saint Realty's website and navigated to the page with the agents' bios. Unsurprisingly, Andi Hart's entry was short and sweet, giving nothing away other than the basics. It didn't even carry a photo of her. What it did claim, though, was that she had "more than fifteen years' experience as a Realtor."

So either she had lied on her résumé about her work history when she joined Saint, or she was first licensed as a real estate agent someplace that wasn't New York.

If she'd falsified her résumé, it could be a first step to discrediting her. It wasn't exactly a bombshell revelation, not like, say, hiding a criminal record, but it was a start. Probably not a fireable offense, given David's embarrassing schoolboy crush on her, but if she'd lied about her employment history, what else had she lied about?

Hunter then considered the second option, that Andi was telling the truth about having fifteen years' experience as a Realtor, which meant she'd first been licensed in a different state altogether. If so, where? And why never mention working anywhere other than New York?

He tapped his fingers on the table. Emptied the wineglass. Got up and made his way into the kitchen for a refill. Like a lot of folks' refrigerators, his was covered with magnets and tickets and reminder notes and photos. As he opened the door, Hunter's eyes went to an LA Lakers magnet holding a photograph of him and Melissa in place. He poured the wine, and his mind flashed back to Justin Wittman's "game night" pic.

Once he was back in the garden, Hunter opened Wittman's Instagram account again and found the photo. He reread the caption: Game night! Hope me and my girl are still talking later! #goknicks

What did it mean? The hashtag indicated that Wittman was a New York Knicks fan, so did the caption mean that Andi was a fan of the opposition? Hunter searched that year's schedule on the NBA's website. On that particular date, the New York Knicks had lost to Orlando Magic at Madison Square Garden.

Orlando.

Adrenaline began to fizz in Hunter's veins. He found the Florida Department of Business and Professional Regulation website and plugged in Andi's name. He got a hit. She'd been licensed in the state for five years prior to her move to New York. The address given at the time was a brokerage in Orlando that had long since gone out of business.

Part of Hunter was disappointed because Andi hadn't lied to David and Diana Saint about her real estate credentials when she'd joined the agency. But a bigger part of him was intrigued. He guessed she'd have been around twenty-one when she first gained her license in Florida, so that's where she likely grew up too. So why never mention it? Why all the secrecy?

He opened a Google search page and typed "Andi Hart Realtor Orlando" and got no relevant hits. He deleted "Orlando" and replaced it with "Florida." He scrolled past all the sponsored links and irrelevant garbage. Then he came to a bunch of newspaper stories about a woman by the name of Patti Hart who was a Realtor from Florida. Coincidence? Probably, but he clicked on one of the links anyway.

The headline read: Tragic Death of Popular Local Realtor Ruled an Accident.

The subheading read: Body of Patti Hart was found by distraught daughter at their Kissimmee home.

There was a photo of Patti Hart with her daughter. Patti was attractive in a *Stepford Wives* kind of way. Big blond hair and trim figure and sparkling smile and smart skirt suit. But it was the daughter who caught Hunter's eye. The girl was fifteen or sixteen and wore a surly expression and a Foo Fighters T-shirt. The story was from twenty years ago, meaning the photo was old too. Even so, there was no doubt that the teenager in the photograph was Andi Hart.

Except the newspaper article and picture caption said differently. The "distraught daughter" wasn't called Andi Hart. She had a different name altogether. Hunter felt a prickle of excitement.

He now knew two key facts about his secretive coworker—she hadn't been honest about where she came from, and she had lied about her real name.

Hunter closed the laptop, sat back, and drank the wine. Yes, it had been a good day all right.

21

KRYSTAL
BEFORE

The hotel was perched on the rocky coastline with views of the ocean that would make an artist weep. In the distance, the lights from Malibu Pier reflected off the inky water below, and dusk painted the sky in blazing orange and lilac.

The view was stunning, but Krystal wanted to make sure all eyes in the hotel bar were on her rather than the vista outside the window.

She knew she looked great. When David and Diana had left soon after David's tense discussion with Andi, Krystal had made the most of the opportunity by clocking out earlier than usual herself. She'd then spent two hours teasing her long hair into loose curls, applying makeup, and picking out the perfect dress. She'd opted for a little black number that emphasized her slim figure, offered a glimpse of cleavage, and showed off her shapely legs. Sexy without being trampy.

Micah had still been at a lunch meeting with Al Toledo (according to the GPS tracker, he was actually telling the truth this time), and Krystal had taken great pleasure in leaving a note for him on the kitchen counter.

Work dinner. Potential new client. Don't wait up.

No "Hi, honey" at the beginning or kiss at the end.

Now, as she walked across the room, Krystal knew she'd achieved her aim. All eyes were on her—including the ones that mattered. Nolan Chapman sat at the bar with his back to her and watched in the mirror behind the shelf where the good whiskies were kept as she approached the empty stool next to him.

"Is this seat taken?" she asked.

There were several other vacant stools that she could have chosen but didn't. This wasn't lost on him. Chapman took a casual sip of his martini and turned to her with a smile. He was late fifties, with a tennis player's physique, a surfer's tan, and a strong jawline that brought to mind Robert Redford. He had ice-blue eyes and blond hair that was turning gray. His jeans, shirt, and shoes were subtly expensive, the Breitling watch not so subtle.

"It is now." He indicated the seat next to him. "Please, sit. Can I buy you a drink?"

"Champagne, please."

He caught the bartender's eye and ordered a glass of Henriot for her and another vodka martini for himself. They clinked glasses, and Krystal noticed him noticing her platinum-and-diamond engagement and wedding rings. He wore no ring himself.

"What's your name?" he asked.

"Krystal. Krystal Taylor."

If he recognized it, he didn't show it.

"Nolan." He didn't offer up a surname or a hand to shake. They weren't doing formal. "Are you here on your own, Krystal?"

She held his gaze. "Definitely alone."

He nodded. "In town for business or pleasure?"

"Both."

"Staying long?"

It was time to cut to the chase.

"I'm not a guest at the hotel," Krystal said. "I work for Saint Realty."

A look of surprise briefly crossed Chapman's face before he regained his composure. "Working on anything interesting?" he asked lightly.

"I think you know I am. Malibu Beach Drive."

Chapman smiled, but his eyes were pure ice. "So I guess you being here is no happy accident. How did you know where to find me? How do you even know about me?"

"I'm very resourceful."

"Is that so? How?"

"I know you're based in New York, so you'd likely be staying in a hotel. This is one of the best in Malibu, and it's not too far from the property."

Krystal didn't tell him she'd already tried two other hotel bars this evening before getting lucky on the third attempt. That wouldn't sound resourceful, just desperate.

"How did you know I'd even be in town? My business partner is dealing with Malibu Beach Drive."

"I assumed you'd want to be here now that the house is finished and ready to go on the market. You'd want to oversee the important stuff, like offers and potential buyers. You don't strike me as the type of businessman who'd leave those details to someone else. And I was right. Here you are."

"Here I am," Chapman said. "But why seek me out? Why not just deal with Marty? He's very capable, and he's also the public face of the project and the brokerage's contact."

"I guess I wanted to have a drink with a handsome man."

Chapman grinned. "Ouch. Poor Marty."

They seemed like an odd pairing to Krystal: the rich and charismatic Nolan Chapman and the guy who looked like he shopped at the supermarket for his clothing along with his food. Maybe they were buddies on top of working together. Maybe she'd just insulted his best friend.

"Are you and Mr. Stein friends as well as business partners?" she asked.

"I guess so. We knew each other back in Florida twenty years ago when we both worked in construction. Marty moved to LA soon after the breakup of his marriage, and I eventually relocated to New York. When I got interested in this project a few years ago, I looked Marty up. He was also in the real estate game by then and had all the right contacts out here. He seemed like a good fit."

"I'm sure he's a great guy."

"Do any of your coworkers at Saint know about me?" Chapman asked.

The sudden change of subject caught Krystal off guard. "Um, not that I know of."

"Good. Let's keep it that way."

"Why?"

"I'm a very private man."

"Don't worry." She placed a hand on his knee and left it there. "I'm good at keeping secrets."

He nodded. "Tell me about them."

"Who?"

"The people you work with."

Krystal withdrew her hand. She shrugged, annoyed. "There's not much to tell. There are five of us. All you need to know is that I'm the one who's going to bring you a buyer for Malibu Beach Drive."

He smiled, amused. "What about Andi Hart?"

Krystal bristled. "What about her?"

"David Saint tells me she's his best agent."

"That's his opinion."

"Based on results, apparently. Not opinion."

"Andi is very good at selling properties to the young Hollywood crowd. But she doesn't have clients with the wealth to write an offer on Malibu."

"And you do?"

Krystal smiled mysteriously over the rim of her champagne flute. "Maybe."

It was true. Ryoko Yamada's office had gotten back to Krystal to say the tech magnate wanted to discuss the property further.

"Good to hear. You don't like her, do you? Why is that?"

"Who?"

"Andi Hart."

Krystal sighed. "We work together. Whether I like or dislike her doesn't really matter."

They were getting off track. This wasn't what she'd had in mind.

"She moved here from New York, didn't she?" Chapman pressed. "Do you think she's—?"

Krystal cut him off. "I think we've had enough shoptalk for one night, don't you?"

Chapman's cheek twitched. Maybe anger or amusement. "Okay, what do you want to talk about instead?"

Krystal tried to arch an eyebrow, then remembered her forehead was frozen. She settled for a playful tone instead. "Who said anything about talking?"

Chapman glanced at her rings again. "What does your husband think of you drinking with strange men in hotel bars?"

"He doesn't know. And he's not expecting me home any time soon."

"Another drink, then?"

Krystal's champagne glass was empty. "I thought you'd never ask."

"Same again?"

"Why don't we order a bottle and have them send it to your room?"

Chapman smiled the cold smile again. "I thought you'd never ask."

22

VERONA
BEFORE

Verona spent an hour happily helping her sons with their home-work at the kitchen table and felt the anger from the confrontation with Hunter Brooks drain away.

Eli was ten now and looked more like his daddy with every passing day. He was working on a history project, and Verona found herself wrapped up in his essay about past presidents. It had been her favorite subject at school. She'd always loved learning about the ways in which people did—and did not—learn from the past.

Lucas, two years older than his brother, had a math assignment to complete, which was less fun. Verona was pretty good at simple arithmetic and could work out her commission payments at the click of a finger, but seventh-grade algebra was far trickier. Even so, she gave both boys equal time and attention, while Richard did the washing up.

The three loves of her life all in one room together.

The only things that mattered.

Not Hunter Brooks.

Not Malibu Beach Drive.

Her three boys. That was all.

When they were done, she sent Eli and Lucas upstairs to brush their teeth and change into their pajamas. They were allowed to read for half an hour before bedtime, although Verona knew full well that Lucas would go straight for the Nintendo Switch rather than reach for a book.

Richard came over to where she was sitting, put his hands on her shoulders, and gently massaged them.

Verona closed her eyes. "That feels good, baby."

"You're all bunched up with tension. Everything okay?"

There was concern in his voice, even though he was trying to keep the tone light and conversational.

"Rough day at work, that's all."

Richard had known something was up when he'd arrived home from picking the kids up at their after-school activities to find her napping upstairs in the bedroom. After walking out of the office, she'd gone straight home, shut the blinds, swallowed an Advil, then lay in the darkened room until sheer exhaustion overtook her.

"Want to talk about it?" Richard asked.

"Not worth dwelling on." She reached up and squeezed his hand, then brought it to her mouth and kissed it. "But thank you."

"You know I'm here any time you do want to talk."

"I know, baby."

Verona had been thirty-six when she met Richard King, and he'd turned her whole world upside down.

She'd been fully focused on her career until then, still unsure whether a husband and kids were going to be part of the plan. She'd grown up with the love of Aunt Mimi but didn't know if she was missing the maternal instinct that Verona's mother had not possessed.

Richard had come out to check the electrical on a dump she'd bought cheap back when she was flipping houses as well as selling real estate. He was two years older, divorced, no kids, and had asked her to dinner five minutes after showing up at the house.

Lucas had been a blessing, and Eli had been a surprise. Both of them were adored. Verona was relieved. She was not her mother after all.

Richard said, "Why don't you pour yourself a glass of wine, run a bubble bath, and have a nice long soak in the tub?"

She turned and gave him a knowing look. "Meaning you want to crack open a beer and watch the game."

He grinned, and his eyes crinkled in that way that she loved. "Am I that obvious?"

"I know you too well, Richard King. You go watch your game. I think I'll just take a quick shower and have an early night. Make sure the boys don't stay up too late."

"Just call me the pajama police." He kissed her softly on the lips. "Night, baby."

"Night."

Verona trudged upstairs and, hearing the sounds of a video game, shook her head with a smile. No matter how hard she tried, she was never going to get Lucas interested in reading. Eli was the little bookworm of the family.

She went into the en suite and undressed. Got under the hot stream and relished the pummeling of the water on her tired muscles. Richard was right, she was all bunched up. As she lathered up with shower gel, Verona's hand went to her left breast, and her fingers lingered on the tiny lump there.

It was the size of a pea, but its potential significance was as big as the moon.

Her legs felt weak all of a sudden, like they couldn't carry the weight of her and her burden. She slid down until she was sitting in the stall, knees drawn up to her chest, back against the tiled wall. Then Verona let the tears fall, mixing with the shower water.

Breast cancer had claimed Aunt Mimi at the age of forty-eight. Verona had nursed her through those final months, had witnessed every step of the disease's terrible journey. How it had transformed Aunt Mimi from a lively, vivacious woman to a frail collection of bones who'd seemed to age three decades in the space of eighteen terrible months. She'd been a ghost long before she was dead.

Verona didn't know if there was some kind of cancer gene that ran in her family. Aunt Mimi had no children. She'd taken Verona in as a baby and raised and loved her as her own. Verona had no idea if her mother had gone on to suffer a similar fate as her sister, if she was alive or dead. Probably the latter. Dolores Johnson had chosen booze and pills and men over her infant daughter almost fifty years ago, and Verona guessed addiction would have gotten her long ago if cancer hadn't.

After a while, Verona got up, turned off the shower, and pulled on a bathrobe. Tomorrow she would see Dr. Fazli, and no matter what he had to tell her, Verona would fight like hell. She would not give up on Richard or her boys or herself. She was not her mother.

It was all quiet upstairs now. Verona padded down the hallway and peeked into Lucas's room. The lights were off, and he was snoring like his daddy did after too many beers. She went to Eli's room next. He still slept with a night-light, and the stars-and-moon pattern swirled over the walls and ceiling. He'd fallen asleep with his Harry Potter paperback tucked under his pillow. Verona smiled in the soft light. She went over and slid out the book, then placed it on the shelf above the bed.

She could hear the faint burble of the TV downstairs as she went back to her own bedroom. Her cell phone was on the nightstand, and she picked it up to set the alarm. The screen showed a missed FaceTime call from Myles Goldman. Verona frowned.

It was after ten, and Myles rarely contacted her outside working hours.

She considered ignoring it but knew curiosity would gnaw away at her if she did. Verona returned the call, and Myles's face quickly filled the screen. He looked kind of pale, but maybe it was just the lighting on the phone.

"Hey, Verona. Thanks for getting back to me. I didn't wake you, did I?"

She remembered she was wearing her robe. "No, not at all. I was in the shower."

"How're you doing? You okay?"

"I'm fine."

"We were all worried about you when you left the office earlier and didn't come back. That was a mean stunt Brooks pulled. Guy's a total jerk-off."

Verona wondered if she'd slipped into some sort of parallel universe where Myles Goldman gave a damn about other people and called them up to ask after their well-being.

"You're right, he is a jerk-off. But I shouldn't have reacted the way I did. It was unprofessional. But I'm okay now. Thank you for asking."

"Well, guess what? You weren't the only one to fall victim to one of Brooks's dirty tricks today."

"What do you mean?"

Myles waved his hand across the screen, and she saw he was wearing a cast. "This is what I mean. A broken wrist."

"What happened? Are you saying Hunter did this to you?"

Myles nodded. "An accident during our squash game earlier. I would do air quotes around the word 'accident' with my fingers, but it hurts too much. Accident my ass. The guy is crazy. He should be in jail."

"You need to tell David," Verona said, appalled. "Hunter can't get away with this. Messing up a lunch meeting is one thing, but this? This is assault."

Myles shook his head. "Waste of time. It would be his word against mine. No witnesses. No way of proving it was intentional. But if Brooks thinks this"—he held up the cast again—"is going to stop me from getting my hands on that commission, he's dead wrong."

"You're still going to work?"

"Damn straight I am. I haven't even taken the meds the doctor gave me, even though my wrist hurts like a bitch. I need to be sharp and on my game. Especially now that I know what Brooks is capable of. It's starting to itch like a bitch too."

"Knitting needles," Verona said.

"Huh?"

"To scratch the itch."

Myles rolled his eyes. "Oh, sure, Verona, let me just go find my latest knitting project. I'm sure I left it lying around here someplace. You do realize I'm a twenty-eight-year-old man and not an eighty-year-old grandma, don't you?"

Verona shrugged. "Just trying to help."

"Do you think Postmates or Uber would deliver knitting needles tonight?"

"Probably not."

"Anyway, the reason I called. I need your help. I was wondering if you'd take a look at something for me?"

Verona bit back a smile. This was more like it. Myles looking for a favor. Normal service had resumed. "Sure, what is it?"

"A video of Brooks with a woman. Don't ask me how—or why—I have it. That's not important. It's just that I'm sure I recognize the woman, but I can't place her, and it's been driving me nuts. I thought maybe you might know her?"

"Okay, I'll take a look."

"Great. I'll send it over now. Call me back when you've watched it."

Myles disconnected before she could respond. Her email alert pinged, indicating a new message. She opened it and clicked on the file Myles had sent. The video showed Hunter in a park—Verona guessed Echo Park Lake—sitting on a bench with a dark-haired woman who had a stroller next to her. Verona recognized the brunette immediately.

Carmen Vega.

She was an interior decorator who'd staged a bunch of properties for Verona before taking time off to have a baby. She guessed Carmen's maternity leave was now over, and Hunter wanted to discuss some new projects with her, although a park was a strange place to hold a meeting. Then she realized Hunter was cradling Carmen's son in his arms. Verona watched the video again and then called Myles on FaceTime. He answered immediately, like he'd been waiting with the phone in his hand.

"Did you watch it? Do you know the woman?"

"Sure, I know her. It's Carmen Vega."

Myles's face scrunched up. "Who?"

"Saint uses her to stage homes. She's worked on several of my properties here in the Valley."

His blank expression changed to one of recognition. "Oh yeah, I know who you mean. Dreadful taste in decor. I used her once and then hired my own decorator. I can give you his number by the way if you want me to hook you up. He's way better than the Vega woman."

"I'll keep that in mind."

"It makes no sense, though. Brooks sneaking off to meet the stager at Echo Park Lake."

"Maybe he wants to hire her?" Verona suggested.

"But why's he snuggling up to her kid?"

"Yeah, I did wonder about that too," Verona admitted.

"If you'd told me she was a successful businesswoman or married to a rich dude, I'd have assumed she was a client, and he was trying to get in her good graces by pretending to like kids. I mean, if he's willing to snap someone's wrist for a paycheck, he's going to have no problem cuddling a baby for a few moments. But a *decorator?*"

Myles let the question hang in the air for a few seconds.

"Unless . . ."

"Unless, what?" Verona asked.

"Is Carmen Vega married?"

"Nope. At least she wasn't when I last saw her."

"Boyfriend?"

"I don't think so. The last time we spoke, she was dating a few guys but nothing serious. I remember being surprised when I heard she was pregnant. I assumed she'd met someone and . . ." Verona stopped talking. She stared at Myles. "Wait. You're not thinking . . . ?"

Myles grinned. "That's exactly what I'm thinking, Verona."

"Wow. I guess it's possible."

"If only there was a way to find out the kid's name and date of birth."

Verona was friends with Carmen Vega on Facebook, and she was almost certain the woman had posted about her son after giving birth. One of those black-and-white photos that showed a tiny hand or foot. But Hunter was married. If she and Myles were right, exposing a secret like that could have catastrophic consequences for his marriage.

Which was clearly what Myles had in mind.

Verona didn't want to hurt anybody, but Hunter Brooks hadn't given a damn about her, or her marriage and kids, when he'd sabotaged her best shot at financial security for her family. An image of hospital appointments and medical bills piling up flashed through her mind. Verona felt a spark of anger and knew it hadn't really gone away. It was still smoldering away just below the surface.

She said, "I think I know a way to get hold of that information."

23

ARIBO
AFTER

The Lost Hills station was a single-story red brick building on Agoura Road on the edge of Calabasas and a stone's throw from the 101 freeway.

Aribo and Lombardi arrived to find a woman in the waiting area. She was slim with short platinum hair and wore a white blouse and matching floaty pants. She appeared to be very agitated.

"The lady over there wants to speak to whoever's in charge of the Malibu murder," the officer at the front desk told them. "She says she already gave a statement at the scene, but she insisted on waiting here for a detective."

"Who is she?"

The officer consulted his notes. "Diana Saint. She's the one who organized the party."

They went over to where the woman was sitting, anxiously checking her cell phone.

"Mrs. Saint? I'm Detective Aribo and this is my partner, Detective Lombardi. You wanted to speak to us?"

She sprang out of the chair like a jack-in-the-box. "Are you in charge of the investigation?"

The woman was British and sounded like the actress Emma Thompson.

"Yes, we're investigating the death at Malibu Beach Drive," Aribo said. "Do you have some information for us?"

"Have you identified the body yet?" she asked. "Is it him?"

"Is it who, Mrs. Saint?"

"My husband. David Saint. He left the brokers' open to go for a walk hours ago, and I haven't seen or heard from him since. He's not answering his phone. Is it him? Is he the body in the pool?"

"If you'll excuse us for just one moment please, Mrs. Saint."

The detectives stepped away from the waiting area.

Aribo said, "We know the victim isn't David Saint, but we still need to speak to her. Do you want to take her out back and see what you can find out? She might be able to tell us if any of her staff were planning a trip to Malibu last night. I'll make a start on what we have so far from the door-to-doors."

"Sure thing," Lombardi said. "Once I'm done with her, I'll do some more digging on the vic. I've requested cell phone and bank records."

After they'd gotten a provisional ID from the driver's license in the wallet, they had run the name through the system and discovered the deceased had a bunch of speeding tickets and had also been charged with a couple of misdemeanor offenses. In both cases, the charges were dropped when the complainants withdrew their statements. Aribo guessed they'd been paid off. That's what a shit ton of money did for you.

Lombardi took Diana Saint down the hallway to an interview room, and Aribo headed for the squad room, where he found Alex Garcia. The captain was in his early fifties, with a shaved head to conceal his premature hair loss and designer stubble to compensate for it. His uniform was stretched tight across broad shoulders, and his belt hung heavy on his hips.

Garcia's mouth twitched—same as Lombardi's had—when he saw Aribo.

"Yes, Captain, this is how I dress for an anniversary lunch and no, I won't be getting laid tonight, before you ask."

Garcia broke into a grin. "I wouldn't dream of it, Jimmy."

Aribo filled him in on what was happening with the investigation and then got settled at his cubicle. He listened to a recording of the 911 call.

Dispatcher: 911, what is your emergency?

Hart: I'm at a property at Malibu Beach Drive. There's a body in the pool. Please send help.

Dispatcher: Is the person still in the water? Are you sure they're dead?

Hart: Yes, they're dead. No, wait. I don't know. I think they're dead.

Dispatcher: Have you attempted CPR?

Hart: No.

Dispatcher: Do you want me to talk you through doing CPR?

Hart: No, someone else is trying to get them out of the pool. Please, just send help.

Dispatcher: An ambulance is already on the way.

The next thirty minutes were then spent combing through footage from doorbell cameras that had been collected during the neighborhood canvass since there was no CCTV on the street. Some of the footage showed the victim walking alone along Malibu Beach Drive toward the house, which explained why there were no car keys among the items recovered from the body. But it didn't explain who else had shared the champagne or what had happened to the bottle and the flutes.

Lombardi returned from the interview with Diana Saint carrying two chilled bottles of water and candy bars from the vending machine. He handed a water and a Snickers to Aribo. "Don't say I don't spoil you, Jimmy."

"Have a listen to this and tell me what you think."

Aribo played the 911 call.

When it was finished, Lombardi said, "Interesting. She's telling the operator the person is dead and that she's made no attempt to help them. Then she changes her mind and says she *thinks* they're dead."

"Exactly. She doesn't sound too upset either."

"Shock, maybe? She's asking for help to be sent right away. That's in her favor."

"Not if she already knew the stiff had been in the pool overnight," Aribo countered.

"True. Find anything interesting on the cameras?"

"Our vic walked to the house. Didn't drive."

"Walked from where?"

"I'm still trying to figure that out. I ran the plates for all the cars that were in the area during the time frame Delgado gave us. Three stood out."

"Three?" Lombardi said. "Why'd they stand out?"

"All three cars are owned by agents who work for the listing agency."

"Do any of those cars belong to Hunter Brooks?"

"Yep. A black Rolls-Royce Ghost. I'm telling you, Tim, we're in the wrong line of work. We should be selling houses to rich folks instead of busting our asses trying to catch criminals."

"And miss out on all the fun?" Lombardi flipped through his notepad. "Diana Saint just gave me a list of everyone who had a reason to be at the house last night. By the way, she was at home all evening with her husband. Says they had friends over for dinner.

I'll check with the friends, but it looks like they're both in the clear. Oh, and the husband finally returned her calls. He's in a bar and sounds very drunk. Apparently, he's had a rough day."

"Haven't we all? Tell me about this list."

Lombardi said, "It's very short. Only one person on it—and that's Hunter Brooks. According to Diana Saint, he'd arranged for a Silicon Valley guy by the name of Don Garland to have a private showing. She says Hunter left straight from the office to go pick up the client, and they drove to the house together. She thinks they would have gotten there around seven. She also thinks Garland was planning on staying overnight in a hotel in Malibu."

"Meaning Brooks would have returned to LA alone. No one else had any showings scheduled?"

"Not according to Diana Saint. What other cars showed up on the cameras?"

Aribo said, "A red Porsche 911 registered to Krystal Taylor."

"Who—Diana Saint says—called in sick for the brokers' open."

"And a blue BMW registered to Andi Hart."

"Who made the 911 call and then disappeared."

Aribo said, "And neither one of them had any reason—that we know of—to be at Malibu Beach Drive last night."

24

ANDI
BEFORE

On Thursday morning, Andi made the trip to Malibu without a flat tire or AAA guy in sight.

She drove with the windows down, the radio cranked up, the wind in her hair, and the company of a sea breeze that she could taste as well as smell. On days like this, she didn't even miss New York, with its grit and grime and freezing cold winters and trying not to get mugged on the subway.

Andi turned onto Malibu Beach Drive. It was a dusty, narrow two-lane road overlooked by imposing bluffs topped with dry brush, and not at all what she'd been expecting.

A silver Honda Civic that she didn't recognize was parked outside the house. David hadn't mentioned any other scheduled visits this morning. Andi wondered if Marty Stein had decided to drop by unexpectedly to give her the grand tour that she'd missed out on a couple of days ago. She hoped not. Andi would prefer to film her videos for Walker Young without an audience present.

From the street, the frontage was almost modest considering the hefty price tag. Only one level was visible, along with an unremarkable front entrance and access to the triple-bay garage. It didn't look too different from a million other white box dwellings in Southern California, but Andi knew the beachside view would be a different story altogether. That's where the wow factor would be.

She went to unlock the door and saw that it was already unlocked. The alarm panel inside had been disabled. The large open-plan living area was spacious and impressive—and she was vaguely aware that it had been staged—but Andi barely noticed her surroundings. She was too preoccupied with the idea of someone else being in the house to stop and admire the decor.

"Hello?" she called out. "Is there anyone here?"

There was no response. Total silence other than the soft whirr of the AC and the crashing of waves outside pocket doors that were wide open. Andi ventured farther into the vast space. The living, dining, and family rooms were all unoccupied. So was the kitchen. There was no one outside on the balcony either. The three closed doors, she knew from studying the floor plan, provided access to a mud room, powder room, and theater room.

"Hello?" she called again.

"Hi there."

Andi gasped. Her heart thundered. If she were able to speak, the word *fuck* would have been the one she'd have reached for. She spun around, her hand clutching her chest. It took a second for her to recognize the brunette who was standing at the bottom of the stairs wearing an apologetic smile.

Carmen Vega.

"Carmen," she breathed. "It's you."

"Shit. I'm so sorry, Andi. I didn't mean to startle you." Carmen gestured to the offending items on her feet. "I'm a sneaker gal these days. Super comfortable, great for running around after a kid, and—unfortunately for you—also perfect for creeping around big houses."

154

Even though she was wearing sneakers, skinny jeans, and a plain white tee, Carmen was still a total knockout.

Andi said, "It's okay, I no longer feel like I'm about to have a heart attack. I wasn't expecting anyone to be here, is all. Then I saw the car outside and the door was unlocked. When no one answered, I guess I was a little freaked out."

"I was just taking care of some finishing touches to the staging. The photographer's shoot was supposed to be this afternoon, but he's double booked, so it's taking place on Saturday instead. Not ideal as it's now going to be after the brokers' open, so hopefully no one spills red wine everywhere before the photos! I'm done now, so the place is all yours."

"It looks fabulous, you've done a really great job. I didn't realize you were back at work already."

Andi remembered Carmen had taken some time off last year to have a baby.

"I started taking on some projects around a month or so ago," Carmen said. "I was going stir crazy at home all day, just me and the baby, so I'm loving being back. And I totally lucked out when David asked me to work on this place. Fifty million dollars, huh? Can you imagine living in a place like this?"

"Yeah, in my wildest dreams. The same dreams where I get to marry Jake Gyllenhaal. How's the baby?"

Carmen's beautiful face lit up. "Oh, he's great. A little poop machine but a real sweetheart. He's sleeping through the night now, which is a total game changer. Here, do you want to have a look?"

She pulled her phone from the back pocket of her jeans and handed it to Andi. On the screen was a photo of a little boy around six or seven months old. Andi wasn't big on babies, but she had to admit this one was gorgeous. Then again, he'd hit the jackpot with the genes he'd inherited from his mother.

"He's a real cutie," Andi said, handing the phone back. "What's his name?"

"Scout. Scout Vega."

Andi figured the daddy wasn't on the scene, then.

Carmen said, "Do you have a showing here this morning?"

Andi nodded. "Kind of. A virtual one. My client is in New York, so I said I'd film some video to send to him. It's a real bonus having the place staged now, it really does make all the difference."

"I hope your client loves the house and writes a big, fat, juicy check. I'll let you get on with your filming. You okay to lock up and set the alarm when you leave?"

"Sure, no problem."

"Fantastic. I'd better go drop off my set of keys with the developer now that my work here is done."

"Marty Stein, right?"

Carmen frowned. She opened her mouth to say something, then her phone rang in her hand. "I have to take this. I'll catch you later, Andi. It was good seeing you."

Andi heard the front door close, followed by the sound of an engine starting up outside. She found her own phone in her purse and set it to record.

As she walked through the main level, filming and providing a narration about the fixtures and finishes and dimensions and so on, Andi could fully appreciate just how magnificent the house was. It was huge, for a start, and the views were incredible. You didn't even have to know that the kitchen island was quartzite or the cabinetry was walnut to understand that everything was top tier.

Carmen Vega had opted for a largely muted palette of cream, mauve, and sage, and a sleek modern aesthetic throughout. Andi had, for the most part, been telling the truth when she'd told Carmen she'd done a great job staging the house. It was only now that she was starting to notice some of the "finishing touches" that weren't to her own personal taste. Odd wall sculptures and garish cushions and throws that weren't really needed, in Andi's opinion.

Upstairs was styled similarly to the main level. Soft pastel tones in the bedrooms, glass and chrome and wood in the home office, and marble in the bathrooms, which had all been accessorized with fresh orchids and Aesop bath products. The primary en suite had a freestanding tub tucked into a corner wall of glass so you could gaze out at the Pacific while you scrubbed yourself clean.

Andi paused the recording and sat on a sumptuously quilted footstool at the end of the bed in the primary suite. The floor-to-ceiling pocket doors and windows framed the kind of vista that would make waking up in this room a joy every single morning. Foamy waves rolled over the rocks below, and farther along the beach, she could see a half dozen surfers riding the waves.

Once finished on the upper level, she ascended again to the rooftop terrace and shot another video of the firepit and Jacuzzi and permanent planters filled with wildflowers in lush greens and purples.

The sun beat down on her, hot and fierce. Again, it was all about the views up here. This time, 360 degrees' worth, taking in the ocean, bluffs, and other multimillion-dollar homes nestled along the coastline. She gazed over the perimeter fencing onto Malibu Beach Drive, and for a weird moment expected to see a boxy gold car down below. But the street was empty save for her old Beemer.

Andi made her way back downstairs to the main level. There was one place she hadn't yet seen, and she could put it off no longer.

She went out onto the balcony and turned a corner to where the pool deck was located.

Her heart began to beat fast again, like it had when Carmen Vega startled her. Andi closed her eyes. She focused on her breathing, and the calming rhythm of the waves, and the smell of brine in the air. The images came anyway, stark and bright and vivid, like the video she'd just filmed for Walker Young.

The whoomph of the ceiling fan. The broken vase. The lamp knocked to the floor. The empty vodka bottle and the overturned kitchen chair.

The back door.

Andi always awoke before she reached that door, but she knew exactly what horrors lay beyond it. The dreams were more than just dreams. They were memories with sharp teeth and claws that bit into her flesh and clung and refused to let go no matter how hard she tried to move on from what happened all those years ago.

She opened her eyes.

Told herself it was just a pool.

Andi held up her phone and started filming again: the custom tiles, the sun-dappled aqua water, the two outdoor chaises perfectly positioned on either side of a decorative table with an ugly gold ornament on top, the gate providing direct access to the beach.

She ended the recording and emailed the video files to Young's personal assistant, Gretchen Davis. It was almost noon, the sun hotter than a tanning booth, the temperature well into the nineties. But Andi felt a coldness that chilled her all the way to her bones.

She turned away from the pool and walked quickly back into the house.

25

MYLES
BEFORE

Myles took great pleasure in witnessing Hunter Brooks's surprise at his turning up at Saint Realty at exactly nine a.m. just like every other morning.

True, he'd had to suffer the indignity of needing Jack's help to get into his slim-fit jeans and Prada shirt and Italian leather loafers—and the ugly cast didn't exactly have the same aesthetic appeal as the diamond Rolex on his other wrist—but he'd made it to the office, and that was all that mattered.

Smooth-talking Hunter Brooks actually seemed at a loss for words for once. "Myles . . . ," he stammered. "I didn't . . . are you . . . ?"

"Surprised to see me?"

Hunter masked the surprise with a fake smile. "How are you, buddy? Sorry I didn't stay at the hospital until you were done. Melissa needed me at home, and . . . Well, anyway, it's good to see you up and about."

Myles settled at his own desk. "I broke my wrist, I didn't have open-heart surgery." He smiled to show his retort was good natured. It wasn't.

A nurse had informed him that "his friend" had hung around the ER's waiting room until he'd learned that Myles had broken his wrist. Then he'd vanished. It seemed like his "friend" had only waited around long enough for confirmation of the damage he'd done.

Hunter craned his neck now—so far Myles thought he might break it, with any luck—trying to see out the window.

"You didn't drive, did you?" he asked. "I don't think you're supposed to get behind the wheel wearing a cast. Wouldn't want you wrapping that beautiful Lambo around a lamppost."

Oh, you'd love that, wouldn't you?

Myles swiveled in his chair and pointed with the cast.

"See that Bentley out there? My father owns that car. And behind the wheel is George, who's my father's driver. George has thirty years of experience, has never had a ticket, and, more importantly, isn't wearing a cast. So you really don't have to worry about me, Hunter. I'm in very safe hands until this thing comes off. Which means I won't have any problem hopping onto the PCH to show Malibu whenever I want to. And I expect old George is going to be pretty busy, seeing as I have three interested parties lined up already."

If Myles could have taken a photo of Hunter's face at that exact moment, he would have framed it and hung it on his wall.

"That's great," Hunter said insincerely. "Gene Goldman comes through once again."

"He certainly does."

Diana said, "This is fabulous news, Myles. We really appreciate you making the effort to even be here after such a horrific injury. Don't we, David?"

David grunted from behind his laptop screen. He looked about as happy as Hunter did. Krystal appeared tired and not as well put together as she usually was, but she also seemed suspiciously happy despite Myles's announcement. No, not happy. Smug. Andi and Verona weren't at their desks.

"No Andi or Verona today?" he asked.

He thought Verona would have enjoyed seeing Hunter's jaw hit the floor at Myles's unexpected appearance.

Diana said, "Andi is having a look around Malibu Beach Drive this morning. Verona has a personal appointment. Both will be in the office later."

"Good, good," Myles murmured, booting up his laptop. It was only for show. He couldn't operate the trackpad properly or type with his left hand. He would make some calls to his father's golf buddies later when everyone else was out of earshot.

Hunter went back to his own work, looking like a kid who'd dropped his ice cream.

Myles had already landed one sucker punch, and he was hoping the next would be the knockout blow. Verona had texted last night with the information Myles wanted about Carmen Vega's son. Name: Scout B. Vega. DOB: November 5, last year.

Myles had a good idea what the *B* stood for.

Myles packed up his things around lunchtime and clocked out for the day. He made a vague reference to some client meetings to explain leaving early, but no one questioned him because he'd already gone above and beyond by even showing up with a broken wrist.

George drove him to Blue Jay Way, and Myles told the old driver to head back to his father's home in Beverly Hills. He would call if he needed him. But Myles would not be requiring George's services for where he had to go later. His father could never know about what he was going to do, and even though he had known the man his whole life, Myles knew George's loyalty was to Gene Goldman first and foremost.

Once he'd retrieved the mail he'd hidden from Jack in the sideboard drawer, he placed those envelopes on the dining table along with all the others stamped "Past Due." A familiar sickness settled in his gut. Every single day, the nausea and guilt did battle with the compulsion. And every single day, the nausea and guilt lost out. Only when he relented, when he promised himself "just one game," could Myles breathe easy again.

He had never considered himself to be someone with an addictive personality or impulse-control issues. If anything, he took pride in always being in control, just like his father.

Myles didn't smoke or vape (both disgusting and unsociable), he'd never been interested in drugs (not even pot because that was for deadbeats and hippies), and he didn't feel the need to watch an unhealthy amount of porn (and when he did indulge, it was never at an inappropriate time or place). Similarly, he enjoyed a glass of fine wine or an expertly mixed cocktail, but he had never once been blackout drunk. Falling out of bars and clubs with puke on his designer sweaters was not his style.

It had been on a weekend trip to Vegas two years ago that Myles had discovered his weakness, the thing that did get his blood pumping, that gave him the kind of rush booze and pills never had.

Money.

He'd made the long drive to Nevada to hook up with a guy he'd spent three weeks chatting to on a dating app only to decide half an hour into their date that there was zero chemistry between them. Myles had made his excuses and left and then did what everyone else did when they were in town—hit the casinos.

He had never known anything other than great wealth throughout his life. Gene Goldman owned his own law firm, and Myles's mother had come from old money. He had grown up in a large Mediterranean villa on Alto Cedro, drove a Porsche when he was sixteen, attended Beverly Hills High School, and had an allowance as a college student that was more than most men made after working fifty hours a week.

But sitting in that poker room, his fate resting on the turn of a card, the chips stacking up on the felt next to him, it was like nothing he'd ever experienced before. He ended the night $500 up—paper-route money to someone like Myles—but when he'd cashed in those chips, the feeling was better than the best sex he'd ever had.

What started in a poker room in Las Vegas quickly moved online. He would play for an hour or two before bed, snatch a few games between calls at the office, even have a couple of spins on the roulette wheel in the restroom while out for dinner with his parents.

Blackjack, roulette, slots, keno—jeez, he'd even resorted to bingo for a fix—it didn't matter. Myles would play them all.

He removed the statements from the envelopes and spread them all out on the table. They filled the entire space. Swallowing down the bile in his throat, he went through each one and made a note of the money he owed.

A grand total of $252,065.

And $22,654 due immediately or already overdue.

He'd all but emptied his checking account, maxed out his credit cards, taken out every loan possible with the legit companies before they started rejecting him. At least he'd never gone down the route of loan sharks. Myles valued his looks and limbs too much.

His trust fund, after buying the house and car, was long gone. Selling Blue Jay Way or the Lamborghini were options he'd already considered and dismissed. What was he going to do? Rent a condo in the Valley next door to Verona? Drive an old banger like Andi Hart and pay it off in monthly installments? His credibility would be shot. He would never sell a house in Beverly Hills or Bel Air again.

In this town, it was all about appearances.

And what would his father say? Myles would rather die than admit he was broke—or the reason he was in so much trouble.

Myles's gaze fell on his good wrist and the platinum Rolex that encircled it. The diamonds sparkled in the sun streaming through the kitchen window. It had been a gift from his parents for his twenty-first birthday. He wore it every day and felt naked without it. But he assured himself the absence of its comforting weight would only be temporary.

Myles opened a Google search page on his cell phone and painstakingly typed with his left hand the words "Pawn Shops Los Angeles Rolex." He took a screenshot of the results.

The watch had been purchased and insured by his father, and Myles was concerned that if he went to a reputable jeweler on Rodeo Drive, they would consult Gene Goldman before sanctioning any sale. In any case, Myles didn't want to sell; he just needed a quick cash fix. A place that didn't ask too many questions. A brief reprieve from the demand letters until Malibu Beach Drive solved all his problems.

Next, Myles searched his contacts and found an entry for a private eye down in Venice that his father used occasionally to carry out background checks on potential employees.

"MAC Investigations."

"Matt Connor?"

"Speaking."

"It's Myles Goldman here. Gene's son."

"Hey, how are you doing, Myles?"

Apart from being a quarter of a million dollars in debt and suffering agonizing pain from a broken wrist deliberately inflicted by a coworker?

"I'm good."

"And the old man?"

"He'll outlive us all. Listen, do you think you'd be able to do a very quick and discreet job for me?"

"Depends what it is."

Myles told him.

Connor blew out air on the other end of the line. "I don't know, Myles. It sounds kind of hinky. Are you thinking this kid could be yours?"

"Is that a serious question?"

"Even more hinky, then."

Myles said, "But you do have the contacts to check it out?"

A pause.

"Yeah, I do."

"And you do still want my father to keep sending paychecks your way?"

Another pause. Another heavy sigh.

"Okay," Connor said. "When do you need it by?"

"Yesterday. Oh, and Connor?"

"Uh-huh?"

"Send the invoice to my father. He's paying."

26

ANDI
BEFORE

Jeremy Rundle's bike was chained to the staircase when Andi got home. She knocked on his door.

There was movement inside and what sounded like a lot of locks being undone before the door opened a crack and Jeremy peered out. His eyes bugged out when he saw her. The crack got bigger, and she saw that he was kind of rumpled looking, with messy hair and a T-shirt that had never met an iron.

"Andi?" The word ended on a high note, like he was asking a question. Or maybe he was just really surprised to find her on his doorstep.

"Hi, Jeremy," she said. "I got your note. Sorry I missed you."

He appeared confused for a moment, and she wondered if he'd been napping and wasn't fully awake yet. Then a light bulb went on and he said, "Oh yeah, the note. That's right, I have something important to show you."

He stared at her, and she thought maybe he was high instead of sleepy.

"So . . . what did you want to show me?"

He opened the door all the way. "It's on my cell phone. Do you want to come inside?"

Andi really didn't want to go inside. He noticed her reluctance and did a weird laugh. "Heh heh, it's okay. I'm not a serial killer. Promise."

Like he would tell her if he was.

She followed him inside. It was the first time she'd been in his apartment. The layout was identical to her own, but that's where the similarities ended. Hers was light and airy, with a mix of IKEA furniture and thrift-store finds. His was downright gloomy. Dark painted walls were accessorized with framed Marvel movie prints. A guitar was propped in a corner that she'd never heard him play (she did hear him farting and snoring, though). A futon bed was folded up into the seat position, which she thought was a strange choice of sofa as she'd never known him to have any friends over, let alone overnight guests.

The place smelled of old socks, but she wasn't getting the sweet telltale aroma of weed, and there were no bongs or joints smoldering in ashtrays anywhere, so she figured he wasn't high after all. Just naturally dopey.

"Take a seat," he said.

The only place to sit was the futon. "It's okay, I'll stand."

"Can I get you a drink? Glass of water?"

"I'm good."

Jeremy stared at her again, and Andi wondered if it was the first time he'd had a woman in his apartment. Then she wondered if anyone would hear her if she screamed and decided probably not, seeing as she was the only neighbor nearby. He blinked and picked up his cell phone from a coffee table.

"I want to show you a video," he said.

"I hope it's not R-rated," she quipped, trying to bring his intensity down a notch.

It didn't work.

Jeremy blushed all the way to the tips of his ears. "It's not that kind of video."

"Relax, Jeremy. I was yanking your chain."

He nodded. His hands were shaking as he searched through the phone for whatever video he wanted her to see. "It's footage from one of the two cameras outside. Specifically, the one outside your front door."

Now it was Andi's eyes that bugged out. "What? Whoa. Back up a second, pal. What cameras? I don't know anything about any cameras."

He looked up from his phone. "The cameras I installed. One outside my front door. The other outside yours. It's concealed behind the hanging planter. Not easy to spot."

"No kidding, seeing as I had no idea it was there."

He smiled. "Yeah, I did a pretty good job, if I do say so myself."

"I think you're missing the point here, Jeremy." Andi pointed to her face. "This here is the face of a very pissed woman."

His smile disappeared. "Oh."

"What the hell were you thinking? A camera outside my door? Do you realize how *creepy* that is? Is it even legal?"

"Uh, I didn't think to check the legality. A situation arose, and I decided to act. I wasn't spying on you."

"A situation? What situation?"

Jeremy said, "You know I work from home, right? With computers. The bedroom has been converted into a home office, and the desk is positioned in front of the window, which looks out onto the front of the property."

"I know, I have the same apartment, remember?"

"Right. Anyway, I notice what goes on in the neighborhood. For example, the elderly gentleman with the toupee goes out for a power walk at ten every morning. The, ah, attractive blond lady who lives in the pink building walks her dog—an aggressive Chihuahua—twice a day. And Mr. Herbert across the street tends his flowerboxes every Monday without fail.

"I also know all the cars that belong here, such as your 2018 BMW coupe. So I notice the ones that don't belong. When I kept seeing the same unfamiliar car—that didn't appear to be a new purchase by any of the neighbors—I got concerned. I was worried about vandalism or, even worse, theft. My bike is worth a lot of money, you know."

"So you installed the cameras?" Andi said, still not pleased.

"That's right. That way, if anything suspect did happen, I would have a visual recording of it. The camera outside your door is really to cover the area where my bike is chained, although I guess if someone grabbed you on your doorstep, it would also be useful evidence for the police."

"Gee, that makes me feel a whole lot better."

Jeremy nodded, missing the sarcasm completely. "My bike is a Pinarello," he said.

The name meant nothing to Andi. It just looked like an orange-and-black bike to her.

"Um, okay."

He seemed disappointed that she wasn't more impressed. "A lot of the pro cycling teams ride them. Mine cost more than three grand, and it took me six months to save for it."

"Three grand? For a bike? Really?"

"Yes, really. And the last thing I want is for it to end up in the trunk of that gold car and then show up on Craigslist a week later."

Andi's blood turned to ice. "What gold car?"

"The one I just told you about. The unfamiliar car I keep seeing driving past the apartment."

"Do you have any video of this gold car?"

"I sure do." Jeremy got busy on the phone again. "This clip is from Camera 1—that's the one outside my door, which has a better view of the street. Here, look."

Andi watched the clip. The date and time stamp showed 9:10 p.m., exactly a week ago. The car was a big boxy vintage thing with a long hood and trunk and a hard top. Sepia-tinted windows. Exactly like the one she'd seen outside her office. That had been creepy enough. If this was the same car, it wasn't just creepy, it was stalking.

Jeremy said, "I did some digging around online and found out that it's a Plymouth Road Runner. They were produced in the US between 1968 and 1980, and my guess is that this one is first generation, so '68 to '70. Plymouth licensed the name from the Warner Bros. cartoons, and if you look real close, you can just about make out the cartoon character on the side of the car. However, I can't confirm if this guy still has the distinctive 'beep-beep' horn because, so far, I haven't heard him sound the horn."

Andi handed the phone back. She said, "The license plate is visible in the clip."

"I know. I have a note of it in my street journal."

"Street journal?"

"It's where I keep a record of all the comings and goings in the neighborhood."

Andi didn't know whether to be alarmed or comforted.

"So now we can find out who the driver is, right? Maybe it'll help us figure out why he's been cruising around the neighborhood. And I'm going to go out on a limb here, Jeremy, and say it's not because he wants to steal your bike."

"It's a very covetable bike." Jeremy frowned. "But I don't see how we can find out who the driver is when we don't have access to DMV records."

"Can't you just hack into their system?"

Jeremy's eyebrows jumped all the way to his receding hairline. "How, exactly, do you expect me to do that?"

"You said your job has something to do with computers."

"It does. That doesn't mean I'm a hacker."

"You're very secretive about it. Like it's top-secret work. Like hacking."

Jeremy looked embarrassed. "I maintain and update databases for local libraries. I'm not a hacker."

"Why all the secrecy?"

"It's not a very sexy job."

"No, it isn't," Andi agreed. "So we have no way of finding out who this guy is who's been stalking the neighborhood?"

Jeremy shrugged. "I guess not. But that's not what I wanted to show you." He tapped and swiped at the phone again. "This is what I wanted to show you. It's from Camera 2—which is the one positioned outside your door. I didn't watch the recording until later, otherwise I would have told you about it when we bumped into each other Tuesday morning. It's from the night before."

Andi took the phone from him. The time stamp was just before midnight. Framed in the shot was Jeremy's apparently very expensive and covetable bike next to the staircase and Andi's not-so-expensive and covetable Beemer.

She watched as a figure dressed in dark clothing with a hood pulled all the way up approached her car. The night vision gave the scene a weird alien glow. Goose bumps popped up on her arms and the flesh on her scalp prickled. The figure bent down in front of the tire and produced something from a pocket—Andi couldn't tell if it was a screwdriver or a knife or some other tool—and pushed it into the tire sidewall. The person got up and glanced around, and that's when Andi saw their face.

She tapped the screen to freeze the image. Tried to take in what she was seeing.

She sank onto the futon and must have looked shocked or dazed or something because Jeremy said, "Do you recognize the person who trashed your tire?"

Andi looked up at him. "Yes, I do. I know exactly who it is."

27

ARIBO
AFTER

Aribo turned up the volume on the TV in the squad room when he spotted the beachfront property on the news.

"Shit," he said.

Lombardi came over to join him. "What's up, Jimmy?"

"That's what's up." Aribo pointed with the remote. "Goddamn reporters."

The news channel was showing an aerial shot of the house. The chyron running along the bottom of the screen read: *"Murder" at $50 million Malibu mansion.* The other residents of Malibu Beach Drive were going to be absolutely thrilled. The shots were live, and thankfully, the body had already been removed from the scene. The media didn't have the victim's name either, which was also a blessing because Aribo and Lombardi had not yet made the death notification to the next of kin.

The picture changed to Mitch O'Malley—chief reporter and chief pain in the ass—outside the house. He was telling viewers how an as yet unidentified male had been found dead in the pool during a brokers' open. Sources close to the investigation had supposedly told O'Malley that the death was being treated as a homicide.

Lombardi said, "I'm not sure you'd even class the house as a mansion, but I guess they like their alliteration. With so many people at the party, it was always going to be impossible to keep a lid on this one."

"It just pisses me off that they're already telling the world it's a homicide. 'Sources close to the investigation' my ass. *We* don't even know for sure that it's a homicide yet. Not until Delgado does the cut."

"Yeah but 'possible accidental death' isn't as sexy. It's all about the viewing figures with these people. Anyway, dinner's here."

Aribo muted the TV, and they both returned to their desks. Lombardi had ordered a couple of pizzas from Domino's.

"Italian twice in one day for you," he said. "Told you I was spoiling you."

"It's not exactly Toscanova, but it'll do."

Denise had texted to let Aribo know that her best friend, Susan, would be using the spare Howard Jones ticket, and they would be making a night of it with a few drinks after. Aribo was glad. Susan was great fun and loved to dance and sing along loudly with her favorite songs. Unfortunately, she was also completely tone deaf. He'd texted Denise back: Thoughts and prayers with whoever's next to Susan at the gig.

The detectives ate and swapped notes on the progress they'd each made so far.

Lombardi said, "The developer, Marty Stein, was having dinner in Woodland Hills last night. I checked with the restaurant. He's a regular there and was paying the check around the same time the vic's watch stopped."

Aribo said, "I tracked down the two women who left the brokers' open early. One of them was Carmen Vega, who's an interior decorator and who staged the property. She was at home all last night with her baby son and her mom. The mom stayed overnight because she was babysitting this weekend while Vega was at the party. The other woman was Melissa Brooks, wife of Hunter. She had a sleepover at her folks' place in Bel Air last night. They confirmed she was nowhere near Malibu until the party this afternoon. Hunter Brooks was the guy who was booted by the Rock look-alike."

"If the wife wasn't at home last night, does that mean Hunter Brooks doesn't have an alibi for the rest of the evening after leaving Don Garland?"

Aribo swallowed a mouthful of pizza, then said, "I don't know. I haven't been able to reach him. His phone is off, and I've left a bunch of voice messages. The wife doesn't know where he is."

"You speak to Garland yet?"

"Yep. He confirmed what Diana Saint told us. He hitched a ride out to Malibu with Brooks in the Rolls. They got there around seven, had a look around for half an hour or so, then left. He claims they didn't crack open a bottle of champagne, so they weren't the ones quaffing the Cristal. Brooks dropped Garland off at a nearby hotel. Garland said a guy had appeared as they were leaving the house and spoke briefly with Brooks while he was locking up. Garland didn't know who the guy was, only that he wasn't another potential buyer."

"Description?"

Aribo told him.

"You think Brooks is our perp? You think he's in the wind?"

Aribo took another bite and chewed while he thought about Lombardi's questions. Other than the victim, Brooks and Garland were the only two people they knew for sure had been inside the death house last night. The venture capitalist had spent the rest of the night in his hotel's restaurant and bar. There was still a big question mark over Brooks's movements.

"Maybe," he said. "He could have returned to the house after leaving Garland at the hotel. We don't have another sighting of the Rolls on Malibu Beach Drive later on, but that doesn't mean he didn't approach on foot and dodge the doorbell cameras."

Lombardi finished the last of his pizza, wiped his hands, and balled the napkin. He reached for his notepad. "I spoke to Krystal Taylor's husband, Micah, who said she was in bed and too sick to talk on the phone."

"*The* Micah Taylor?"

"The very same."

"Damn. What a player he was. One of the finest wide receivers of his generation. Let's pay Mrs. Taylor a visit at home tomorrow and see what she has to say for herself."

"You're not going to embarrass yourself and ask for a selfie with the husband, are you?"

Aribo grinned. "Maybe just an autograph. Any luck with Andi Hart?"

"I just got off the phone with her. She's coming into the station tomorrow at lunchtime. She sounded kind of drunk."

"Let me guess, she had a rough day too? I just hope she remembers the appointment."

28

MYLES
BEFORE

Bobby Gee's pawn shop was located in a neighborhood that Myles had never visited, in a part of town that he didn't frequent. The premises looked different in real life than they had in the photos online. And not in a good way.

He'd picked this particular establishment out of all the ones that specialized in Rolex watches because its name wasn't a pun on the word *porn* (Hardcore Pawn, Pawn Stars, and so on) and it didn't have signage with inaccurate apostrophes ("Guitar's! Camera's! Rolex's!").

Myles was now regretting his lack of research. Apparently, proper use of punctuation was not a guarantee of quality.

He should have known something was up when the Uber driver was nervous. When he'd picked Myles up outside his home, the man had asked if the destination was accurate. Myles had assured him that it was, indeed, the correct information. The driver had eyed Myles up and down and asked again if he was sure. Myles had told him he was sure, and he was also in a hurry to catch the store before it closed for the night. The guy had shrugged and muttered something in a language Myles didn't understand. Now he was thinking it had probably been along the lines of "Don't say I didn't ask" or "It's your funeral, pal."

Myles thought about getting back in the car and coming up with another way to pay off the debt, but the Uber driver had already taken off. No doubt worried if he spent any longer than thirty seconds curbside, his nice silver wheel covers might end up in the pawn shop's window.

Bobby Gee's was smack-dab in the middle of a dirty block that housed hair salons, vape shops, and nail bars. A clairvoyant was right next door. On the other side was a vacant unit that looked like it had lain empty for years. The pawn shop had signs in both English and Spanish and big metal bars on grimy windows. Lots of flashing lights and fizzy neon, trying to tempt broke passersby. They reminded Myles of the online casinos. But the colorful lights couldn't disguise the fact that the place was a dump.

Myles clutched the messenger bag that held his watch tighter to his body. He should really order another Uber and get the hell out of there. But one of the LED lights spelled out the word "Rolex" in red dots, and Myles told himself it had to be a legit enterprise if it was dealing in luxury brands. Plus, he needed the money really fucking badly.

He pushed open the door. Flinched as a loud buzzer announced his arrival. Blinked in the harsh glare of a strip light that appeared to have a load of dead bugs trapped inside. The shelves were filled with televisions and power tools and keyboards. Guitars hung on the walls, and golf clubs were stacked in a corner. Glass cabinets displayed jewelry and handbags. The jewelers on Rodeo Drive kept chilled champagne out back to offer to customers perusing engagement rings or special birthday gifts. Myles guessed Bobby Gee kept a baseball bat or pump-action shotgun under the counter.

Behind the counter stood a skinny man with long gray hair and wrinkled skin the color of old library-book pages. His fingernails were dirty, and his too-big slacks and button-down shirt screamed Goodwill. His eyebrows raised a fraction as he took in Myles's preppy appearance. The man wasn't wearing a name tag, so Myles didn't know if he was Bobby Gee or someone of lesser importance.

He didn't want to linger any longer than necessary, so Myles decided to skip the preamble with small talk about the weather and get straight down to business.

"I'd like to pawn a watch," he said.

"You've come to the right place."

"How does it work? Pawning something, I mean."

The old man grinned. "First-timer, huh? It's pretty simple. You bring us an item, and we decide if we want it. If we do, we agree on a price and pay cash. For larger amounts, it's an electronic transfer straight into your checking account. You get a ticket and a grace period of a month to buy the item back. If you don't, we sell it to whoever wants it. That's it. Simple."

"The sign outside says you buy and sell Rolex watches."

The man licked thin dry lips. "That we do."

Myles took the Rolex from the messenger bag. It was in its original green leather presentation case. He opened the case and spun it around for the cashier to see. The watch was nestled in soft beige velvet lining. The platinum shone, and the diamonds winked in the mortuary glare of the dead-bug strip light, and the skinny man's eyes lit up just as brightly. He let out a whistle between his teeth that grated like a fork scraping a plate.

"Very nice. May I?"

Myles didn't want the dirty fingernails anywhere near the watch, but he nodded. The man picked it up, squeezed an eye shut, and turned it over in his hands to examine it.

"Seems like the real deal," he said, placing the watch back in the presentation box.

"Of course it's the real deal," Myles said indignantly. "Do I look like the kind of person who purchases forgeries from hawkers on Venice Beach or the trunks of cars in strange parking lots?" He aimed the cast at the watch. "That is a work of art. A very generous gift from my parents."

The other man's eyebrows lifted again, and Myles knew what he was thinking.

And yet here you are trying to sell it in a dump like this.

What he said was "I didn't mean any offense. We run a legit business here. We have to be sure about what we're buying and selling, that's all."

Myles rummaged in the messenger bag and pulled out an envelope. "Here's the authenticity paperwork. Original purchase receipt and warranty card and owner's manual. You can check it out for yourself."

"Again, I don't wish to cause offense, but a good forger can fake those papers just as easily as the watch itself. We see it all the time."

"Are you saying you don't want to buy the watch?"

"That's not what I'm saying," the man said quickly. "Bobby Gee is the expert, is all, not me. Once he gives it the once-over, I'm sure we'll be happy to do business."

"How much?"

The skinny man ran his eyes over the Rolex again and shrugged with his mouth. "Maybe twenty-five."

"Twenty-five grand? It cost four times as much!"

"Like I said, Bobby Gee is the expert, not me. Every chance he'll be willing to do a nice deal for you. Pay a bit more."

"And where is Bobby Gee right now?"

"He's gone for the day. You could come by again tomorrow if you want? No, wait. Shoot. He's off tomorrow. You want to try Monday instead? Bobby Gee will be here for sure from ten on."

Myles didn't want to make a return journey to this hellhole unless he was collecting his watch again. And he didn't want several more days to tick by without paying any of the money he owed. What if the credit card and loan companies sent people to his house to take his stuff? His car? In front of the neighbors? He felt himself start to sweat.

"I can't wait until Monday," he said. "It has to be today."

The skinny man nodded slowly. "Okay. Let me see what I can do." He disappeared through a back door and returned a couple of minutes later. He pushed the watch case back toward Myles.

"Well?" Myles asked.

"Bobby Gee will see you in an hour. Come back then with the Rolex."

There weren't a whole lot of options for passing an hour in the neighborhood, unless Myles wanted a bad haircut or a fake psychic to read his one good palm.

He took off down the block and spotted a strip mall across the street that comprised a liquor store, a pharmacy, a shoe repair store, and a fast food joint. He headed for the restaurant.

"What can I getcha?" asked the teenage server.

It was almost dinnertime, and Myles was hungry but not hungry enough to eat fried chicken from a greasy cardboard box.

"Do you sell coffee?"

"Yeah."

"Blond vanilla latte?"

"Sorry, this ain't Starbucks."

"Is there a Starbucks nearby?" Myles asked hopefully. A soulless multinational coffeehouse chain would be a big improvement on his current location.

"No."

"Okay. Just a black coffee, then."

Myles grabbed a bunch of napkins from a dispenser and took his black coffee to an empty table that was farthest away from the ones where families with noisy children were seated. He wiped the sticky surface with the napkins and got the lid off the takeout cup with some difficulty to allow the lava-hot drink to cool.

It was going to be a long hour.

Myles wished he'd brought a book or a magazine with him. All he had for entertainment was his cell phone, which was a dangerous weapon in the hands of a bored person with a gambling habit. He took it out of the messenger bag anyway and laid it on the table in front of him. Saw that he had a text from Jack.

Hi honey, how's my favorite patient? Hope you're not in too much pain! I'm stuck at an after-work drinks thing but will escape SOON and swing by to help you out of those jeans xx

Myles groaned. He should have realized Jack would want to check in on him after the struggle to get dressed this morning. Myles took what felt like forever to tap out a response with his left hand. At least it passed some time.

Hey honey. I'm staying over at my parents' place tonight. George will take me straight to Malibu from here tomorrow morning. You enjoy your drinks xx

A quick reply from Jack: You mean I don't get to take those jeans off? DEVASTATED!! Speak to you tomorrow. Love you xx

Myles sent a kissing-face emoji. It was quicker than the left-handed texting. He shut down the text app, and his gaze fell on the gambling apps. He expected the usual tightening in his gut and the quick breathing that happened when he needed a fix, but there was only a rush of anger.

His clothes were likely ruined with the stink of chicken grease, he was about to hand over a much-loved gift to an old hustler for a quarter of what it was worth, and he had just lied—yet again—to the sweetest man he'd ever met. Myles did what he should have done months ago and deleted the apps. One by one. Fifteen in total. Then he sat back in the booth and closed his eyes, breathing hard.

An email alert sounded on his phone.

Myles's eyes snapped open. It was from Matt Connor at MAC Investigations. The message was short and to the point.

Myles.

The information you requested. Remember, this didn't come from me.

MC

There was a single attachment. Myles opened it. It was a photo of a birth certificate that had been issued by the Los Angeles County Department of Public Health the previous November. Myles pinched the screen to zoom in on the important bits.

Name of Child: Scout Brooks Vega

Name of Father/Parent: Hunter Matthew Brooks

Myles grinned. "Gotcha."

He'd already set up a fake email account and found out that Brooks's wife, Melissa, had a cute little floristry business with a cute little website and an email address on the contact page.

He opened a new message, slowly typed the words "Hunter Brooks" in the subject line, and then attached both the birth certificate photo and the video he'd filmed of Brooks with Carmen Vega and the kid at Echo Park Lake. Then he hit "Send."

Myles checked the time on his phone.

Forty minutes to go.

Myles waited for a break in the traffic, then jogged across the street.

The hair salons and vape shops and nail bars were all shuttered. He had a moment of panic, thinking the skinny guy had gotten rid of him so he could also lock up for the night. Then he saw red and green flickering lights up ahead and a jaundiced yellow glow spilling onto the black sidewalk, and he breathed a sigh of relief. Bobby Gee's was still open.

The relief quickly turned to apprehension. There was no one else around. Not even much in the way of passing cars. He quickened his pace, moving faster along the empty block. His good hand gripped the strap of the messenger bag so tightly it hurt almost as much as the throbbing in his broken wrist. As he passed by an opening between two storefronts, Myles heard movement from the shadows. His first thought was a stray dog. Then he realized it had been the fast scuffle of boots on gravel.

His arms were yanked painfully behind him as he was dragged roughly into the opening. Myles tried to scream, but a big meaty hand clamped over his mouth, muffling his cries for help. The grip on his arms remained tight. He guessed there were two assailants.

Panic exploded inside him. Myles tried to kick out and lost a loafer. He squirmed and thrashed and fought as hard as he could, but he was hauled farther into the alleyway, past overflowing dumpsters and puddles of stinking piss and graffiti-tagged walls.

The dragging finally stopped, and he was thrown to the ground behind one of the dumpsters, landing among a pile of trash bags. His messenger bag was wrenched from him. Myles still hadn't gotten a look at the guys who had grabbed him. He tried to stand on shaky legs, then felt something solid smash across the back of his knees. He dropped to the ground. The pain was so sudden and shocking and excruciating that he couldn't even scream. He was struck again. Then a third time.

Myles curled into the fetal position and whimpered. His blood and tears pooled on the gravel along with old urine and stale milk from a discarded carton.

Then came a blow to the head and there was nothing but darkness.

29

ANDI
BEFORE

Andi paced the floor of her living room.

Every time she thought of the familiar face frozen on Jeremy's phone, she wanted to punch the wall or scream. But that would only alert the one-man Neighborhood Watch Committee downstairs. Give him something else to stick in his street journal.

She went into the kitchen and poured a glass of wine instead. Drank it down in two gulps and refilled the glass. She'd been right. She couldn't trust anyone at Saint Realty. She couldn't trust anyone in this whole damn city.

Andi wasn't a big fan of confrontation, but this one was going to be unavoidable—and it was going to be horrible. What had made a respectable and responsible person act like a criminal? And why target Andi? She had to know.

But she'd have to forget the tire sabotage for now. There was a more pressing matter to be dealt with first.

The gold car.

Jeremy might not be able to hack into the DMV's computer for confirmation of the driver's identity, but Andi had a pretty good idea who was behind the wheel of the Plymouth Road Runner. What was it that Jeremy had said? Probably first generation. Built between 1968 and 1970.

Always those old muscle cars from the '50s and '60s.

Andi took the wine into the living room and settled onto the couch with her laptop. She opened Google and searched for "Petronia Property Group." They didn't appear to have an official website. What she did find was a public database that contained information on millions of companies registered in the US— including Petronia Property Group.

There were two directors listed. Marty Stein was one of them. The other was the chief executive officer. His name was Nolan Chapman.

Just as she'd thought.

Andi kept reading. PPG's jurisdiction was given as California (US). She guessed Chapman would have another company in New York, maybe even still have one registered in Florida. PPG's incorporation date was a little under three years ago. Just after Andi had moved to Los Angeles.

The familiar memory crashed into her brain again, like a scene from a gruesome horror movie that was stuck on repeat.

The whoomph of the ceiling fan. The broken vase. The lamp knocked to the floor. The empty vodka bottle and the overturned kitchen chair.

The back door.

Chapman had followed her to Manhattan. Now he had followed her here.

She remembered the note she'd written him on the day she'd left twenty years ago.

Don't try to find me or I'll tell them what you did.

She'd changed her name, unofficially and then officially. She'd moved cities and then states. And then she'd had to move again.

That had been the hardest move of all. The one that had cost her everything. The one that had taken her away from Justin.

Andi had known she wouldn't be impossible to find. She had a life and a job and an online footprint whether she wanted one or not. She was not going to hide herself away completely. She was not the one who had done wrong.

And Chapman had found her. He hadn't listened. He had known her threat was empty, that she couldn't prove anything. Andi had hoped guilt—if not fear—would keep him away. But he was always there. Skulking in the shadows, hiding behind tinted windows, following her, watching her. How long had he been in New York before she'd spotted him by chance in that diner? How about LA?

Jeremy had only started noticing the gold car in the last few weeks, so Chapman likely hadn't been in town for long. But the plan had been set in motion three years ago when Petronia Property Group was formed and work began on Malibu Beach Drive.

Malibu Beach Drive.

Andi thought about David Saint's frustration at her missing the tour, the pressure he'd been putting her under to find a buyer. It made sense that he wanted to double-end the deal and take a brokerage fee on top of his own selling agent's commission. But he'd get the same brokerage cut if Hunter or Verona or Krystal or Myles found a buyer. It didn't have to be Andi.

Now it was all starting to make sense.

Saint Realty landing the listing for the Malibu house had been no happy accident or stroke of luck. Then Andi considered her own good fortune.

Walker Young.

The ideal candidate for a multimillion-dollar beachfront property in Southern California, whose email had dropped into her inbox at exactly the right time. She went back to the laptop. When she put the two names together, it didn't take too long to find a photograph of Young and Chapman together at a black-tie fundraiser in Manhattan. Andi's cheeks burned.

She fired off a short email to Gretchen Davis informing her that she would no longer be able to act as Walker Young's real estate agent. She didn't give a reason why.

Then Andi called Nick Flores. After a couple of rings, his voice mail kicked in and she left a message. It was straight to the point.

"Twenty-seven dollars per square foot for Santa Monica. Best and final."

Andi thought of the conversation with Carmen Vega and how she'd mentioned the developer visiting the house to assess the staging ahead of tomorrow's brokers' open. Carmen had not appeared to recognize Marty Stein's name. She was expecting someone else to be at Malibu Beach Drive tonight.

Nolan Chapman.

Andi got up from the couch and found her car keys.

She was done with running away.

30

HUNTER
BEFORE

Melissa still wasn't picking up.

Hunter had sent her a text earlier, reminding her that he was showing a house this evening and wouldn't be home for dinner. She hadn't replied. He'd sent a follow-up text. Then he'd tried calling before hitting the PCH, and it had rung and rung before going to voice mail. Hunter had left a voice message. Now he was parked on Malibu Beach Drive and his anxiety levels were spiking with each monotonous ring as he tried calling again.

Hi, this is Melissa. I can't get to the phone right now. Leave a message and I'll call you right back!

But she hadn't called him right back, and it wasn't like her at all. It'd been over an hour since his first text. Melissa was never without her cell phone. She never left a message unanswered.

Maybe Dr. Kessler's office had been in touch again with more bad news. Hunter thought back to the bloody scene in the bathroom a few nights ago. Melissa's phone had rung, so it wasn't out of range or out of juice. What if she couldn't answer? What if she'd hurt herself again? What if it was much worse this time?

"You done?" Don Garland asked from the passenger seat.

Hunter looked up from his phone. "Huh?"

"I don't know about you, Harrison, but I don't have all god-damn night. You showing me this place or what?"

"Yes. Yes, I am. Let's go."

They got out of the car, and Hunter could tell from his puckered expression that Garland wasn't exactly bowled over by his first glimpse of the property.

"What did you think of the drive over?" he asked. "Pretty nice, huh? And definitely doable in under an hour depending on the traffic."

"The conversation left a lot to be desired but, yeah, great scenery. Nice route." Garland nodded to the Ghost. "A sweet ride like that helps."

Hunter grinned. "I'm sure you have a whole fleet of cars that are a joy to drive."

"I don't have one of those."

"Treat yourself. I'll hook you up with my dealer."

Garland made another face as he sized up the house again. "As pleasant as the drive was, I'm not convinced this house is going to be worth it."

"It will be."

The house had been staged since his visit a few days ago, and Hunter thought the decorator had done a fantastic job. The soft pastel color palette was perfectly offset by carefully selected artwork and home furnishings that added interest. Conversation pieces. It was exactly how Hunter would have staged the property himself. Garland was trying to give nothing away, but Hunter could tell he was impressed.

"Better?" he asked.

"We'll see," Garland said.

They toured the three levels, including the rooftop terrace, and Garland made a lot of noncommittal "hmmm" noises as Hunter pointed out the house's major selling points. He could tell the man had zero interest in who'd made the kitchen appliances or where the walnut tub had been shipped in from, but two things did manage to break through the poker face—the spectacular views and the triple-bay garage.

Once they'd returned to the main level, Garland wanted to go back out onto the balcony for another look at the beach now that it was washed in the violet of twilight, and Hunter knew that he was sold.

"You see all those twinkling lights along the coastline?" Hunter said. "Apparently, it's called the Queen's Necklace."

"Why's it called that?"

"I guess because it looks like a string of jewels?"

"Yeah, I know. I was kidding." Garland pulled a fat cigar from the inside pocket of his blazer. "Is it okay to smoke this out here?"

Hunter shook his head. "Once this place is yours, you can smoke as many Cubans as you want. You can stand out here naked and scream at the moon all night. You can even take a piss in the pool if that's your thing. But until you write that check, there's no smoking anywhere on the property. Not even in the outside areas."

"In that case, let's go. I'm jonesing for a smoke."

Garland headed out to the street to light up, while Hunter hung back and tried calling Melissa again. She still hadn't responded to any of his messages. He got her voice mail again, same as before. His excitement over Garland's possible offer was tempered by growing concern for his wife. He went through the house making sure all the pocket doors were secured, the lights were off, and the alarm was reactivated.

Hunter locked up and turned to find a man he didn't know standing on the doorstep with a set of keys in his hand. He was dressed casually, but expensively, in cream chinos, a pink Ralph Lauren polo shirt, and brown leather boat shoes. He was probably late fifties and very tan, with fair hair going gray, and pale blue eyes. He could have been Hunter in twenty years' time.

"Sorry, I didn't realize there was a showing this evening," the man said. "I'm not interrupting, am I? I can come back later."

"It's okay, we were just finishing up." Hunter had no idea who the guy was. He wondered if someone else at Saint had a showing tonight. "Are you a buyer?"

"No, no. I'm the developer."

"The developer, huh? Well, I met him a couple of days ago, and guess what? He wasn't you."

The other man smiled without warmth. "Marty Stein is my business partner. We run Petronia Property Group together."

Nice one, Brooks. Just offend the guy who built the big-bucks house you're trying to sell, why don't you?

"Sorry, I didn't know Mr. Stein had a partner. I'm Hunter Brooks. I work for the listing agency."

The other man hesitated a beat. "Nolan Chapman."

Hunter stared at him.

Chapman.

He knew that name. He'd read it in the newspaper article about Andi Hart's mom just last night.

Chapman's cell phone buzzed, and he said, "Sorry, I have to take this. It was good meeting you, Hunter."

Nolan Chapman went inside, and Hunter walked slowly toward his car. Garland was leaning against the Rolls, surrounded by a cloud of thick smoke, the red tip of his cigar glowing in the dusk.

"Who's the guy?" he asked. "Don't tell me he's my competition?"

"No, he's not a buyer."

"Glad to hear it. I gotta hand it to you, Harrison. You did good. The house is terrific."

"Yeah, it is."

Hunter's mind was whirring. Marty Stein had been visibly disappointed when Andi failed to show for the tour. David Saint seemed desperate for her to find a buyer. And now Stein's business partner, whom everyone had failed to mention even existed, turned out to be a guy called Chapman—the same name that appeared in an old newspaper story from twenty years ago.

Hunter felt sick.

Garland said, "I don't think I'll be taking up surfing any time soon, but the wife is going to love the beach. I'll speak to my accountant tomorrow, go over the financials. Then we'll see about writing an offer. What do you think? Forty-five?"

Hunter nodded. "Forty-five sounds good."

He was barely listening. Any buzz he'd gotten from showing the venture capitalist around the beach house earlier was gone. He didn't know what was going on—but he knew Andi Hart was right at the middle of it all.

31

ANDI
THE BROKERS' OPEN

Waitstaff in black-and-white uniforms weaved through the crowd offering vintage Dom Pérignon in crystal flutes and tiny canapés from Nobu on little napkins. A dozen more bottles of champagne were chilling in silver ice buckets on the quartzite kitchen island.

Saint Realty had hired two luxury coaches to ferry brokers and their guests to and from Malibu so they could get happily smashed without the worry of picking up a DUI on the way back to Los Angeles.

The pocket doors had been thrown open to allow for the calming sound of the ocean as a backdrop to the conversation and a cool breeze to flow through the large room. There was the occasional excited squeal of "Dolphins!" but no one was venturing out onto the balcony because it was hotter than hell out there, and the sun was bad for wrinkles.

Diana had done a fantastic job putting the event together, and everybody seemed to be having a good time. Everyone except the agents from Saint Realty.

Hunter was having a very intense conversation with Carmen Vega. They were talking in low voices so as not to draw the attention of other guests, but both seemed very pissed. They reminded Andi of a bickering married couple.

Verona was watching Hunter and Carmen with an inexplicably anxious expression. Her hand kept fluttering nervously to her mouth, and she hadn't touched the champagne in her other hand. Andi wondered why Verona was so concerned about Hunter arguing with the stager.

There was no sign of Myles or Krystal anywhere.

Andi had considered not showing up herself after last night's discovery and finally making the decision to quit Saint Realty. But she didn't want to let Diana down, and she didn't want her unexplained absence to come across as unprofessional to other brokers she'd want to work with on future projects with her own brokerage.

She stood by herself in a corner, eating and drinking, and trying her best to avoid David, who was too busy schmoozing a couple of old country-club types anyway. The bubbles fizzled pleasantly on her tongue, and the salmon rice cakes and sea bass lettuce cups melted in her mouth. Andi wondered if this was what it felt like to be rich, washing down canapés from the best restaurant in town with $200 bottles of champagne while enjoying a multimillion-dollar view. She figured she might as well enjoy it while she could. Once she'd signed the lease on the unit on Santa Monica, she'd be living on peanut butter and jelly sandwiches for the foreseeable future.

Andi smelled Nick Flores before she saw him. He really should lay off the cologne. He swooped into her space, clinked a glass against her own, and said, "Congrats, again! You must be *so* excited."

He'd called this morning to confirm her offer on the lot had been accepted, at which point she'd had to admit that she, herself, was the client.

Andi smiled. "Yeah, I am."

She *was* excited. Her own brokerage. It had always been the dream. It was happening a little sooner than planned—and definitely with less cash in the bank than she would have liked—but she was determined to make it work. And she was determined to make LA work too. Andi had spent too long pining for her old life back in New York. Her former clients had moved on, Justin had definitely moved on with Janie, and it was time for Andi to move on too.

Flores said, "I'll send over the paperwork first thing on Monday morning. It should be fairly straightforward. Once everything is signed, it'll be official—LA's hottest new brokerage!"

"Fantastic. Can't wait."

Flores nudged her. "A dog-grooming business, huh?"

Andi grinned. "Yeah, sorry about the little white lie. But I am hoping for lots of celebrity clients, so at least that part was true."

She saw David approach, and her smile vanished. He was running his hand through his hair agitatedly and looking generally harassed.

"Sorry to interrupt," he said. "Andi, have you seen Myles at all?"

"I haven't seen him all day."

"No, neither have I."

"I'm sure he'll be around here somewhere. It's a big house."

"I don't know." David frowned. "I've just spent half an hour entertaining his clients. He was supposed to be meeting them here."

"I haven't seen Krystal either. Maybe they're together."

"Krystal texted this morning. She's sick. Diana has been babysitting her client."

Andi noticed Diana on the other side of the room with a small Japanese woman who had a fierce black bob and was dressed in a puffy smock dress and neon sneakers.

"Maybe Myles's driver broke down on the way?" she said.

"I've tried his cell phone, and he's not picking up."

"If I see him, I'll let him know you're looking for him."

"Thanks, Andi. Sorry again for butting in."

Flores stuck out a hand. "I don't think we've met. Nick Flores."

David shook his hand, still scanning the room for Myles. "David. Good to meet you, Nick."

"We were just celebrating Andi's good news."

"Good news?" David asked, still distracted. "What good news?"

Andi said, "I haven't—"

Flores said, "She's opening her own brokerage. Isn't that fantastic? We've just agreed to the lease on the premises."

Shit.

That got David's full attention, the search for Myles now forgotten. "There must be some mistake. Andi already has a job, and she doesn't have a broker's license in any case."

"Actually, I do."

"What? When did this happen?"

"I got the license a couple of months ago. I've been working on it for a while."

"And you didn't think to tell me?"

"No, I didn't."

Flores said, "Um, did I say something I shouldn't have?"

Andi said, "David is my boss. He doesn't know I'm leaving. At least, he didn't until now."

"Oh, crap," Flores said. "Me and my big mouth."

David glared at her. "Can I have a word, please? In private."

Flores mouthed "Sorry" as David steered her away. He opened the door of the theater room and ushered her inside. Andi noticed Diana watching them.

The theater room had a 150-inch projector screen, thick carpeting, and two rows of huge leather armchairs with individual drink holders. Framed vintage movie posters hung on the walls, including one for *Glengarry Glen Ross*. The movie was about a team

198

of sales reps at a real estate firm, competing with each other for sales and trying not to get fired. Andi wondered if Carmen Vega's choice of poster had been deliberate. The chairs looked really comfortable, but she didn't sit.

David closed the door. "What the fuck, Andi?"

"I'm sorry. I didn't want you to find out like this."

"Your own brokerage? A rival firm? Why?"

"It's best that I leave," she said. "You know it is."

"Is this about what happened between us?"

"Partly."

"Jesus, can't we just move on? It was just a stupid kiss!"

"I am moving on. From Saint Realty and from you."

"Bloody hell, Andi. When were you going to tell me? Does Diana know?"

"No, she doesn't. I was going to tell both of you once the papers were signed on the lease for my premises. I'm happy to work one month's notice as per my contract and fulfill the live listings that I already have. But you should know that I won't be bringing you a buyer for this house. I'm done with Malibu Beach Drive."

"What?" David yelled. "You'd better be bloody joking."

"I'm not laughing."

"Fuuuuuck." He ran both hands through his hair and paced the room. Stopped pacing and looked at her. "What about your client? The one who wants to buy this place? You can't just screw him over too."

Andi's eyes narrowed. "What client?"

"The rich guy in New York."

"I never told you about any rich guy in New York."

"Yes, you did. How else would I know?"

"I'm guessing Nolan Chapman told you."

David stared at her. His mouth opened and then closed again.

"I think you'd better tell me everything," she said. "About the listing. About Nolan Chapman."

David fussed with his hair. He pushed his glasses farther up the bridge of his nose. He sighed and nodded. Finally, he said, "Chapman approached me a while back about listing the house. As you can imagine, I was ecstatic. I couldn't believe it. A fifty-million-dollar property. You know we've never had anything close to that price before at Saint. He told me the listing was mine, but he had two conditions. One—he was only prepared to sell to a buyer who was represented by you. And two—you could never know about his involvement. He already had a buyer lined up in New York, and he said this guy was going to hire you as his Realtor. It all seemed so . . . simple."

"And you didn't think it also seemed—I don't know—very odd? You didn't ask why this guy was interested in me?"

"Well, no. But I . . ."

"You wanted the money." Andi held up a hand. "Let me just do the math . . . Five percent commission split fifty-fifty between the listing agent—which would be you—and the buyer's agent—which, apparently, would be me. Plus, the twenty percent brokerage cut you'd take from my fee means you'd be walking away with one and a half million. Not too bad for selling out one of your own staff."

"It wasn't like that," David said. "You'd be making a lot of money from the deal too. You still can. We both can."

Andi shook her head. "You're pathetic, do you know that? Actually, I think it's best that I don't work my notice period at Saint. I'm done. Outta here. I quit, effective immediately."

She went to push past him, and he grabbed her arm, his fingers digging into the flesh. "You can't do this to me. I won't let you."

"Take your fucking hand off me."

David didn't loosen his grip. His eyes burned into hers. "I mean it. You can't do this."

The door opened, and Diana stuck her head inside. "Everything okay in here?"

Andi shook free of David's grasp. "Everything's fine. I was just leaving."

She squeezed past Diana, into the living area. Diana went into the theater room and said something about "a situation" to David before closing the door behind herself. Andi gulped down some air. She was vaguely aware of a weird atmosphere in the room. One of the waiters was brushing broken glass into a dustpan. Her arm throbbed where David had grabbed her, the skin mottled and red. It was going to bruise.

Nick Flores was over by the pocket doors leading to the balcony, watching her. He was with two older female Realtors, who were chatting excitedly. He frowned and mouthed, "You okay?" Andi nodded. She grabbed a glass of champagne from a passing waiter and drank it down in one gulp.

She wasn't okay, but she'd feel a whole lot better once she was out of this house, with Malibu Beach Drive and David Saint firmly in her rearview mirror.

But first there was something she had to do.

32

HUNTER
THE BROKERS' OPEN

Hunter strode over to where Carmen Vega was deep in conversation with a young guy wearing Buddy Holly glasses and skinny jeans with a saggy butt. They were standing next to a $10,000 sideboard and a huge abstract canvas of the ocean.

She was dressed in a seashell-pink satin dress that hugged her curves and complemented her complexion. Hunter might have enjoyed the view if he wasn't freaking out so much. He stared at Buddy Holly until he got the message and slinked away.

"Okay, that was seriously rude," Carmen said.

"What are you doing here?" Hunter hissed.

"It's nice to see you too, Hunter," she said. "I was invited by Diana, that's what I'm doing here."

"Why would Diana invite you?"

She pointed to the canvas. "See this abstract right here? I sourced it from a gallery in Topanga Canyon. And the L-shaped couch over there that everyone's raving about? I picked that out too. The Missoni cushions on the couch? Me again."

"Wait, you staged this house?"

"That's right."

"You didn't mention you were working on Malibu Beach Drive when we spoke at the park," he said accusingly. "All you said was you'd taken on some projects. This is a hell of a project to keep quiet about."

Carmen gave him a pointed look. "You didn't mention Malibu Beach Drive either."

"You can't be here," Hunter said urgently.

"Sure I can. My mother has Scout overnight, so I get to do something fun for once." Carmen took a sip of champagne. "And this bubbly is *good*."

"Melissa is coming to the brokers' open. There's no way the two of you can be in the same room together."

"Why? Melissa doesn't know about me. What's the big deal?"

Carmen's tone was nonchalant, but she looked worried.

"What's the big deal? This is a fucking nightmare scenario." Hunter noticed both Andi and Verona watching them, and he lowered his voice again. "I didn't even know she knew about the brokers' open. Diana must have invited her too. They've known each other for years, ever since I first started working at Saint."

"Why isn't she here already? You didn't travel from Brentwood together?"

Hunter shook his head. "No. Something's up. She stayed at her folks' last night. I found a note when I got home from showing this place. It said she'd be coming here today. She hasn't been answering her phone. When I tried calling her folks' house, the line was busy all night." Hunter stared at Carmen. "You didn't tell her, did you? You didn't show up at the house again?"

"Of course not. You told me you'd get the extra money, and I believe you. Although I don't like that you lied to me about this listing."

Hunter watched as David Saint and Andi went into the theater room together. Neither of them looked happy.

"I didn't lie to you," he said. "I just didn't tell you. I don't have to tell you about every listing I have. In any case, it's not my listing, it's David's. And I wouldn't bet on any of my clients having an offer accepted anyway."

"Why not? You said you had a showing last night."

"Shit," Hunter said.

Melissa had arrived. She stood on her own awkwardly, searching the crowd of faces. The floral Oscar de la Renta dress she was wearing had always been one of his favorites, but Hunter noticed it hung loose on her now, and even from across the room, he could see how drawn and tired she looked, as though she hadn't slept at all the previous night.

Her eyes landed on him, and the awkwardness changed into something that looked a lot like hate. Her gaze then switched to Carmen, and there was a flash of recognition followed by unmistakable anger. Hunter's stomach lurched.

She knows.

Melissa stalked over to where they were standing, almost knocking over one of the waitstaff, who, thankfully, recovered quickly enough to avoid upending a tray full of drinks.

"Well, isn't this cozy," she spat. "Mommy and Daddy here together. Where's little Scout? Is he here too? Is it a perfect family day out? Don't tell me I'm ruining all the fun by showing up?"

Fuck.

Hunter felt like he was going to throw up, like the seafood canapés he'd scarfed earlier were suddenly a very bad idea.

"Melissa, I . . ."

"What? You can explain? Is that what you were going to say? Yes, Hunter, please do explain how you were screwing the decorator and getting her knocked up, while your wife was going through hell trying to get pregnant for the last five years."

Carmen looked at him. "What? You never told me."

Melissa said, "Oh, would that have made a difference? Would you have made a bigger effort not to sleep with my husband if you'd known we were trying for a baby? That's real big of you."

The guests closest to them had stopped talking and were staring in their direction. Melissa noticed too.

"That's right, folks," she said loudly. "While my husband and I were going through IVF and he was pretending to be as heartbroken as I was, he was actually playing house with this whore bitch and their secret kid."

Most of the nearby guests dropped their eyes to the floor.

A broker by the name of Marcia Stringer said, "Oh my. What a mess."

Betsy Bowers said, "You dirty dog, Hunter Brooks."

Carmen said, "Okay, that's enough, Melissa. This isn't the time or place for this discussion."

Melissa's response was to snatch the crystal flute from Carmen's hand and throw the champagne in her face. There was a collective gasp from the onlookers.

Hunter said, "Melissa! What do you think you're doing?"

She turned to him with a mixture of hurt and fury in her eyes. "You're seriously taking *her* side?"

Melissa dropped the champagne flute, which shattered on impact with the tiled flooring. Then she was on him. Pummeling his chest with her fists, then clawing at his face with her nails. Hunter stood with his arms by his sides. He didn't try to stop her. It was what he deserved. No, he deserved much worse.

It was Diana who hauled Melissa off him and folded her into a hug, stroking her hair like she was a child. She glared at Hunter and Carmen over Melissa's shoulder. "I think you should both go."

"*What?*" Carmen said. "I'm the one with Dom Pérignon all over my face and dress."

"Just go," Diana said. She signaled to the guy at the door who had been tasked with scanning everyone's QR code invites on their cell phones upon arrival. He looked like Dwayne Johnson in a tux that was straining against the muscles.

Melissa pulled away from Diana. "It's okay. I'm leaving. My father is waiting outside. I just came here to tell my husband that the locks on the house have been changed, his bags have been packed, and I plan to take him for every cent I can in divorce court."

She kissed Diana on the cheek and then stalked out of the house.

Diana turned to Hunter and Carmen. "You two are out of here too."

The Dwayne Johnson look-alike gestured to the open front door. "You heard the lady."

Carmen left. Hunter stood rooted to the spot, stunned by what had just happened.

How did Melissa find out? How did she know Scout's name?

"How could you, Hunter?" Diana asked softly.

He shook his head. He had no answer for her.

Outside, there was no sign of Carmen. Four plastic suitcases and a Louis Vuitton duffel bag that Hunter recognized as his own were stacked by the roadside.

Melissa's father's car was on the dirt shoulder on the other side of the street, engine idling, the driver's-side window all the way down.

Buck Grover leaned out and yelled, "I hired Gene Goldman this morning. You might have heard of him—he's the best divorce lawyer in town. You broke my daughter's heart. Now I'm going to destroy you, you fucker."

Melissa stared straight ahead, refusing to look Hunter's way. Then Buck took off, leaving a cloud of dust in their wake.

33

VERONA
THE BROKERS' OPEN

Verona was in the powder room trying to repair the damage to her makeup. She cleaned up the mascara and eyeliner smudges with a tissue, but her bloodshot eyes betrayed her earlier tears.

She was still shaken by what she'd just witnessed. Melissa Brooks was a broken woman, no doubt about it. Verona hadn't known about the couple's struggles to become parents. It wasn't something Hunter had ever discussed with the people he worked alongside. She knew the woman's distress was ultimately because of her husband's infidelity—that Hunter was primarily to blame along with Carmen Vega. But Verona also had to acknowledge the part that she and Myles had played in the bloody battlefield that was now the Brooks's marriage.

And where was Myles anyway? He'd casually dropped a grenade into the lives of three people—four if you counted little Scout—and now he was nowhere to be found. Didn't have the balls to show up and face the consequences of what he had done.

Verona spritzed some perfume, as though that would help, and flushed, even though she hadn't used the toilet. When she opened the door, Andi was standing outside.

"Can we talk?" she asked. She didn't look friendly.

"Sure," Verona said.

"Not here. Somewhere more private."

Verona followed Andi upstairs to the primary suite. She perched on the edge of the bed and put her purse on the night-stand next to an ugly gold figurine. The bed reminded her of those found in fancy hotel rooms, soft yet firm at the same time, with high-thread-count bedding and a small mountain of pillows and cushions. The furnishings in the large room were sparse, just the super-king bed, bedside tables, footstool, and a small table and chairs positioned just so on a rug. The view was all the adornment the room needed.

Andi sat on the footstool at the end of the bed. She was quiet for a moment, watching what was going on outside the windows as some dolphins slipped in and out of the waves. The bright blue waters weren't calming her, though. She appeared troubled.

Finally, she said, "I know what you did."

Verona's tears came again. Shame burned her skin. She said, "I know I shouldn't have gotten involved, but I was just so angry after what Hunter did to me. And then I found out what he did to Myles, and I don't know . . . I just didn't think. Poor Melissa. You must think I'm a terrible person."

Andi stared at her. "What are you talking about?"

"Helping Myles prove that Hunter is the father of Carmen Vega's son. Isn't that what you meant?"

Andi frowned. "Carmen's baby . . . Hunter is the father?"

"Yes. I guess you must have missed the showdown that just happened between Melissa, Hunter, and Carmen?"

"I guess so. I've just finished talking to David in the theater room. So you and Myles outed Hunter as the kid's father? That's a really shitty thing to do, Verona."

Verona dropped her head and clasped her hands on her lap. "I know. I have no idea what I was thinking. I don't think I *was* thinking."

Her tentative relief at Dr. Fazli's initial assessment of the lump in her breast was tempered by the guilt of blowing up other people's lives in some sort of twisted quest for revenge. Now Verona had a different reason for not being able to sleep at night.

Andi said, "That's not what I wanted to talk to you about. I know it was you who trashed my tire and stopped me from coming here for the tour."

The tire.

With everything else that was going on, Verona had completely forgotten about what she'd done to Andi's car. Now a fresh wave of shame washed over her.

She'd been out late, one of her midnight drives, moving aimlessly through the empty city streets, when she'd found herself in Andi's neighborhood in Laurel Canyon. Like everyone else at Saint Realty, Verona had seen how David had focused all his attention on Andi when announcing the listing for Malibu Beach Drive, how he had made it clear he expected—and wanted—her to be the one who earned the commission.

The life-changing commission.

Money that Verona needed way more than her single, dependent-free, worry-free younger coworker.

Being an electrician, Richard insisted Verona always keep a tool kit in the trunk of her car along with the first aid kit. "You never know when a screwdriver or wrench could come in useful!" he liked to say.

Verona had felt like she was operating on autopilot as she parked outside Andi's apartment, pulled up the hood of her sweater, got out of the car, opened the trunk, and found the screwdriver. As she approached the BMW, knelt down, jammed the tool into the tire's sidewall, and listened to the satisfying hiss of the air escaping.

She was exhausted and consumed with worry and resentful of Andi's carefree life. But Verona realized now, it was no excuse for vandalizing the woman's car. Just like there was no excuse for what she'd done to Melissa Brooks. When had she become this horrible, spiteful person?

"How did you know it was me?" Verona asked.

Andi tossed her cell phone across the bed. On the screen was a frozen image of Verona crouched down next to the Beemer with the screwdriver in her hand, lit up by the night-vision glow of a camera she'd been unaware of.

Andi said, "My downstairs neighbor installed cameras outside both of our front doors for security purposes. I have a recording of the whole thing."

"I'm so sorry," Verona whispered.

"What I don't understand is why? Why did you do it, Verona? I thought we were friends."

It all came out then, about finding the lump in her breast and Aunt Mimi's battle with cancer and Verona's fears that she could suffer a similar fate. How she'd been desperate for the money to make sure she would not become a burden to Richard and the boys if she did get sick, that she would know they'd be looked after when she was gone. How David Saint's obvious favoritism toward Andi, combined with Andi's successful sales record, had made her feel threatened.

"I'm sorry," she said again. "I feel like I've lost my mind these past few weeks."

"Oh, Verona." Andi's hard expression had softened. "Have you seen a doctor yet?"

Verona nodded. "Yesterday. He thinks it's benign, probably a cyst, but wants me to have a breast ultrasound to be sure, given my family history. The worry hasn't gone away, and it won't until I get the results of the ultrasound, but it has lessened."

"I really hope it's good news."

Verona held up Andi's phone. "Are you going to show this to David? Take it to the police? You have every right to. What I did was wrong."

Andi shook her head. "I'm going to delete it. No one has to see it."

"Thank you." Verona returned the phone. She hesitated a beat, then said, "I hope we can still be friends."

Andi smiled sadly. "Maybe."

Verona just nodded.

Andi said, "There's something else you should know. I'm leaving Saint. Well, actually, I've already left. I quit, effective immediately."

Verona had noticed things between Andi and David had been strained for a while, and she suspected something similar to what had happened with Andi's predecessor, Shea Snyder, was going on.

"Really? Why?"

"It's a long story, for another time."

"What will you do?"

"I have plans." Andi got up. "Take care of yourself, Verona."

Andi left the bedroom, and Verona sat for a moment. She felt drained all of a sudden and wanted nothing more than to go home to her husband and her boys. It was time to have the talk with Richard. She picked up her purse from the bedside table. The figurine on top really was butt ugly.

As she moved to the doorway, Verona heard voices in the hallway outside. They belonged to Diana and Andi. She paused and listened.

Diana was saying, "I know why you're leaving, Andi. I know about your affair with David."

34

ANDI
THE BROKERS' OPEN

Andi wanted this nightmare day to be over.

"I'm not having an affair with David," she said in a low voice. "And Verona is right through there in the primary suite."

Diana nodded but her expression remained grim, and Andi knew the nod was an acknowledgment of their coworker's presence nearby, rather than an acceptance of Andi's denial.

"Follow me."

Andi did as she was told and followed Diana down the stairs and through the packed living space. The Japanese woman was still there, deep in conversation with an actress who was starring in the new Spielberg film. Andi was glad she wouldn't have to endure Krystal's spiteful glances while having the world's most awkward conversation with her boss.

Diana led her out onto the balcony. It was hot outside, but a brisk breeze coming off the ocean provided some respite from the intensity of the sun.

Diana was stylishly dressed in a sleeveless white chiffon shirt and matching wide-legged pants. Her short platinum hair had been freshly highlighted, and her makeup hadn't budged despite the heat, but her features were pinched with tension. She put her hand to her face as a makeshift visor. "Okay, what's going on with you and David? And I want the truth."

"I already told you the truth," Andi said. "I'm not sleeping with him."

"But something's going on. That's why you're leaving."

"I'm leaving for a bunch of different reasons."

"And one of them is David."

It was a statement rather than a question, and Andi didn't offer up an answer. She wanted to get out of the sun and this beautiful house and Malibu and go home and prepare for the next chapter in her life. She didn't want to be having this conversation.

"You're not the first, you know," Diana said.

Andi nodded. "Shea Snyder."

"You know about Shea?"

"Not really. I know something happened and that's why she left Saint, but no one wants to talk about it. Except Krystal. She'd talk for sure, but she didn't join until after I did, so she's probably as much in the dark as I am."

Diana was quiet for a moment. The sounds of chatter from the living room drifted outside. The surf crashed onto the beach below. The silence that stretched between them felt as wide as the ocean.

Finally, she said, "Only Verona and Hunter saw what happened that day—Shea's last day. Myles was at a showing, so I guess he doesn't know the full story if he's never spoken to anyone about it. You know how discreet Verona is. And I've known Hunter for a very long time, so he's probably kept quiet out of respect for me."

Andi squinted against the sun so she could look at Diana. "What happened?"

"You remind me a lot of her." Diana smiled sadly. "Young, pretty in a natural way, ambitious. She was from out of town too.

Ohio rather than New York. Less wise in the ways of the world than you are, though. She'd been at Saint for around six months when I suspected David was having an affair. All the classic signs were there—working late, making more of an effort with his appearance, text messages that he didn't want me to see, a sudden lack of interest in sex. Well, with me anyway."

Diana flushed hard, and Andi knew she was deeply embarrassed to be discussing this kind of stuff about her personal life. This talk was as hard for Diana as it was for her. Harder.

Diana went on. "It soon became obvious that the other woman was Shea. She was awkward around me, and she could no longer look me in the eye. And she couldn't take her eyes off David. She followed him around like a lovesick puppy. The others noticed too. Hunter even told me about his suspicions that they were having an affair."

"What did you do? Did you confront David?"

Diana shook her head. "I decided to let it run its course—which I was sure wouldn't take long. David would get bored, and Shea would move on somewhere else. I was right. It didn't take long before David tried to end it."

"'Tried'?"

"Shea didn't take it well at all. She threatened to tell me everything if David didn't leave me for her. He refused, so that's what she did—told me about the affair. Then she showed up at our house screaming and shouting. When that didn't work, she turned up at the office covered in blood. She'd cut her wrists. They were superficial injuries, but it was very distressing for everyone who witnessed it."

"Was she okay?"

"Yes, thank God. We got her to a hospital and called her parents, who flew out to LA immediately. She moved back to Ohio, quit the real estate game altogether. I check in on her occasionally on Facebook and Instagram. She's married now. She has a little girl. So, the thing is, Andi, you and David . . . I've seen it all before."

"I swear to you, I never slept with him."

"But he wanted to?"

Andi nodded.

"Did you?" Diana asked.

"No. Maybe. I don't know."

Diana stared at her, waiting for her to say more. Andi sighed. Her head was starting to pound from the sun and the stress.

She said, "We were working late one night on a listing. We were in David's office. After a while, he said we needed a break, and he opened a bottle of wine. Maybe I should have known then that something was up, but I didn't. We drank the wine and chatted."

David scooted his chair closer and topped off Andi's wineglass. "Thanks again for staying so late to get this done, especially on a Friday night. You should be out on a date instead of stuck here with an old codger like me."

"I don't mind." Andi smiled. "I didn't have anywhere else to be anyway."

"Oh? No boyfriend on the scene?"

"Nope."

"I don't believe it. Someone as gorgeous as you, they should be forming a queue around the block."

Andi laughed. "Yeah, right. I'm practically beating them off with a stick."

David didn't laugh. He'd taken his glasses off and fixed her with an intense stare. She was aware of how close he was to her now. She could feel the heat radiating from his body. The wine was making her feel a little woozy.

"I mean it, Andi." His voice had dropped to a low murmur. "You're a very beautiful woman."

Was David hitting on her?

Did she want him to?

Andi tried to look away, but she couldn't tear her eyes away from his.

Then his lips were on her own. Soft and tentative at first. She found herself responding, and the kiss grew deeper, more urgent. Her hands gripped his hair, while his hands explored her body.

"We kissed," Andi told Diana. "Then I told him we had to stop, that what we were doing was wrong. That's as far as it went."

"What did David say? I bet he wasn't happy."

Andi pulled away from him. "I can't do this. We can't do this."

"Sure we can. We've both been wanting this to happen for ages. Let's not fight it any longer."

David leaned in to kiss her again. She could smell the booze on his breath. Andi pushed him away. "I said no, David. I don't want to."

Anger flashed in his eyes. "What do you mean, you don't want to? You've been giving me the come-on for months."

"I . . . what? I haven't . . ."

"Of course you have. All the little smiles and looks and jokes. What was I supposed to think?"

"I was being friendly. *I wasn't flirting with you."*

"So I've been misreading the signs all these months? Is that what you're trying to say? I don't think so. I sure as hell wasn't misreading anything two minutes ago when your tongue was in my mouth. You know, there's a name for women like you."

Andi got up. "I should go."

She walked over to the office door. David was right behind her. She could feel his breath on the back of her neck as she reached for the doorknob. He grabbed her wrist.

"Are you going to tell Diana?" he demanded.

Andi looked down at his hand. "Let go of me."

"I mean it, Andi. If you want to keep working here—if you want to keep working in this town—you'll keep your mouth shut."

"I won't say anything."

He let go of her wrist.

"He agreed that it was a mistake," Andi said. "That it should never have happened."

"I won't leave him, you know."

"Okay."

"He's my partner in life and in business. Always has been. We simply don't work without each other. That's never going to change."

Andi didn't know what to say, so she didn't say anything.

"What will you do now that you've left Saint?" Diana asked.

"David didn't tell you?"

"Only that you're leaving."

"I'm setting up my own brokerage."

Diana's eyebrows arched. "I didn't know you had your license. Good for you. New York?"

"No, I've agreed to a lease on a unit on Santa Monica Boulevard."

"You're setting up a rival company just a few blocks from us?"

"That's right," Andi said.

"I see," Diana said tightly. "David failed to mention that part. Well, I suppose we're done here. I should probably go and find him."

"Where is he?"

"I told him to take a walk, cool down after finding out you were leaving the brokerage. You know, Andi, it might be best for everybody if you just left town. Went home to New York."

"I'm not Shea Snyder. I'm not running away."

Diana nodded curtly, then walked back into the house.

Andi stood on the balcony and stared out at the blue water. She felt relieved. No more secrets and lies. No more feeling guilty all the time. Nick Flores had actually done her a favor by blurting out her plans to David. He'd ripped off the Band-Aid for her. Andi went inside.

Flores was still trapped in a little huddle with Marcia Stringer and Betsy Bowers. He threw Andi a questioning look, but she ignored him. She'd talk to him on Monday. She just wanted to go home.

"A place like this has to have a pool, right?" Betsy was saying as a waiter topped off her champagne.

"Who needs a pool when you have the ocean right on your doorstep?" Marcia replied, gesturing toward the balcony and the view of the sun-dappled waves beyond.

"I'm sure they mentioned a pool."

Andi felt a hand clamp around her arm as she walked past the group. The iron grip belonged to Betsy, who said, "You're with the listing agency, aren't you? Be a sweetheart and show us where the pool is?"

Andi suppressed a sigh. All she wanted was to escape this goddamn house, but Betsy was a power player in Beverly Hills, and Andi knew she'd do well to stay on the woman's good side. Ditto Betsy's pal, Marcia.

"Of course," Andi said. "It's around the side of the house. It's custom tiled and really quite stunning. Follow me."

Louboutin and Manolo heels click-clacked on the tiled floor as the trio made their way through the open pocket doors onto the balcony and turned the corner onto the pool deck.

The wind whipped at their hair. The sun momentarily blinded their eyes. A faint smell of salt and seaweed carried on the breeze. The three women walked toward the pool.

Andi stopped. There was a dark red stain on the concrete. That wasn't right. She frowned. It looked a lot like blood. Then her gaze traveled from the blood to the pool. Someone was in the water. They were facedown. Arms outstretched. Fully clothed. Not moving.

Marcia and Betsy both started screaming, but Andi could barely hear them over the roaring in her ears. She couldn't breathe. Her vision started to go black around the edges. The sweat on her back turned to ice. Andi shrank away from the pool.

This couldn't be happening.

Not again.

35

ARIBO
AFTER

It was after midnight when Aribo finally called it a night and went home.

Susan was sprawled on the couch with a blanket half covering her. Her mouth was open, and she was snoring like a bear with a sinus problem. She wore a Howard Jones tour T-shirt over her own top. A *Greatest Hits of the '80s* CD case was on the coffee table, along with an almost empty bottle of red.

Aribo went upstairs to the bedroom. Denise was also passed out. He undressed quietly and climbed in next to her, careful not to wake her. She didn't even stir. The deep slumber of the very drunk. He kissed her softly on the lips, tasting the wine, and whispered, "Happy anniversary, babe."

Within seconds, Aribo was asleep too.

Denise and Susan were both still dead to the world when he left for work the following morning. He placed a couple of Advil and a glass of water on the nightstand next to his wife and did the same for her friend. He didn't envy them the hangovers.

The squad room was quiet this early on a Saturday. Aribo didn't mind the late finish and early start because what he and Lombardi had discovered about both Hart and Taylor last night had changed everything.

Today's interviews were going to be interesting, to say the least.

He got a pot of coffee going and took the mug to his desk. He'd told Lombardi to head straight to the autopsy, which was scheduled for noon.

It would mean Aribo having to fly solo for the interview with Andi Hart, who was expected at the station around the same time, but he was glad of the excuse not to attend the cut. Even after all these years, the process still made him queasy. Aribo could handle seeing dead bodies—and he had seen plenty—but he would never get used to the sight of one being sliced open and all their insides on display.

Lombardi, on the other hand, was more than happy to take autopsy duty. It was an opportunity to be around Isabel Delgado, even if it was the least romantic setting in the world and there was a corpse there as a third wheel. Aribo wished the guy would just ask if he could come along to one of her weekend cookouts and be done with it.

Aribo was prepping for the interview with Andi Hart when his cell phone vibrated on the desk next to him. The number that flashed on the screen belonged to Hunter Brooks.

"Is this Detective Aribo?" Brooks's voice sounded thick, like he'd just woken up.

"Mr. Brooks, I've been trying to reach you since yesterday afternoon."

"My phone's been off. I just picked up your messages and turned on the news. Someone died at Malibu Beach Drive? Wow, I guess they had an even worse day than I did."

Brooks told Aribo he'd been holed up in a hotel in Malibu since an argument with his wife at the brokers' open. He didn't go into details, but it sounded nasty. Melissa Brooks had had the locks changed on their home and had dumped her husband's belongings on the doorstep of the Malibu house. Aribo guessed Brooks had cheated on the wife with Carmen Vega, who'd also been thrown out of the party. Brooks had then retreated to a suite at a five-star hotel to lick his wounds in luxury.

Aribo noticed Brooks didn't ask who the stiff was, and he didn't know if that was because Brooks didn't care or because he already knew because he was the murderer.

"You had a showing at the house the night before the brokers' open with your client Don Garland," Aribo said. "What did you do after the showing?"

"I gave Garland a ride to his hotel, same place I'm staying right now, then I drove home."

"You didn't go anywhere else? Talk to anyone else?"

"Only the developer as I was locking up the house. Why are you asking about Thursday night? Wait. Is that when the murder happened?"

"We're just trying to establish everyone's whereabouts in the hours leading up to the party."

"I told you, I went straight home. Melissa hadn't been answering my calls and texts. Now I know why, but at the time, I was worried sick about her and wanted to get back to Brentwood as soon as possible."

"But she wasn't there when you got home," Aribo said.

"No, she stayed overnight at her parents' place."

"Is there anyone else who can verify your movements?"

"Whoa. Hold on. Am I a *suspect*?"

Aribo didn't answer.

Brooks said, "No, there isn't anyone who can verify my movements. I was alone all night. I didn't know I'd be needing . . . Actually . . . Wait. Yes! There is someone who can confirm I was at home."

"Who?"

"My neighbor. I had an Amazon delivery while I was out, and Jeff next door took the packages. He brought them over not long after I got back from Malibu. Praise the Lord for a pool float and mini waffle maker!"

"Do you have a surname and contact details for this Jeff?"

Brooks gave him the information.

Aribo said, "I'll be in touch. What's the best way to reach you?"

"On my cell phone. I'll be switching hotels to the Waldorf Astoria in Beverly Hills."

"That's where you'll be staying?"

"I don't have anywhere else to go."

Aribo spoke to the neighbor, Jeff Barnes, who confirmed he'd delivered a couple of packages to Brooks's home and they'd chatted a while about football and a show on Netflix they'd both been watching.

Hunter Brooks appeared to be in the clear.

Andi Hart sat at the table in the interview room looking as rough as he imagined Denise and Susan would be feeling about now. She was pale, her skin had the waxy sheen of boozy sweat, and her eyes were bloodshot and puffy.

He handed her a bottle of water straight from the vending machine that was slick with condensation. She took it gratefully and drank thirstily.

"Thanks," she said. "I feel like shit. The water helps."

Aribo smiled. "Heavy night?"

She nodded. "I guess I let the bartender overserve me. It's not every day you find a dead body."

Aribo didn't respond to that comment, just opened a yellow legal pad to a fresh page and clicked his pen, ready for action. His cell phone and a brown bubble envelope were also on the table.

Hart massaged her temples and winced. Her blond hair was dull and lank, like she hadn't showered this morning. She was dressed in sweats and a T-shirt and old sneakers.

"Are you feeling okay?" Aribo asked. "You're not going to hurl, are you?"

"I'm good. Well, not good, but I'm not going to throw up."

"You want to talk me through what happened yesterday?"

Hart provided a similar account to the one given by Flores—Bowers and Stringer asking to see the pool, Hart taking them out to the pool deck, the blood, the body in the water, the 911 call, Flores's vain attempts to revive the victim. Aribo's pen made a scratching sound on the paper as he took notes.

"I listened to the recording of the 911 call," he said when she was done.

"Okay."

"A couple of things bothered me."

Hart's eyes narrowed slightly. "Oh?"

"The operator asked if you'd checked if the person was still breathing and if you had attempted to perform CPR, and you said no to both. Why not? You were one of the first on the scene. Why no attempt to help?"

"Everything happened very fast. Before I could even react, Nick Flores was jumping in the pool to try to save the person, so

I didn't have to. It seemed like a more useful thing to do would be to call 911."

"Flores said you were backing away from the pool when he arrived on the deck, not rushing toward the body."

"I was pretty sure the person was dead already."

"That's the other thing that bothers me. That's what you also told the operator, even though you just told me you didn't go near the body at any point. So how did you know they were dead?"

"The body was submerged in the water, it wasn't floating on the surface. Dead bodies sink. Live ones don't. The dead ones only rise to the surface much later once putrefaction sets in. Something to do with gases in the body."

Aribo's eyebrows lifted. "I'm impressed. You seem to know a lot about drowning."

Hart stared at him for a beat. "I must have read it somewhere."

"Did you know the deceased?"

"I don't know. I already said I didn't see the body once Nick got it out of the pool." She suddenly appeared worried. "It's not someone from Saint, is it?"

"No, it's not."

"That's a relief. I'm leaving the company, but I'd hate to think something horrible like that happened to a coworker."

Aribo said, "Ms. Hart, I'm going to ask you to do something, and I'm warning you now that it's not going to be easy."

She eyed him warily. "What do you want me to do?"

"Would you be willing to look at a photograph of the deceased? It's a close-up shot of the face after they passed. It may be distressing."

"Why on earth would I want to look at a photo of a dead person?"

"We need to make a positive identification, and that's usually done by a family member."

"Yes, I understand that, but why . . ." Hart stopped talking. She stared at him. "What are you saying?"

"We believe the person who died at Malibu Beach Drive was your father."

Aribo studied her face for a reaction. There wasn't much of one. Mild shock that seemed to pass quickly. That was it.

"Okay," she said.

He removed a clear plastic evidence bag from the bubble envelope. It contained the wallet that had been recovered from the body. The wallet was open, displaying the driver's license. The man in the DL photo was in his late fifties, with blond hair going gray and cold blue eyes. Aribo slid the plastic bag across the table to Hart.

"Nolan Chapman. He's your father, right?"

She folded her arms across her chest and looked down at the wallet without touching it. She nodded.

"I need you to make the ID now, Andi. Is that okay?"

Another nod.

Aribo picked up his cell phone and found the photo that Delgado had sent him. The white foam had been cleaned from Chapman's nose and mouth, but it still wasn't pretty to look at. He passed the phone to Hart.

Aribo had seen many different reactions from family members when doing the identification. Some collapsed with shock and grief, some went into denial and refused to accept the loss of a loved one, others got violent and struck out.

Hart did none of those things. She just said, "Yes, that's Nolan Chapman." Her face was impassive. She could have been telling a server that she'd like milk in her coffee or a side of fries with her hamburger for all the emotion she showed.

"You don't seem too upset," he said.

"I'm not," she said. "I haven't spoken to him in twenty years."

"Why not?"

Hart shrugged. Stared at the table. Didn't answer him.

"Is it because of what happened in Kissimmee?" he asked.

Her head snapped up. "You know about that?"

Aribo said, "I've read the police report. You found a dead body in a swimming pool back then too."

36

ANDREA
TWENTY YEARS AGO

Andrea Chapman was feeling pretty good about herself that Friday afternoon as she walked home from school with her best friend, Shelby Talbot.

She'd made the debate team, and everyone thought they had a great chance of reaching the state championship this year. And Blake Westbrook had *finally* asked her out on a date. (Okay, what he'd actually said was "Let's hang out in Old Town tomorrow"— which was totally a date.)

Kissimmee's Old Town was an amusement park and entertainment district that featured old-time shopping, dining, and rides. The thought of making out with Blake Westbrook on one of those carnival rides made her skin tingle.

Andrea couldn't wait to tell her mom about the debate team, but she'd keep the date to herself. She was a junior, and Blake was a senior, and she didn't think her mom would approve. If her father found out, he'd flat out refuse to let her go. She'd have to make sure she wasn't spotted in Old Town with Blake if her father attended the weekly classic car show and cruise with his baby-blue '65 Ford Zodiac, like he sometimes did on a Saturday evening.

She parted company with Shelby at the corner of their respective streets and turned onto Petronia Street. It was a beautiful day, warm but not too hot. Mrs. Prescott was out on her front lawn tending to her roses.

"Hi, Mrs. Prescott."

"Oh, hi, sweetie." Mrs. Prescott removed a gardening glove and wiped her brow. "How's your mom? Hope she's feeling better."

Andrea frowned. "Feeling better?"

"Yes, she's selling my friend's house and they had a bunch of showings booked for today, but Patti called her this morning to cancel because she wasn't feeling very well."

Patti Hart was a Realtor who was well known and popular within the local community. Andrea was about to say that her mom had been absolutely fine when she'd left for school, but Patti was very reliable, so if she'd canceled her appointments, she must have had a good reason.

"Probably just one of those twenty-four-hour things," she said. "I'll tell her you were asking after her."

Andrea continued along the street, hefting her heavy bookbag from one shoulder to the other. When she reached her house, she saw her mom's car was in the driveway. Maybe Mrs. Prescott was right, maybe she was sick. Then Andrea noticed the wooden blinds in the front window were half-closed and her good mood evaporated.

She unlocked the front door and stepped into the hallway. There was shattered glass, spilled water, and scattered flowers on the floor. Andrea knew the broken glass belonged to the vase her mom had picked up at a yard sale last summer, which usually stood on the side table, always stuffed full of fresh blooms. A lamp had been knocked over too.

Andrea dropped her bookbag and closed the door. A knot of tension began pulsing at the base of her skull, traveled down her neck, and settled in her shoulders. There was a horrible stillness to the house, a tension in the air, that she knew all too well. People often spoke about the calm before the storm, but this was what Andrea always thought of as the silence after the violence.

"Mom?" she called out.

There was no answer.

The living room was warm and stuffy and empty. The only sound was the whoomph of the ceiling fan, its blades slicing vainly through stagnant air. The blinds' tilted slats prevented anyone on the street outside from witnessing what went on inside.

Andrea knew what the half-closed blinds meant.

She returned to the hallway and carefully stepped over the broken glass and scattered flowers and puddle of water. The shade on the lamp was askew.

"Mom?" Louder this time.

Andrea stopped to listen.

Nothing.

No response.

All she could hear was the thump-thump-thump of her own heartbeat.

Andrea continued into the kitchen. A chair had been upended. There was an empty vodka bottle on the table. The creeping dread turned to real fear. Only one person in this house drank vodka.

Him.

Sometimes on the rocks. Sometimes mixed in a martini. Always prepared by his wife.

The bottle hadn't been on the table when Andrea left for school. The three of them had had breakfast together as usual. Cereal for her, fruit for her mom (who was always watching her figure), and scrambled eggs and black coffee for him. The dirty dishes, utensils, and cutlery had since been washed and put away in cupboards and drawers.

The back door, which led to the pool enclosure, was ajar. Andrea walked toward it. Her heartbeat continued its too-fast rhythm.

Thump-thump-thump.

She reached for the handle, pulled the door open all the way, and entered the pool cage.

Patti Hart was in the water.

Her blond hair was fanned out around her. Her arms were out by her sides, like she was flying. She was casually dressed in jeans and a bright pink T-shirt, rather than one of the skirt suits she usually wore on a workday, which today should have been.

She was under the water. Facedown. Not moving.

"Mom!"

Andrea jumped into the pool and dragged her mom to the surface, holding her face above the water. Patti's eyes were closed, her skin was deathly pale under the tan, and she was so, so heavy. Andrea managed to pull her up the corner steps and lay her by the side of the pool. She started pumping her mom's chest. She screamed and cried and prayed. But she knew she was too late.

She also knew who was responsible.

Him.

The female police officer was kind and sympathetic and gently probing with her questions. But she asked all the wrong ones.

Had your mom been upset recently?

Was she depressed?

Had she been drinking more than usual?

Did she often drink during the day?

Did she ever hurt herself or have accidents when she'd been drinking?

Andrea tried to tell the cop that her mother wasn't a drunk. That she'd have a glass of wine with dinner, maybe a couple of glasses if she was out for lunch with a friend. Patti Hart didn't get blind drunk and knock stuff over. She never touched hard liquor. And she definitely didn't get so smashed that she fell in the pool and drowned.

As for being depressed? Okay, so her mom wasn't always a ray of sunshine, but it was hard to keep a smile on your face when you were married to a monster. When you lived every single day of your life in fear. But Andrea didn't tell the kindly police officer any of that.

"No, my mom wasn't upset recently," Andrea said. "In fact, she was pretty happy these last few weeks. Happier than she'd been in a long time."

It was true.

"I don't think that's uncommon," the cop said with a sad smile.

"What isn't?"

The policewoman didn't answer the question. All she said was "You've been very helpful, Andrea. I'm so sorry for your loss."

Andrea realized later what the cop had meant. That some depressed people appeared to be happy right before they took their own lives because they'd made the decision and were at peace with it.

It was all bullshit.

Patti Hart didn't kill herself. There was no suicide note, for a start. She would never have left Andrea on her own with *him*. And she absolutely, under no circumstances, would have allowed Andrea to find her body.

But that's what the cops were thinking. Accident or suicide. Patti Hart had gotten tanked on Grey Goose, knocked a bunch of stuff over, and then staggered out to the pool, where she either fell in or went into the water intentionally.

What the cops should have been asking was:

Was there anyone who wanted to harm her?

Why did she have old bruises on her body?

Where was her husband when this "accident" happened?

But the front door had been locked when Andrea returned from school. The windows were closed and locked too. The door leading from the pool enclosure to the backyard had also been locked and was undamaged. None of the neighbors on Petronia Street reported hearing a disturbance or witnessing anyone suspicious hanging around the house. There had been no sign of forced entry.

But a murderer didn't need to force their way into a house when they had a key.

Later, once the body had been taken to the morgue and the police and forensics people were gone, Andrea and her father ate dinner in silence. She didn't do much eating, mostly just pushed the food around on the plate. She tried not to cry, tried not to make him mad. He ate every last bite and washed the meal down with two glasses of wine.

She asked to be excused from the table.

"Not yet, Andrea," he said. "There's something you need to know about what happened today. Your mother had a drinking problem. She drank almost every day. Mostly vodka so you wouldn't smell it on her breath. She hid it from you, and she hid it from everyone else. Everyone apart from me, that is."

The only thing Patti Hart hid from the world was the beatings she endured at the hands of her husband.

Nolan Chapman. Respected construction company owner. Popular country-club member. Competitive tennis partner. Friendly neighbor. Wife beater.

"Can I go to my room now?"

Upstairs, Andrea opened the old jewelry box on her dressing table. The music played faintly, and the tiny ballerina pirouetted jerkily. She lifted out the gold bracelet she'd picked out with her mom for her sweet sixteenth and fastened it around her wrist. The photos taped around the edge of the mirror were mostly of Andrea and Shelby making goofy faces, but there were a couple of Patti too. The tears came then, and this time, she didn't try to stop them.

After a while, Andrea went over to the window and stared down at the pool cage and the still blue water that was visible through the mesh. She would never be able to look at the pool again without seeing her mom's lifeless body.

Then she thought of something else. A memory. A different day. A few months back. Andrea had arrived home early after soccer practice was canceled. Just like today, the back door had been open. She had heard voices. His angry; hers pleading. Andrea had walked over to the door and peered into the pool enclosure.

Her mom had been flat on her belly, hanging over the pool's edge. Her father was on his knees, looming over his wife. He had a fistful of her hair in his grip. Her hair and face and blouse were soaking wet. He was screaming at her. Calling her a filthy whore. Asking who she was screwing this time. She was pleading with him to let her go. Then he'd shoved her face under the water.

"Stop it!" Andrea had yelled from the doorway.

Her father had looked up at her in surprise. He'd let her mother go. Pushed her away from him. She'd lain there by the poolside, coughing and retching and trying to catch her breath.

"Go to your room, Andrea," he'd said, his blue eyes cold with rage.

235

She'd sprinted upstairs. Then she'd heard the rumble of the garage door, followed by the sound of his Zodiac starting up. When she'd looked out the window, her mom had been sitting in the pool cage, knees pulled up to her chin, weeping.

The cheating accusations were ones that Andrea had heard a million times before, even though Shelby had once overheard her mom telling a friend that Nolan Chapman was always screwing around with young women not much older than his daughter.

Andrea's father had always hated the fact that Patti chose to keep her maiden name because of her real estate business. Whenever the subject came up—and it came up often—Patti would try to reason with him.

"Everybody in town knows me as Patti Hart. My business is registered as Patti Hart Real Estate. Ditto my contracts and business accounts and IRS returns. It would have been a nightmare to change everything back then, and it would still be a nightmare now. Then there would be the cost of reprinting my letterheads and flyers, changing my newspaper ads, having new boards made up . . ."

"*Bullshit!* You want people to think you're still single so that men will hit on you and you can flirt with them and fuck around."

"I wear a wedding ring, Nolan! You're being ridiculous."

"A wedding ring can easily be removed. Your husband's name can't. Do you realize how pathetic it makes me look? Do you know what people say about me behind my back? 'How can his wife have any respect for him when she won't even take his name?' That's what they say."

Then the fighting would start for real.

Punching and slapping and kicking.

Screaming and crying and begging.

Andrea stepped away from the window and started to undress for bed, even though she knew she wouldn't be able to sleep. She opened the top drawer of the dresser and frowned. Her pajamas weren't there. A couple of her band tees were folded untidily in their place.

She opened the next drawer—where the T-shirts were usually kept—and found the pajamas stuffed in next to some sweaters. Her underwear drawer was messier than usual too. Bras and panties thrown in haphazardly instead of stacked neatly.

Andrea went into her bathroom. Her shampoo and conditioner bottles were on top of the vanity. She always kept them in the shower stall with the shower gel. She opened the medicine cabinet, and her moisturizer and cleanser were on the wrong shelf. Her favorite perfume was in there too, when it should have been on the dressing table next to the jewelry box.

Andrea crept out to the hallway. The TV was on loud downstairs. It sounded like *Seinfeld*. Her father laughed along noisily with the studio audience. His wife was lying in a freezer at the morgue and he was *laughing*.

She crept into her parents' bedroom and opened the closet where her mom kept her stuff. Andrea could tell immediately that everything was wrong. Patti always grouped the blouses together, then the dresses, then the pants, then the jeans, then her work suits. A blouse had been shoved between two pairs of pants. There were more pants at the end of the rod where the skirt suits were kept. A pair of jeans hung between two suits. Her shoes had been tossed carelessly at the bottom of the closet too. That wasn't Patti at all. Her mom had been a neat freak.

Andrea left the bedroom. Her father was still laughing at Jerry Seinfeld and Larry David downstairs. She went into the guest room. Opened the closet where the spare linen and towels and luggage were kept. She tugged on the cord for the light bulb so she could see better. The suitcases were in the wrong order. She got down on her knees and peered inside. The little dents in the carpet were no longer aligned with the wheels of the luggage.

Andrea thought of the times recently when she'd heard her mom talking in a low voice on the phone in the kitchen when Nolan was working late and she thought Andrea was upstairs doing her homework.

Maybe her father had been right, maybe Patti Hart did have a lover. Or maybe she had a friend who knew the real reason for the bruises and the heavy makeup.

Someone who wanted to help.

Someone who'd told her to get out of her abusive marriage.

Patti Hart had packed a bag for herself and for her daughter. She'd been planning on leaving Nolan Chapman. Taking them both someplace far away from Petronia Street.

She never got the chance.

37

ANDI
AFTER

Aribo said, "If the last time you spoke to Nolan Chapman was twenty years ago, you must have been, what, sixteen at the time?"

"That's right," Andi said.

She'd stuffed some clothing, her gold bracelet, and precious photos into a backpack while her father was at work. Just like her mom had done. The difference was Andi didn't get caught. She didn't wind up facedown in the pool. She'd escaped, and then she'd hitched a ride to Orlando.

Aribo nodded and doodled on the yellow legal pad. She guessed his age to be midforties. He wasn't bad looking, and he was in good shape, like he spent a lot of time in the gym. His voice was soft and conversational, but his brown eyes were alert and watchful.

"He didn't report you missing?" he asked. "Didn't try to find you? There's no record of a missing persons report being filed with the police in Florida. We checked."

Andi thought of the note she'd left for Chapman.

Don't try to find me or I'll tell them what you did.

"You'd have to ask him about that," she said. "Oh, wait. You can't."

A small smile. "What about school?"

"I dropped out."

"Why did you leave?"

"I couldn't stay with him."

"Why not?"

Andi didn't answer. The rapid-fire questions were making her headache worse. Her throat felt like sandpaper. Last night, the tequila shots had taken the edge off a shitty day of awkward showdowns with Verona and Diana and David. Now just the thought of salt and lime made her feel like puking. She uncapped the bottle of water and took another drink. It tasted like the best thing she'd ever had.

Aribo said, "Did you blame your father for what happened to your mom?"

Andi met his eyes across the table. "Yes, I did."

"It was a terrible accident, Andi. No one was to blame. It's all there in the police report."

"The police report is bullshit."

"The inquest ruled it as an accidental death too."

Andi had left Kissimmee by the time the inquest delivered its verdict. She'd read about it in the newspaper. At least they'd dropped the ridiculous idea that Patti Hart had killed herself. Instead, the world thought her mom was a stupid, careless drunk who'd fallen into her own swimming pool.

"That was bullshit too," she said.

"What do you think happened?" Aribo asked. "Do you think your father killed her?"

Andi stared at the table. She didn't want to talk about this stuff. She bit her bottom lip hard. She would not cry in front of the cop.

Aribo said, "Nolan Chapman had an alibi. He was at work. Two of his coworkers verified his whereabouts."

"They weren't 'coworkers,'" Andi said bitterly. "They were his staff, they worked for him, they did what he told them to do." She met Aribo's gaze again. "And they said whatever he told them to say. If he was at work all day, why did Mr. Scovil say he saw the Zodiac driving into the garage around lunchtime?"

"Mr. Scovil was very old. Confused. The investigating officers think he likely got the days of the week mixed up."

"Mr. Scovil was seventy-six and sharp as a tack. He knew what he saw."

Andi figured Chapman had somehow found out about Patti's plan to leave him or had returned home purely by chance and caught her packing. He'd parked the Zodiac in the garage because he never left it out in the driveway in harsh sunlight. There had been a confrontation and a fight. He'd then forced a bottle of his vodka down Patti's throat and drowned her in the pool and made her murder look like an accident.

"Where did you go?" Aribo asked.

"Orlando."

"What did you do there? You were only sixteen."

"Waited tables. Cleaned motel rooms. Worked at the amusement parks. Went to night school and got my GED. Got my real estate license and a job with a brokerage." Andi took another sip of water. "Is there a point to all of this, Detective Aribo? I'd much rather be in bed, nursing a hangover with a Big Mac and a chocolate milkshake, instead of taking a stroll down memory lane in this overly warm room."

Aribo smiled. "I'm just trying to get a sense of your relationship with the victim. But you're right, it *is* kind of hot in here."

"I've seen enough TV shows to know that's what cops do, right? Literally crank up the heat in the interrogation room to try to sweat a confession out of the suspect."

"Do you have a confession to make?" he asked lightly.

"Am I a suspect?" she shot back.

"You moved from Florida to New York, and you changed your name. Why was that?"

"Why move to New York, or why change my name?"

"Both."

"I always wanted to live in New York. I didn't want Chapman's name. You know, it was him who wanted to call me Andrea? My mom never had a say. She liked Emily. So I shortened Andrea to Andi and took my mother's maiden name." She laughed. "Believe me, that would have *really* pissed him off."

"Why did you leave New York?" Aribo asked.

"He moved there, so I moved here."

"But not long after you moved to LA, Nolan Chapman purchased the lot at Malibu Beach Drive. I checked the sale records. Then he hired the brokerage you work for to sell the house."

"That's right."

"Seems to me like he wanted to reconnect with you," Aribo said. "And yet you say you hadn't seen him in twenty years."

"I said I hadn't spoken to him in twenty years. I saw him in New York once. Through a window. That was enough. And he didn't want to 'reconnect.'"

"No? What did he want?"

"With Nolan Chapman, it was all about control," Andi said. "Control and power. He controlled his wife, his workers, even his friends. He controlled me until I was sixteen years old. He wanted that control back. He wanted to know where I was and who I was with and what I was doing. He followed me to New York, and then he followed me here."

"When did you find out he was the owner of Malibu Beach Drive?"

"Thursday night."

"The same night he died."

Andi felt her insides turn cold. She stared at the detective. She had a pretty good idea where all this was leading now. "I thought he died at the brokers' open."

Aribo drilled her with a stare. "Did you really?"

"Yes."

"He didn't. He died Thursday night. Did you kill him?"

"No."

"Maybe you wanted revenge for your mother's death? Or maybe you just wanted him out of your life for good?"

"Or maybe he got good and drunk and fell in the pool. An 'accident' just like my mother. Karma. That's what they call it, right?"

"No, Andi, they call it murder. Nolan Chapman was struck twice on the back of the head before he went into the water. Did you inflict those blows?"

"No."

"But you were at the house around the time of his death."

Not a question. There it was. What Detective Aribo had been leading up to. Get her talking, nail the motive, then place her at the scene. A thick cold sweat settled on her back. She wetted dry lips. "I don't know what time he died."

Aribo told her. "We have video of your car on Malibu Beach Drive shortly beforehand."

"I went to the house Thursday night, but I didn't go inside, and I didn't see or speak to Chapman."

"So you drove out there and just . . . sat in your car?"

Andi nodded. "When I found out Chapman owned the property and that he'd been following me around for weeks, I was mad as hell. I jumped in the car and drove to Malibu to confront him. The decorator had told me he'd be there to check on the place before the brokers' open. When I got there, all the lights were on. I sat a while and watched the house."

"Why didn't you confront him?"

"I didn't get the chance. It's like I said, I hadn't seen him in two decades. I was working up to it, trying to decide if I really wanted to speak to him after all this time. Just when I'd decided that, yes, I did want to tell him to his face to get the fuck out of my life, another car showed up. I drove off. Went home."

"Which route did you take?"

"I drove farther along the street and made the first turn I came to. From there, I found my way back to the highway. Then I headed north through the mountains and got on the 101 at Calabasas."

"Did you recognize the other car?"

"Sure, it was Krystal's Porsche."

"Did you see Mrs. Taylor?"

"Yes. Just as I was about to make the turn, I looked in my rearview mirror. She'd gotten out of the car and was reaching back inside for something."

"What was she reaching for?"

"I couldn't say for sure, but it looked like a bottle. She was holding it by the neck. Knowing Krystal, it was probably champagne."

Aribo seemed to sit up a little straighter in his chair. "Does she have a favorite brand?"

"Cristal," Andi answered immediately. "She loves it because it's expensive, and it sounds like her name."

38

ARIBO
AFTER

Lombardi got back from Nolan Chapman's autopsy just before two.

"Delgado has concluded that the two wounds to the back of the skull *were* inflicted with a blunt instrument," he announced. "We officially have ourselves a homicide investigation."

Aribo nodded. "She say how?"

"She believes the first blow happened when he was in a standing position. It would have been unexpected and enough to daze him. He dropped to his knees, and the perp smashed him on the head again. This cut was deeper and would have done more damage. Lots of blood and a loss of consciousness. We still don't know how he wound up in the pool."

Aribo briefly filled his partner in on the interview with Andi Hart, then said, "Fancy paying a surprise visit to the indisposed Krystal Taylor?"

They stopped off on the way for a quick takeout lunch at the Jack in the Box on Agoura Road. They ate outside in the lot, using the hood of Aribo's Mustang as a makeshift table for the food and drinks.

Aribo had the Cluck Sandwich, while Lombardi opted for tacos and curly fries that he wolfed down in about two minutes flat. Aribo watched him and said, "How can you even eat so soon after an autopsy?"

"I have a very strong stomach. And I'm starving after skipping breakfast. That's the secret to getting through an autopsy without throwing up—don't eat beforehand. That way, if you do need to barf, there's nothing to come up."

"I bet Delgado has a strong stomach too, but even she skips her neighborhood cookout right after doing a cut." Aribo eyed him slyly. "Speaking of your favorite DME, have you asked her out on a date yet?"

Lombardi wiped taco sauce off his chin with a paper napkin and shook his head. "No way."

"You'll happily chase after armed criminals and hunt down murderers, but you won't ask a woman out to dinner?"

"Don't forget rescuing kittens from trees."

"You've never rescued a kitten from a tree in your life."

"According to my Tinder profile, I have."

They trashed their wrappers and paper cups, got back in the car, and hit the 101. The Saturday-afternoon traffic was lighter than weekday rush hour, but the freeway was still crammed.

"I finally found the missing Myles that everyone was looking for," Lombardi said. "He's in the hospital with a concussion, two broken legs, and a broken wrist."

"Holy shit. What happened?"

"Assault and robbery the night before the brokers' open. They took his Rolex, wallet, cell phone, and even his clothes. He was found in an alleyway in the early hours of Friday, wearing only his boxers, by a transient who was pissed off that someone had stolen his patch. Apparently, the boxers were Calvin Klein, so it's a wonder the assailants—there were at least two of them—didn't make off with those too. When the homeless guy realized Goldman was seriously hurt, he found a pay phone and called 911. He keeps asking about a reward. The broken wrist didn't happen during the assault, by the way. That was a couple days earlier."

Aribo glanced at Lombardi. "Wow. Either Goldman is really clumsy or really unlucky."

"Squash injury. A particularly competitive game with Hunter Brooks."

"Those agents at Saint Realty are starting to make the inmates at the county jail look like kindergarteners."

Lombardi said, "Seeing as Goldman was half-naked and unconscious in a pool of piss and blood in a stinking alleyway when Chapman got whacked, I guess he's off the suspects list. You still liking Hart for it after what she told you earlier? It sure sounds like she hated Chapman enough to do it."

"She has motive and she was at the house. None of the doorbell cameras on Malibu Beach Drive captured her leaving the scene, but even if they did, it proves nothing either way. The time she says she spent sitting outside the house contemplating a family reunion was long enough to knock Chapman unconscious and shove him in the pool."

"What about Krystal Taylor?" Lombardi asked. "We know her Porsche was there Thursday night too. And Hart thinks she saw her with a champagne bottle."

"That's what Hart says anyway. Maybe she was the one who brought the champagne? A pretend peace offering for Chapman, a way to get inside the house and get him relaxed. Then she hit him with the bottle and cleaned up after herself. Maybe Taylor didn't actually enter the house because Chapman was too dead to answer the door."

"Only one way to find out," Lombardi said.

Aribo took the Coldwater Canyon Avenue exit, then continued south on Mulholland and into Trousdale Estates. They pulled up in front of Krystal Taylor's house, and Lombardi let out a low whistle.

"Not bad."

"You got everything we need?" Aribo asked.

Lombardi held up a manila folder. "It's all right here."

Krystal's red Porsche and her husband's Aston Martin were in the driveway. A white soft-top Jaguar F-TYPE was parked on the street outside their house.

"Looks like the Taylors are both at home," said Lombardi.

"And they already have company," said Aribo.

Micah Taylor answered the door, filling most of the frame with his impressive bulk. He eyed them the way he used to eye the opposition. The detectives introduced themselves and asked to speak to his wife.

"Krystal is sick. She's not up to visitors right now."

Lombardi said, "We won't take up much of her time. We just need to check her off our list."

"I don't know . . ."

Aribo said, "Man, I can't believe we're actually standing here talking to Micah Taylor. Wait until the guys at the station hear about this."

"You a Rams fan?"

"Go to most of the home games when the work allows." Aribo shook his head in admiration. "I was there for your sixty-yard punt return for that touchdown against the Bengals. What a night that was."

Taylor smiled at the memory. "Yeah, it was pretty cool. Hey, let me see if Krystal is well enough for a quick chat."

Aribo winked at Lombardi as they were led into a neat, sparsely decorated living area where everything from the couches to the furniture to the rug was white. A man was sitting on a white leather easy chair. He wore a white linen suit, a pink T-shirt, and slip-on shoes and clearly took his style inspiration from *Miami Vice*, except it wasn't the '80s anymore, and the guy was at least fifty.

Taylor said, "This is my agent, Al Toledo. Al, these gentlemen are Detectives Aribo and Lombardi from the LASD. They're here to speak to Krystal. I'll go get her. See if she wants to talk."

Toledo nodded but made no move to get up and offer a hand-shake. He made no attempt at small talk either to fill the awkward silence.

A few minutes later, Krystal Taylor followed her husband down a floating staircase. She was barefoot and dressed in leggings and an oversized turtleneck sweater despite the hot weather. Long blond extensions hung around a face so white it matched the furniture. She settled next to Micah on a couch. The detectives took the matching one facing them. Lombardi was on note-taking duty again and produced a pad and pen from his back pocket.

Aribo said, "Thanks for agreeing to talk to us, Mrs. Taylor. Especially as you're so unwell. Although it might be best if we spoke to you alone?"

Before she could answer, Toledo piped up. "Krystal isn't being formally questioned, is she? It's just an informal chat, right?"

"That's right," said Aribo.

"Then I think it's best that Micah and I stay."

Aribo turned his attention back to Krystal Taylor. "A body was discovered at a property on Malibu Beach Drive yesterday during a brokers' open that was being hosted by your employer."

"Yeah, we saw it on the news," Toledo butted in. "Krystal wasn't there."

Aribo glared at him. "We're here to talk to Mrs. Taylor, not you."

Toledo held his hands up and sat back in the chair, but he didn't look happy.

Krystal said, "Al's right. I saw it on the news. I wasn't at the brokers' open. I was sick."

"The deceased was a man named Nolan Chapman. He was the property's developer. How well did you know Mr. Chapman?"

She hesitated. "The developer I met was called Marty Stein. He's the one who showed the agents around the house on Tuesday."

"That's correct, but tell me about your dealings with Mr. Chapman. You did know him, didn't you?"

A longer pause this time. "No. I don't think so."

"I'd like you to take a look at this photograph."

Aribo signaled to his partner, and Lombardi opened the folder and took out a blown-up version of Chapman's driver's license photo. He placed it on a coffee table between the two couches and pushed it toward Krystal Taylor. Aribo noticed her hand trembling as she picked it up.

"That's Mr. Chapman in the photo. Are you sure you don't know him?"

She glanced at the image and shook her head. "I've never met him." She returned the picture to Lombardi, who withdrew three more photos from the file. He laid one of them in front of her. Krystal's eyes widened when she saw what it was.

Aribo said, "This is a still from one of the cameras at the hotel where Mr. Chapman was staying. That's you sitting with Mr. Chapman at the bar on Wednesday evening. He bought you a drink, you chatted for a while, and then you left together."

Al Toledo puffed out air noisily. Micah Taylor frowned at the photo on the table and then at his wife. Krystal Taylor stared at the image of her and Chapman like she was hoping it would suddenly change into something else. She didn't say anything.

Lombardi placed the other two images on the glass tabletop, like he was dealing cards. It was another hand that she wasn't going to like.

Aribo said, "CCTV from the hotel's corridor this time. You and Mr. Chapman entering his suite. Then you leaving alone, just under two hours later."

"Oh, jeez," said Toledo.

"What the fuck, Krystal?" said the husband.

"It was a business meeting," she mumbled.

"In his fucking hotel suite?" Taylor yelled, and she flinched.

Aribo said, "Clearly, you did know Mr. Chapman. Why lie to us, Mrs. Taylor?"

Toledo said, "You don't have to answer that, Krystal."

Aribo shot him a warning look. "Mr. Toledo, please."

"I didn't recognize him from the picture you showed me, okay?" Krystal said.

"You spent an evening in his company—including a considerable amount of time in his hotel suite—and you didn't know his name either?"

"I guess I forgot," she said, her chin jutting out defiantly now. "I'm terrible with names."

"Where were you between the hours of seven p.m. and eleven p.m. on Thursday night?"

"I . . . um . . . let me think."

Toledo said, "Why are you asking about Thursday night? The news said this Chapman guy was bumped off yesterday at the brokers' open."

Aribo wondered why Krystal hadn't asked the same question. He said, "Nolan Chapman died the evening before the party."

"Krystal was at home all night," Micah Taylor said. "She was sick."

Lombardi said, "Were you here all evening too, Mr. Taylor? Can you personally vouch for your wife's whereabouts?"

"Well, no," he admitted. "I had a business thing with Al. But I know she was in bed sick all night because that's what she told me when I got home. Right, babe?"

"Right." Krystal was eyeing Lombardi's file like he might show her something else that she didn't want to see. He didn't disappoint.

This time it was a still of her Porsche 911, captured on one of the doorbell cameras on Malibu Beach Drive.

"This is your car, right?" Aribo asked.

The license plate was clearly visible.

Krystal Taylor wrapped her arms around her slim body. "I'm sorry. I have a terrible migraine. I can't even think straight. Can we stop now?"

Aribo ignored her. "This image is from Thursday night, shortly before Mr. Chapman died in the pool at his property. You were there, weren't you? You were with Mr. Chapman the night he died?"

"Hey, my wife already told you she was here all night," Micah Taylor said. "I think we're done here."

Aribo made no move to get up. "We need to establish how her car was at a crime scene when she claimed to be at home at the same time."

"Maybe the car was stolen. Did you think about that, huh? Maybe someone else was driving." Taylor's voice was getting louder with every word. "Your stupid photo doesn't show who's behind the wheel, does it?"

"The Porsche is in the driveway outside," Lombardi pointed out.

"Maybe whoever stole it brought it back. Maybe they were kids. Joyriders. I don't know." He stood up, towering over them, and pointed to the door. "Now get the hell out of my house. We. Are. Done. Here."

Aribo spoke to Krystal. "Were you at Malibu Beach Drive when Nolan Chapman was murdered?"

"I . . . no . . . I wasn't."

"We have a witness who saw you at the house."

Krystal looked up at her husband, wide eyed, but it was the agent who came to her rescue.

"Don't say another word, Krystal," Al Toledo ordered. He turned to Aribo. "Mr. Taylor has asked you to leave. If you want to speak to Krystal again, you'll have to do so with her lawyer present. I'll show you both out."

Toledo got up out of the chair, buttoned his jacket, and started toward the front door.

Lombardi snapped his notepad shut and collected the photos.

Aribo said, "We'll be in touch."

Toledo watched them from the doorway as they walked across the lawn to the Mustang. They got in and fastened their seatbelts, and the agent closed the door.

Lombardi said, "Well, that was interesting. She did look kind of sick, though."

Aribo said, "Sick, my ass. Krystal Taylor lied to us twice—about knowing Chapman and about being at the Malibu house. You ask me, the only thing that's wrong with her is a guilty conscience."

39

KRYSTAL
AFTER

The front door slammed shut and Krystal jumped. Her nerve endings were like live wires. Al Toledo returned to the living area. "They're gone."

He walked across the room and settled back into the chair. She'd hoped he would leave too, but he clearly had no intention of going anywhere, and Micah wouldn't make him. Her husband was still standing. He looked furious. His hands were bunched into fists. She knew he wouldn't hit her—he never had and he never would—but she was worried he might take his anger out on the wall. Hurt himself.

"Sit down, Micah," she said. "We need to talk."

His jaw worked and his fingers flexed. He nodded. "Damn straight we do." He went to the couch the cops had just vacated. "Let's start with what you were doing in some old dude's hotel suite?"

"Now an old dead dude," Toledo said.

"Zip it, Al," Micah snapped, his eyes never leaving her. "You'd better answer me, Krystal."

"It was work, just like I told those cops. You heard what they said, he owned one of the properties Saint is supposed to be selling. I was doing my job. That's all."

"Do you think I'm stupid?" he asked quietly.

Krystal didn't answer.

"I said—do you think I'm stupid?"

"No, of course not."

"So I will ask you again—what were you doing in the dead guy's hotel suite?"

"I told you—"

"You were screwing him."

"No!"

"How old was he? Sixty? Older? Are you really that desperate?"

"It was work. And he was fifty-eight."

"Women don't go to dudes' hotel rooms for work meetings. They go there for sex."

"Oh, you'd know all about that, wouldn't you?" Krystal spat. She couldn't help herself.

If Micah caught her meaning, he didn't show it. He kept on talking, as though he hadn't heard her. "You're disgusting, do you know that? Once a tramp, always a tramp."

Krystal jumped up and yelled at him, "Don't you dare talk to me like that, you stupid asshole."

Micah sprung to his feet too and screamed, "Did you screw him?"

"Yes, I screwed him!" she screamed back. "And it was fucking fantastic."

"Oh boy," Toledo said.

Micah looked like he'd been slapped. He dropped back onto the couch and put his head in his hands.

Krystal hadn't been lying earlier about having a headache, and now it felt like her skull was being crushed in a vise. Her legs were

255

shaky, and she was sweating in the oversized turtleneck. She sat back down.

"How could you do this to me?" Micah looked up at her, his eyes wet.

The only time she'd seen him cry before was when he'd lost the Super Bowl. Krystal should have felt shame or regret or remorse, but there was only more anger. This whole mess was because of Micah's own cheating.

"I did it because of your affair," she said.

"Huh?" Toledo said.

"What affair?" Micah said.

"I know, Micah. I've known for months."

"Know what? There is no affair."

"I've been following you. There's no point trying to deny it."

"You've been *following* me? What the fuck, Krystal?"

"Yes, and I've seen you with her."

"Seen me with who? There is no 'her.' You're crazy, woman!"

"The redhead. The one you've been meeting in hotels all over town." She checked each one off on a finger. "The Sunset Tower. The Pendry. The Chateau Marmont. The Moment."

Micah looked confused.

She went on. "Five-two. Late thirties. Drives a Mercedes. This ringing any bells yet?"

Toledo said, "Oh shit. I think she means Vanessa."

Micah leaned back and pressed his hands to his eyes and laughed, but there was no joy to the laughter. "Oh, man. Vanessa."

"You think this is funny?"

"I think it's fucking hilarious. Vanessa Tanner isn't my lover. She's my biographer."

"Your what?"

"She's writing my book."

"It's true," said Toledo.

"You're lying," Krystal said. "There is no book. We talked about this already. Right after the Super Bowl. We both agreed to turn down the deal."

Not long after he'd retired, Micah had been offered $500,000 by a big New York publishing house for his autobiography. Al Toledo had been very keen, of course, because he'd only been thinking about his 15 percent cut. Krystal had hated the idea. She knew what those books were like. Everything would come out—all the women Micah had had before her, Krystal's refusal to have children, even though Micah was desperate for a son, her failed Hollywood career, her poor upbringing in Texas.

There had been a few newspaper stories over the years, reporters trying to dig up dirt on both of them, and those had been bad enough. A book would be much worse. There would be no denying the ugly truths that she'd worked so hard to gloss over all these years. As far as Krystal was concerned, $500,000 was nowhere near enough for the world to know their secrets—*her* secrets. She'd pleaded with Micah to turn down the offer, and he'd reluctantly agreed.

Now he was sheepish. "I did turn them down, but then they came back to us about six months ago and offered even more money, and well, Al convinced me to go for it. We figured it'd be best to keep it secret for a while, just until the first draft was done. Then, once you'd read it, you'd realize it wasn't so bad. You'd be okay with the book, and we'd have a nice big paycheck in the bank."

Toledo said, "We decided Micah and Vanessa Tanner should conduct their interviews in the privacy of a hotel room. They couldn't meet here at the house for obvious reasons. Public places were out too, because Micah didn't want the paparazzi snapping pics of him and Vanessa together and speculating about an affair. And we didn't want anyone overhearing sensitive information being discussed as part of those conversations. Not with all that money at stake."

"I thought work meetings didn't happen in hotel rooms?" Krystal countered. "Why should I believe a word either of you are telling me?"

Toledo got up from the chair and showed her his phone. On the screen was a photo of the redhead. It was a page from her website, detailing her work as a writer. She'd worked on autobiographies with a number of film and sports stars. He said, "I have the contract at my office. I can show you that too."

Krystal flashed back to the document she'd seen Micah with, in his study. A horrible sense of dread settled in the pit of her belly. What had she done? It had all been for nothing.

"You really thought I was having an affair?" Micah asked.

She nodded. "You were out all the time. Being super secretive."

"And you slept with this Chapman guy for revenge? To get back at me?"

"No, not revenge."

"Then why?"

The hurt on Micah's face was almost unbearable.

"The commission for finding a buyer for Malibu Beach Drive was one million dollars. The other agents at Saint had clients who were interested, so I had to win Chapman over, do whatever it took for him to accept my client's offer. I needed that money. Badly."

"Sure, a million bucks is a lot of green, but I don't get why you needed it so badly. We have at least five times that much in the bank. And more coming in all the time with my endorsement deals."

"No, *you* have that money in the bank. I don't. In any case, you signed a book deal for less money than the potential Malibu commission."

"It's a book deal! It's talking to a writer, telling my own story in my own words. It's not having sex with someone for money." He gestured around him, and his tone softened. "Is this not enough for you? Do I not give you enough? You have to sleep with old dudes for money again?"

"I thought you were going to leave me, okay? Leave me for the redhead. Leave me with nothing. I . . . I couldn't go back to being *her* again. I couldn't go back to being poor."

"Oh, Krystal . . ."

She thought of something. "You didn't want to be spotted with this Vanessa woman by the paparazzi, but you were with her at Grandmaster Recorders a few nights ago. I saw you. You didn't care about photographers then."

Micah sighed. "It was a celebratory dinner. The interviews are over, and the first draft is almost complete. Al was supposed to be there too. He got held up and joined us at Vanessa's place in Studio City for drinks later."

"Why not have drinks at the restaurant? Why her place?"

"She has a fourteen-year-old son who was at a friend's house. She had to be home by ten because that's when he was being dropped off by the friend's mom."

"It's all true," said Toledo.

Micah said, "I would never leave you, Krystal. I love you. Don't you know that by now?"

She started crying hard then. Micah sat down beside her and held her. She clung on to him. His big arms had always made her feel safe, and she wondered how she could have doubted him. How she could have betrayed him. How she could have . . .

Micah said, "I hate what you did, but I shouldn't have lied to you about the book deal. We can fix this, okay?"

Toledo said, "First, we have to fix this situation with the cops. They're going to come back, you know. They're going to want to know why the Porsche was in Malibu the night Chapman died."

Micah pulled away and stared at her. "Why *was* your car there? You were at home all night, right? Just like you said."

Krystal turned away.

"Krystal? Look at me."

She shook her head. She wouldn't look at him. There was a fresh wave of tears. Her chest heaved.

Micah said, "You say you've been sick for days, but I haven't seen you throw up once. No fever. No coughing or sneezing either."

"She told the cops it was a migraine," Toledo said, but he didn't sound too convinced.

"Krystal doesn't get migraines. And she said she'd been vomiting. A stomach bug or a virus. That's why her clothes were in the washing machine when I got home, because she'd thrown up all over them. That is why you were washing them . . . right?"

She still didn't answer him.

There was panic in Micah's voice now. "Why have you been wearing that old sweater all the time too? It's almost a hundred out. Everyone's broiling in this heat, and you're all covered up, and you're never all covered up."

Krystal finally looked at him. She could taste her tears. Her head felt like it might shatter into a thousand pieces. "Micah . . ."

"Take off the sweater, Krystal."

"Please . . . I'm so sorry . . ."

"Take it off. Now."

She took off the sweater.

Toledo said, "Oh fuck."

Micah said, "What have you done?"

40

ARIBO
AFTER

Sunday morning.

Aribo and Lombardi were in the conference room at the Lost
Hills station, providing an update to Garcia. The captain sat at the
head of a long white table with the two detectives on either side
of him.

When Aribo and Lombardi had gotten back to the station
yesterday after the visit to Krystal Taylor's house, Nolan Chapman's
cell phone records had been waiting for them. They'd gone through
all incoming and outgoing calls in the days leading up to the murder. Chapman had spoken to Marty Stein and David Saint a number of times, which was to be expected considering his working
relationship with both of them. He hadn't spoken with either man
on his cell on the day of the murder. Ditto Andi Hart. They could
find nothing to suggest she'd had any contact at all with her father
prior to his death.

Krystal Taylor was a different story. A call had been made from
her cell phone to Chapman on Thursday at 7:52 p.m. The call had
lasted under a minute. Seven minutes later, her Porsche was seen on

Malibu Beach Drive. Around forty minutes after that, Chapman's watch had stopped when he was attacked.

They laid it all out for Garcia. He didn't seem impressed. He sat back in his chair and stroked the stubble on his chin, appearing troubled.

"Follow up with Taylor," he said. "Nail her down on her whereabouts and her car being in Malibu. And ask her to explain the phone call she made to Chapman shortly before the murder. But right now, it's very thin. Too thin."

Lombardi said, "CSU got a couple strands of blond hair from one of the chaises. It could belong to Taylor."

"One of the *whats*?" Garcia said.

"He means an outdoor lounge chair," Aribo said. "Apparently, rich people call them *chaises*."

Garcia said, "Even if the hair does belong to Krystal Taylor, she was at a tour of the house a few days before the murder, remember? She'll say the hair got on the chaise then. It's not enough, Detectives. Not even close. Do we have a motive? Do we have any reason why Krystal Taylor would want Chapman dead?"

"Crime of passion?" Lombardi suggested.

Garcia said, "We don't even know that there *was* any passion involved. Maybe they did just discuss business in his hotel room Wednesday. And even if they did do the horizontal tango, it doesn't mean that she bashed his skull in twenty-four hours later."

Lombardi sighed and ran his hands through his hair. Aribo knew how his partner was feeling. Tired and frustrated. They had two suspects—Taylor and Hart—and nothing concrete to tie either one of them to Nolan Chapman's murder.

The captain was still talking. "We have to tread very carefully with this one. Micah Taylor is still a big name. The last thing we want is to arrest his wife and then have to let her go because we have nothing but very circumstantial evidence and a hunch that she did it. We don't need this case to become a bigger media circus than it already is."

"Speaking of which." Aribo held aloft his cell phone, displaying an incoming call from the TV reporter Mitch O'Malley. "The biggest clown in the circus."

He rejected the call.

Garcia said, "What about the daughter?"

Aribo said, "We found out the Malibu house now belongs to Hart—or at least it will once all the legal stuff is dealt with. Chapman's other finances are a bit more complicated. Lots of cash tied up in various companies and shares and so on. That's going to take longer to untangle and find out who else benefits financially from his death."

"So Andi Hart has motive—and plenty of it," said Garcia. "She blamed Chapman for her mother's death, she didn't like him showing up wherever she was, and she's about to become a very rich young woman now that he's dead."

Aribo said, "The business partner, Marty Stein, didn't think Hart knew anything about the inheritance. And we can't place her inside the house with Chapman. Only outside in her car before Taylor got there."

"Bring me something solid, Detectives," Garcia said. "Preferably the murder weapon with a nice set of prints on it."

Lombardi said, "We still have deputies out searching every drain and dumpster in the area. The beach and bluffs too. Nada so far."

Aribo's phone vibrated with a text. He glanced at it and frowned. "It's a message from O'Malley. He's asking what the press conference is about."

Now it was Garcia's turn to frown. "I didn't authorize any press conference. What the hell is he talking about?"

"Probably making stuff up as usual," Lombardi said. "The guy has made a career out of it, after all."

Aribo said, "He says it's happening on the front steps of the station in thirty minutes' time. He's asking if there's been a breakthrough in the case."

Garcia pulled his phone from his pocket. "I'll see what media relations has to say about—"

There was a knock at the door, and a deputy stuck his head into the room.

"Sorry to interrupt," he said nervously. "But I thought you'd want to know that Krystal Taylor is at the front desk with her lawyer. She says she's ready to talk about the night of the murder."

41

KRYSTAL
AFTER

Krystal was taken to an interview room that was too warm.

The two detectives who'd come to her home—Aribo and Lombardi—faced her across the table. She declined the offer of water because she wanted to give the impression of being cool and calm and composed when, really, she was finding the claustrophobic environment stifling.

Next to her sat her lawyer. She'd never met the man before last night. Al Toledo had hired him. Larry Carmichael had a long face, bald head, and pallid skin that spoke of a serious vitamin D deficiency. He wore wire-rimmed spectacles and never seemed to smile.

It was also Al's idea to voluntarily come to the Lost Hills station to make a statement, show that she had nothing to hide, that she was willing to cooperate with the police, and that she had an answer for all their questions and concerns.

Aribo, the one who seemed to be in charge, started off by advising her that the interview was being recorded. Neither of the detectives were wearing a jacket, and both of them had their shirt sleeves rolled up to the elbows and their top buttons undone. Carmichael was wearing a three-piece suit and didn't seem to notice the heat. Krystal's fingers instinctively went to loosen the silk scarf she wore around her neck before she realized that would be a bad idea. She clasped her hands together on the table instead.

Aribo said, "You wanted to talk to us about the night Mr. Chapman died."

"That's correct."

"What would you like to tell us, Mrs. Taylor?"

She glanced at the lawyer for guidance, and he nodded once curtly, giving his permission for her to speak.

"I was there," she said. "At the house in Malibu. With Nolan. That's why you have a photo of my car on Malibu Beach Drive."

Lombardi raised his eyebrows a fraction and scribbled some notes on a legal pad. Aribo kept his eyes on her. She made a point of meeting his gaze and showing him that she wasn't going to be intimidated.

"Why did you tell us you were at home all night?" he asked.

The lawyer answered for her this time. "When you spoke with my client yesterday, you were told that she was feeling unwell. Mrs. Taylor had been suffering from a rather severe migraine, which caused her thought processes to become cloudy."

Lombardi said, "Mr. Taylor also seemed to be under the impression that his wife had been at home all of Thursday night."

The lawyer again. "Mr. Taylor accepts that he may have mis-remembered their conversation. Mrs. Taylor had taken unwell on Thursday evening following her return from Malibu. She was in bed when Mr. Taylor got home, and he acknowledges now that he *assumed* she'd been in bed ill all evening. He's happy to make a clarification in a formal statement."

Lombardi made a snorting sound.

The lawyer said, "Did you have something you wanted to say, Detective?"

Lombardi said, "Nope. Please carry on."

Aribo said, "Talk us through how you came to be at the property with Mr. Chapman."

Krystal said, "I had a buyer for Malibu Beach Drive who was willing to pay the full asking price. This was before the property had even gone on the market. Naturally, I was very excited and decided to drive out to Malibu to tell Nolan in person. I took a bottle of Cristal champagne with me from the wine cellar at home. I called Nolan to let him know I was on my way to his hotel and had good news. He told me he was at the house and to meet him there instead. So that's what I did."

Carmichael opened his briefcase and pulled out a sheet of paper. He passed it across the table to the detectives. "A copy of an email from Mrs. Taylor's client, Ryoko Yamada, confirming her interest in submitting an offer for Malibu Beach Drive."

Lombardi read the email and then passed it to his partner.

"What time did you arrive at the property?" Aribo asked.

"Around eight."

"Then what happened?"

"It was such a beautiful night. Nolan suggested we go sit out on the pool deck and take in the view while enjoying the champagne. I told him the news about Ryoko Yamada's offer, and he was just thrilled. He popped open the champagne. I think he'd already had a couple of drinks at the hotel earlier in the evening. I had maybe half a glass and started to get a headache, so I didn't have any more champagne. Nolan drank the rest of the bottle."

"Are you saying Mr. Chapman was drunk?"

She shrugged. "I don't know. A little, I guess."

"So Mr. Chapman got drunk. Then what? A nice evening took a nasty turn? Things got heated and then got violent and you struck Mr. Chapman over the head? Is that what happened?"

"No, of course not. There was no argument or altercation of any kind. I told you, it was a celebration. Nolan was perfectly fine when I left."

"If he was perfectly fine, how come he was found dead in the pool just hours later with two serious head wounds?"

The lawyer held up a hand to stop her from answering. "Finding out how Mr. Chapman came to be injured is your job, Detective. Mrs. Taylor is here to give you the facts, not to offer speculation."

"What time did you leave, Mrs. Taylor?"

"Just before eight thirty. I didn't stay long."

"What happened to the champagne bottle and flutes?"

"I took them with me."

"Why would you do that?"

"Nolan asked me to get rid of them. The bottle was empty, and he didn't want any mess ahead of the brokers' open the next day."

"Why not just put them in the trash at the house? Why go to the bother of taking them with you?"

Krystal smiled. "I knew Diana had ordered Dom Pérignon for the party, and everyone knows I drink Cristal. I didn't want any of the other agents to spot the Cristal bottle in the trash and know that I'd been at the house with Nolan. And I definitely didn't want them to know what we were celebrating. Not until Ryoko Yamada's offer had been accepted. It's a very competitive agency."

"What did you do with the bottle and flutes?"

"I stopped on the way home and tossed them in a dumpster."

Aribo frowned. "A dumpster? Not your own trash at home?"

"My husband could have found them there and asked questions about who I'd been drinking champagne with. Believe me, the dumpster was easier."

"And you trashed the flutes too? Glass flutes?"

Krystal swallowed. "That's right."

"Seems a little odd that you didn't take them home and wash them. That's what most people would do, right?"

She forced a laugh. "I don't do washing; it wrecks my manicure. And they were just regular flutes. Nothing fancy. Easily replaceable."

Aribo stared at her a beat, then asked, "Do you remember which dumpster?"

Krystal pretended to think about it. "I think it was on Coldwater Canyon just after I got off the freeway."

Aribo gave a slight nod, and Lombardi got up and left the room. Krystal knew he'd gone to dispatch some poor rookie cop to the dumpster to trawl through the garbage before it was taken to a landfill.

Aribo said, "Did you strike Mr. Chapman over the head?"

"No, I did not."

"Did you push Mr. Chapman into the pool?"

"No, I did not."

"Did you kill Mr. Chapman?"

"No. I already told you, Nolan was absolutely fine when I left. I'd just told him about a fifty-million-dollar offer on his property. I was about to make one million in commission from the sale myself. Why on earth would I want Nolan Chapman dead?"

Aribo didn't say anything, and she knew it was because he didn't have an answer to that key question.

Carmichael said, "I think we're all done here unless you have any other questions, Detective?"

Aribo didn't have any other questions.

Krystal and the lawyer made their way out of the stuffy room and along a much cooler corridor and finally outside to where the press had gathered on the front steps. Al Toledo had tipped off the reporters about an impromptu press conference. He seemed to think it would make her look less guilty if she faced the cameras as a star witness as opposed to being named as a potential suspect by a "police source" later.

Micah had been waiting in his car and joined her now outside the front entrance of the station. That had been Al's idea too. The reporters jostled for position, pushing and shoving each other and thrusting their microphones in her and Micah's faces. Photographers snapped dozens of shots. Questions were thrown at them.

Krystal had taken a leaf out of Verona's book when selecting her outfit. A pink fitted dress that fell just below the knee and heels that were midheight as opposed to skyscraper. A little more demure than usual. The pink-and-white silk Hermès scarf tied around her neck was a perfect match for the dress—and the perfect way to hide the bruising on her neck that had been inflicted by Nolan Chapman.

Krystal smiled at Micah as he slipped a protective arm around her shoulders and bantered with the reporters.

The lawyer didn't know about the bruising. Only Al and Micah had been told how Chapman had turned violent and grabbed her by the throat and started throttling her. How she'd fought him off, and he'd fallen and struck his head on the ground but had still been very much alive when she'd fled. Al thought it best that the lawyer didn't know that version of events.

Just as Krystal had thought it best that Micah and Al didn't know what really happened the night Nolan Chapman died.

42

ANDI
AFTER

Andi Hart found Detective Aribo halfway along Malibu Pier, sipping a takeout coffee and watching the surfers riding the waves off Surfrider Beach. It was a good spot, with sweeping views of the coast studded with impressive houses, and a stiff breeze to take the heat out of the midafternoon sun.

Aribo handed her a takeout cup and pulled some sugar and creamer packets from his pocket. "I wasn't sure how you took it."

She thanked him and dumped a packet of each into the black coffee. The drink was still hot and burned the tip of her tongue. She said, "That was quite a performance Krystal Taylor and her husband put on for the cameras a few days ago."

Aribo smiled wryly. "It was certainly unexpected."

"The police didn't know about it?"

He shook his head. "By the time the captain got hold of media relations on a Sunday—and confirmed there definitely wasn't a press conference scheduled—it was already underway. It wouldn't have been a great look to bring an appeal for information to a halt in front of all those cameras."

Krystal had told reporters how she'd had a brief professional relationship with the property developer, Nolan Chapman, and had been absolutely devastated to learn of his death. She hadn't been present at the brokers' open when his body was discovered, but she was, of course, assisting the police in any way that she could. She'd then made a heartfelt plea for anyone with information to get in touch with the Los Angeles County Sheriff's Department and had ended the brief statement by saying she hoped the killer would be caught and brought to justice.

"What did you think of it?" Andi asked. "Just plain attention seeking or something more calculated?"

Aribo smiled but didn't answer. Instead, he said, "Why did you ask to meet me, Andi?"

"I wanted to show you something."

She fished in her purse for her cell phone. Thumbed the screen until she found what she was looking for and handed it to Aribo.

"What am I looking at?"

"Footage from a security camera my downstairs neighbor installed outside my apartment. It's from the night Nolan Chapman was murdered. With everything that's been going on, I completely forgot that my building has cameras, otherwise I would have shown it to you sooner."

Aribo watched the video. It showed Andi parking in the driveway next to her apartment and making her way up a staircase to her front door. Her image was bright and clear in the night-vision mode. The date stamp was Thursday night.

She said, "No blood on my clothes. No murder weapon in my hand. And I'd need to be an absolute psychopath to look that calm if I'd just murdered someone. Plus, the time stamp proves I drove back from Malibu when I said I did. That I left as soon as Krystal showed up. That I didn't go back after she left and take a swing at Chapman."

"Can you email this to me?"

"Sure." She took the phone from him and emailed the file. "It helps, right?"

Aribo nodded. "It helps. Let's walk."

They strolled back along the old rough wooden planks toward the pier's entrance. Fishermen lined the deck, their gear spread out on nearby benches and their rods cast in the hopes of catching halibut and corbina and mackerel.

Aribo said, "You know, you could have just emailed me the video file without coming all the way out to Malibu to show it to me first."

"I know. I wanted an update on the case too."

He side-eyed her. "Oh?"

"I figure as next of kin I must have some rights when it comes to being kept informed about the investigation into my father's murder."

"That's the first time I've heard you call him that."

"What?"

"Your father. You've always referred to him as Chapman until now."

"I guess I stopped thinking of him as my father a long time ago."

"So why the change?"

She smiled. "To get information from the police as the grieving daughter."

Aribo said, "If the man meant nothing to you, if he was effectively a stranger to you, why do you care?"

"I know I didn't kill him, and I'm hoping that you know I didn't kill him. But, until you find the person who did, the rest of the world is going to wonder if it was me. You saw those stories in the newspaper?"

Aribo nodded. The press had discovered the family connection between Chapman and Andi and that they'd been estranged for

273

twenty years. They knew she was the one who'd made the 911 call after discovering his body at the brokers' open. And they'd also dug up the old stories about what happened to her mom back in Kissimmee twenty years ago.

She went on. "I don't want suspicion hanging over me for the rest of my life. I'll be opening my own brokerage in a matter of weeks. I need to make a success of my new business. That's going to be a lot harder if people are wondering if I'm a murderer."

"We're still pursuing several lines of inquiry, but there's nothing definite I can tell you right now."

"That sounds like the kind of bullshit line you'd feed to the likes of Mitch O'Malley."

Aribo laughed. "Okay, you got me there."

"Is Krystal Taylor a suspect?"

"She was interviewed the same as everyone else who knew the victim or who worked at the brokerage."

"That's another textbook nonresponse, Detective Aribo. I know she was there that night. I saw her with my own eyes. And I know she didn't hold that press conference out of some sudden desire to fulfill her civic duty. She did it to make herself look less guilty. But kind of achieved the opposite, if you ask me."

Aribo was silent as they continued walking. They exited the pier and turned in the direction of the parking lot.

"Krystal Taylor brought a bottle of champagne to the house the night Nolan Chapman was murdered," he said eventually. "The bottle was missing, so we had been working on the possibility that it may have been used to strike him over the head. The bottle was recovered from a dumpster on Sunday evening. It was exactly where Krystal Taylor told us it would be. I got the lab results back this morning. No hair or blood or skin belonging to the victim. It's not the murder weapon."

"Maybe she wiped it clean. I mean *really* cleaned it. Got rid of all traces of blood?"

Aribo shook his head. "Prints belonging to both Krystal Taylor and Nolan Chapman were lifted from the bottle. It hadn't been wiped."

"So still no murder weapon?"

"It doesn't mean we won't find it, though." They'd come to his Mustang. "Thanks for the video. I'll be in touch with any news."

Aribo got in the car, and she watched him drive away. She thought about how to fill the rest of the afternoon. It would be another couple of days before Andi got the keys to the unit on Santa Monica Boulevard and she could start planning the renovation work. She decided she'd while away an hour at the Malibu Country Mart, a boutique outdoor mall just a few minutes' drive along the PCH.

When she got there, Andi ordered a chili dog and steak-cut fries from a burger shack and ate on a picnic bench before browsing the fashion boutiques and home decor stores and a gift shop selling crystals and stones. She wandered into an art gallery and admired the bold, colorful paintings hanging on stark white walls by local contemporary artists. Her eyes were drawn to a display featuring small ceramic sculptures, and they brought to mind her first visit to Malibu Beach Drive.

She had gone there on her own to shoot some video for Walker Young, before discovering that the New York billionaire was an associate of Chapman's and that the whole thing had been a setup.

Something niggled at her now.

Andi left the gallery, found her phone, and scrolled through her videos until she came to the recording she'd made of the pool deck. She pressed play. The other shoppers around her melted away as she squinted against the glare of the sun and stared at the small screen.

There it was.

An ugly gold figurine on the table between the two outdoor lounge chairs. The day before the brokers' open. Just hours before Nolan Chapman's untimely death at the very same spot.

Andi was sure she'd seen another figurine just like it somewhere else. She closed her eyes and tried to remember. Then it came to her. The showdown with Verona in the primary suite about the slit tire. Another one of those hideous things had been on the bedside table.

Or was it the same one?

If it was, who moved it—and why?

43

THE NIGHT OF THE MURDER

Krystal Taylor arrived home to an empty house and felt a twinge of sadness that Micah wasn't there to share her exciting news with. She missed just talking to him. They never seemed to share anything anymore. Not since the redhead came on the scene. But Krystal was determined not to let his absence ruin her good mood. After all, he was the reason she needed the money so much.

Her potential client, Ryoko Yamada, was currently in New York on a business trip and had found the time in her busy schedule to get on a Zoom call with Krystal earlier. Even with 2,500 miles separating them, the woman had been every bit as terrifying as she had been when they'd met in person at Micah's headphones launch. She had listened impassively while Krystal told her all about Malibu Beach Drive.

At the end of the spiel, Ryoko Yamada had been silent for so long that Krystal feared the connection had frozen. Finally, she'd said, "I sold my house in Los Angeles last year, and I have been looking for a new property in Southern California since then. I like this Malibu beach house very much. I will be in touch."

Then she had ended the call. No thank-you or goodbye. Abrupt, just like Micah's little notes. But Krystal hadn't been offended—she'd been elated. Ryoko Yamada was going to be her ticket to $1 million. Krystal could feel it in her bones. Even her horoscope today had told her to "expect great change."

She went into the kitchen and saw a folded piece of yellow paper on the counter. She didn't bother reading it, just threw it straight in the trash.

After preparing a salad for dinner, Krystal poured a small glass of rosé wine and contemplated what to do with the rest of the evening. Probably indulge in a bit of online shopping (her account with Neiman Marcus had Micah's credit card details stored, so she didn't have to worry about spending money with them) then binge-watch some reality TV shows. Krystal particularly enjoyed the real estate ones and fantasized about landing a part in one of them one day.

A ping from her phone alerted her to the arrival of a new email. It was from Ryoko Yamada. Krystal read it and broke into a smile. "Yes!" she shouted to no one, the word seeming to reverberate around the otherwise empty room.

Ms. Taylor,

I will be flying in from New York to Los Angeles this evening and will attend your brokers' open tomorrow. If I am impressed by the house once I have seen it, I will write an offer for the full asking price. Any offer will be subject to two conditions: acceptance within twenty-four hours and the property not being listed. I do not play games and I do not do bidding wars.

Good day.

RY

A personal email from Ryoko Yamada, not via her office this time. Krystal knew the woman was going to adore Malibu Beach Drive when she saw it for herself. What was there not to love? And full ask! Krystal raised her wineglass and toasted her reflection in the kitchen window. Her salad was still on the plate untouched. She'd lost her appetite. She was too excited to eat or watch TV. She was even too excited to spend Micah's money shopping online.

An idea came to her then. It was a little spontaneous, sure, but she figured Nolan Chapman was the kind of man who appreciated a little spontaneity.

Krystal thought of last night in his hotel suite. It had been a far more pleasant experience than the encounters she'd endured back when she'd first arrived in LA. Overweight men three times her age, fumbling and clumsy and sweating, all for empty promises and bit parts in commercials that only paid a few hundred dollars.

Chapman was different. He had been an accomplished lover and certainly knew his way around a woman's body. He'd made sure her needs had been attended to as well as his own, although she suspected that was due to male pride more than anything else. It had all just been a bit . . . cold. Like the man himself. There had been no tenderness of touch or any real sense of intimacy. Then again, why would there be? It was a business transaction, pure and simple, but one with a far bigger payday than those pet-food commercials.

By the time she'd showered, Nolan had already been asleep. She didn't bother to wake him. When she got home, Micah had also been sleeping. She'd climbed into bed beside him, and he had stirred and draped a big, protective arm over her, but he hadn't woken. Krystal had lain there, staring at the ceiling, still feeling the sensation of another man's hands on her skin, a strange feeling in the pit of her stomach that she couldn't identify. After a while, she'd realized what it was.

Guilt.

That had been unexpected.

Even so.

Krystal went upstairs to the bedroom now and stripped off her work clothes. She picked out some pink lace panties and a matching bra. Pulled on skinny jeans and a cropped sweater that showed off her toned midriff. Not that Nolan hadn't already seen it and much more besides. She finished off the look with Louboutin ankle booties and a dab of Chanel perfume. She stuffed the discarded clothing and underwear into the laundry basket in the bathroom for the housekeeper to deal with.

Back downstairs in the kitchen, Krystal selected a bottle of Cristal from the wine cellar and took two flutes from the cupboard. Tonight was going to be a celebration.

She drove fast through quiet streets and made Malibu in good time. Krystal called Nolan Chapman.

When he answered, there was rustling on the line as though he was moving around. She'd expected him to be drinking a cocktail in the hotel bar but didn't hear the sound of background music or conversation.

"Krystal," he said. "This is a surprise."

She couldn't tell if he was pleased to hear from her or not.

"Guess where I am?" she said.

"Aruba? Antigua? Alaska? Somewhere that doesn't begin with an *A*?"

She laughed. "Try *M*. I'm in Malibu. Are you busy?"

There was silence on his end, only the faint hum of static through the car's speakers. Krystal was worried that she'd come across as desperate, like those pathetic needy women who sleep with a man and then spend days by the phone, willing him to call or text. Krystal Taylor was not one of those women. Then an even worse thought struck her: maybe Nolan Chapman thought she wanted a relationship.

"I have news and I have champagne," she added quickly. "It's a celebration."

"Sounds intriguing. Sure, let's celebrate this mysterious news that you have."

"Are you at your hotel?"

"No, I'm at the house. Meet me here."

She disconnected as she cruised along the PCH and made the turn for Malibu Beach Drive. As she approached the house, a car that had been outside suddenly drove off. It was dark colored and nothing fancy as far as she could tell. Then it turned a corner and was gone. She wondered if Nolan had already had a visitor this evening and what the purpose of the visit had been.

He met her at the door and kissed her lightly on the cheek. She caught a faint hint of booze on his breath that wasn't quite masked by his expensive cologne. He wore cream chinos, a pink Ralph Lauren polo shirt, and brown leather boat shoes. The outfit was a little . . . dated. Not the modern and stylish attire that Micah favored, but she wasn't here to critique the man's fashion sense.

"Krystal, you look stunning. Let me take those." He took the bottle of Cristal and the flutes from her. "It's a beautiful night. Let's drink this outside."

She followed him through the house, admiring the staging that had been done since the tour with Marty Stein on Tuesday morning, and out onto the balcony. They rounded a corner to the pool deck. The underwater lights were on. There were two outdoor lounge chairs and a low table with a gorgeous gold sculpture of a ballerina on top. The piece would look fabulous in her own home. She placed her Hermès bag on the table next to it and went over to the glass barrier. The view was spectacular. Inky water under a darkening sky and hundreds of lights twinkling along the coastline.

Nolan sat on one of the lounge chairs and popped the cork on the champagne. It sounded like a firework going off in the still night. He filled both glasses and joined her at the barrier. The flute he gave her was sticky where the champagne had bubbled over the sides. They clinked glasses.

He said, "Here's to . . . ?"

She smiled. "Fifty-million-dollar deals."

"Oh?"

"Yes."

"Tell me more."

Nolan drank down half his champagne, while Krystal took a small sip of her own. She rarely had more than one glass. Just like desperation, drunkenness was a bad look on a woman.

"I have a buyer for this place," Krystal said. "She's very interested. So interested, in fact, she's flying in from New York tonight so she can attend tomorrow's brokers' open."

Nolan smiled, but it was the same cold smile from last night.

"That's fantastic news. Music to a property developer's ears." He went over to the table and refilled his glass. She turned back to the view.

"Refill?" he asked.

"No thanks."

He came up behind her, pushed her hair to one side, and started kissing the back of her neck.

"Nolan . . ."

"Mmm?"

"We were talking."

"I know what I'd rather be doing."

"I mean it. This is important."

He kept on with the neck nuzzling. Pressed his body against her back and snaked an arm around her waist. Krystal turned to face him so abruptly that he spilled some of his champagne.

"What's wrong?" he asked.

"I want to talk about my buyer. I thought you'd be more interested."

"I thought we were having fun."

His eyes were so cold they could have frozen the ocean down below. Behind him, the aqua pool glowed. In the distance, there was only the shadowy outline of the bluffs.

Krystal said, "First we talk, then we play."

"Okay. Let's sit and talk."

They took a lounge chair each, perching on the edge so they were facing each other. Krystal placed her glass on the table, while he kept on drinking.

"Do you think this buyer will make an offer?" Chapman asked.

"I'm sure she will. Once she sees this place, she'll fall in love with it. But—"

"I was waiting for the 'but.' But she's going to hit me with a lowball offer that you'll try to convince me to accept. Is that what you were going to say?"

Nolan gulped down what was left of his champagne. He didn't offer her a refill this time, just emptied what was left of the bottle into his glass.

"No, not at all," Krystal said. "She's willing to pay the full asking price. Fifty million."

He held his drink in the air in another toast. "Fantastic. Once she actually writes the offer, I'll be happy to consider it along with any other offers that I receive."

"That's the thing," Krystal said. "She'll only pay the full amount on the condition that the house doesn't go on the market. She doesn't want to get into a bidding war."

Nolan laughed. "Oh, I bet she doesn't. I can tell you right now there's no way I'm not listing this house."

The conversation wasn't going as planned. Krystal thought he'd be thrilled, that he would jump at the chance of a quick sale.

"But it's a great offer."

"There is no offer, Krystal. Not yet. There's nothing in writing. She hasn't even seen the property. And there will be other offers."

"My client is good for the money, and she *is* going to write that offer."

He sighed. "Okay, who is she?"

"Her name is Ryoko Yamada. She owns a Japanese tech company."

Nolan's eyes narrowed. "Where's she based?"

"Tokyo."

He shook his head. "I don't like dealing with overseas buyers. Too much hassle. Too many complications."

"She's in New York right now!" Krystal said, exasperated. "She does a lot of business in the States. There won't be any complications. What is wrong with you, Nolan? I thought you'd be pleased."

"Look, I know you're excited Krystal. You did well. If your client makes good with the fifty million, it's a great start. But that's all it is."

"Do you realize how difficult it is to sell inventory in this price range?"

Nolan said, "When I got here tonight, I met your coworker. Guy by the name of Hunter Brooks. He was just leaving after hosting a private showing for his client. I recognized the client from a profile in *Forbes* a while back. He's a big player in Silicon Valley and he has serious cash. And all of it is right here in the States."

Krystal could feel anger and panic battling each other for prominence. The money that she had been so sure was hers was starting to slip away from her.

"Hunter stole that client from another agent," she yelled. "He's not trustworthy. What he did was unprofessional."

Chapman smiled nastily. "And what you did last night wasn't? If this Hunter guy did poach someone else's client, then kudos to him. It's not unprofessional; it's business, sweetheart."

Krystal tried to tamp down the rage. Then Chapman mentioned *her* name.

"David Saint tells me Andi Hart also has a potential buyer," he said. "In fact, I know her client quite well. His offices are on the same block as my own in Manhattan. And, again, his money is right here in the country. So, no, I'm afraid I won't be accepting a preemptive offer from your client in Japan."

"Are you sleeping with her too?" Krystal asked quietly. "Is that why you're so interested in her?"

"Who?"

Krystal thought about the car that had been outside when she'd arrived. Dark in color and shaped like a standard coupe. Not a sports car or an SUV. A car that could have been an old blue Beemer.

"She was here tonight, wasn't she? Andi Hart. You're screwing her too."

"What did you just say?"

"I'm right, aren't I? That little slut is screwing the boss, and now she's screwing you too."

"Shut your filthy mouth. You have no idea what you're talking about."

Suddenly, Chapman was on top of her. He pushed her back against the lounge chair and pinned her arms down with his knees. His hands were around her throat. His face was inches from her own. An ugly mask of hatred and fury. He was screaming at her. His spittle landing on her face.

"You filthy whore! You don't get to speak about her like that!"

His fingers squeezed tighter. Krystal couldn't force any air into her lungs. She tried to wriggle free, but she couldn't move. Her eyes rolled back. She saw flashing white lights.

Then Chapman let her go.

He stepped away from her. She lay there coughing and light headed. She drank in lungfuls of air like someone lost in the desert might drink down water. Her throat felt raw. Krystal looked up at him, expecting to see shock or horror on his face after the unexpected violence. But there was nothing. His expression was blank. His eyes were empty.

"Get out," he said.

When she didn't move, he grabbed her by the arm and jerked her roughly to her feet. She stumbled in the heeled booties, her legs as liquid as water. He started dragging her behind him, like a child with a ragdoll.

"Nolan, stop."

"You know you were never getting that money, don't you? Didn't matter how many times you opened your legs. Andi Hart was always getting the cash. She's worth a million of you. You're nothing. *Nothing.*"

Fear was replaced suddenly by white-hot fury. Krystal Taylor was not nothing. She wrestled free of his grasp. Before he could turn around, before she was even fully aware of what she was doing, she had the gold figurine in her hand. It was heavier than it looked. She swung it at Chapman's head and it connected with a sickening dull thud.

He made a surprised sound. A horrible mixture of a grunt and a gasp and a groan. Then he dropped hard to his knees. She swung again, this time with both hands, and brought the ornament down with force. Chapman fell to the ground. Blood began to pool around his head, thick and dark on the light concrete.

Krystal stood there, breathing heavily. She stared down at the figurine in her hands. Saw the blood on the base where it had connected with Chapman's skull. His blood was on her sweater too. Then she looked at Chapman. His eyes were closed. He wasn't moving. She didn't know if he was breathing. She didn't think so.

Krystal collapsed onto the lounge chair and held the figurine against her body. First came the shakes, then the tears, then the panic.

What had she done?

She was going to go to prison. Her life was over. She wasn't just going to lose Micah; she was going to lose everything.

After a while, the tears stopped, and the panic was replaced by a clarity of thought. No one knew she was here. No one had to know what she'd done.

She could leave right now. Take the champagne bottle and flutes and figurine with her. Toss them in a dumpster. But the cops would look for the weapon, wouldn't they? If they knew the figurine was missing, they would search for it, and they would find her prints all over it.

Krystal carried it into the house and into the powder room. She held it under the faucet until the red-tinged water ran clear. Then she placed it on the toilet lid and dabbed it dry with toilet paper. Wiped around the wash basin with more toilet paper and flushed away the sodden debris. As she went to pick up the figurine, Krystal paused, thinking again about fingerprints. But the cops would assume Chapman's death was an accident, wouldn't they? He'd been drinking, had slipped by the pool, hit his head. All very tragic. Even if they did suspect foul play, the figurine had been washed clean of his blood and would be hidden in plain sight. Krystal smiled. She really was smarter than most people gave her credit for.

She took the figurine up the stairs to the next level and found the primary suite. Both bedside tables were empty and clear of any clutter. Not even a lamp. Krystal placed the figurine on top of one and positioned it just so, like it had always been there. Perfect.

Then she retraced her steps back downstairs and out to the pool deck. Chapman still wasn't moving. There was even more blood now. He was dead. He had to be. But she wasn't going to get close enough to check for a pulse. She wasn't going to touch him.

Krystal swallowed what was left of her champagne and stuffed the two empty flutes and Cristal bottle into her Hermès bag. Then she got out of the house—and out of Malibu—as fast as she could.

44
ANDI
AFTER

Andi went over to the picnic bench where she'd eaten the chili dog and fries earlier and watched the clip of the pool deck again.

She could be getting hyped up over nothing. Maybe the artist who had created the gold figurine had decided to inflict two of them on the world, and the one she'd spotted in the primary suite was the partner of a matching pair. Maybe the crime-scene techs had bagged the pool-deck version and tested it and had already established that it wasn't the murder weapon. Same as they'd done with Krystal Taylor's champagne bottle.

Andi turned her cell phone over in her hands, wondering if she should call Aribo anyway. Tell him about the figurine and let him decide what to do about it. Then she thought of someone else she could speak to. She scrolled through her contacts until she found the number she had stored for Carmen Vega.

It rang for a long time. Just when Andi thought she was out of luck and the voice mail was about to pick up, she heard Carmen's voice.

"Hello?"

The other woman sounded wary.

"Hi, Carmen. It's Andi Hart."

"I know. Your name came up on the caller ID."

There was none of the friendliness that Andi was used to from the decorator either. Then she remembered all the drama she'd apparently missed at the brokers' open—the confrontation between Carmen and Melissa Brooks, the revelation that Hunter Brooks was the father of Carmen's son, the embarrassing exit in front of the other guests.

It had kind of been overshadowed by the discovery of Nolan Chapman's body, but Carmen was clearly still feeling raw from what must have been a horrible experience.

"I wondered if I could talk to you real quick about something?" Andi asked.

"I'm actually in the middle of something right now."

"It'll only take a couple of minutes, I promise."

Carmen sighed. "If you're calling about what happened at the brokers' open, I'd rather not talk about it. I've already had Verona and Diana trying to reach out. I just need some space for a while, okay?"

"Wait," Andi said quickly, before Carmen could hang up. "I don't want to talk about what happened at the brokers' open. That's between you and Hunter and Melissa. It's no one else's business, as far as I'm concerned. I wanted to talk to you about something else."

"Okay, what?"

"Your staging of Malibu Beach Drive."

"What about it?"

"Do you remember when we met last Thursday morning? I was at the house to film some footage for a potential client."

"Uh-huh. I remember."

"There was a gold figurine at the pool deck. It was on a table between two outdoor lounge chairs."

"That's right. It was on loan from a local gallery. I was lucky to get it."

A big man with an untidy beard and a too tight Van Halen T-shirt parked himself at Andi's picnic table with three boys between the ages of seven and ten. They were all noisy. She turned her back to them.

"Were there two of them?" she asked.

Carmen said something, but the dad picked that moment to boom loudly, "What're we having, boys?" And the one who was about ten hollered, "I want fries! I want fries!" Then he started banging his fists on the wooden tabletop.

Andi tutted and glared at them. She got up from the table and walked quickly to a quiet spot under a tree.

"Sorry, Carmen. It's noisy where I am. What did you say?"

"I said there's only one of the figurines. Why do you ask?"

"I saw one just like it in the primary suite during the brokers' open."

"That's weird," Carmen said. "Why would someone move it?"

Exactly—why would they? Andi thought.

She said, "Is it still at the house?"

"I'm not sure. I'd have to check my inventory list. Some of the retailers wanted their stuff back as soon as the crime scene was released to Petronia Property Group. They didn't like their work being associated with a murder house."

"That's understandable."

"Give me two minutes."

Andi heard the phone hit a hard surface, followed by the sound of papers being riffled. Then Carmen came back on the line.

"*The Golden Ballerina* was returned to the gallery," she said.

"The what?" Andi asked.

"That's the name of the sculpture. It's a ballerina. It's actually gold-plated aluminum, rather than real gold, but still worth a fair amount of money."

"Really?" Andi tried not to sound surprised by the revelation that the thing was supposed to be a ballerina or that anyone would pay big bucks for it. "Which gallery?"

"Why the interest, Andi?"

"One of the guests at the brokers' open saw it and loved it. They might be interested in buying it if it's for sale."

"Oh, wow. That's great news. It's the Moonflower gallery just off the PCH. Be sure to mention my name."

"I will. Thanks, Carmen."

Andi ended the call and made her way quickly to her car. The drive took just a few minutes, but by the time she got there, she'd convinced herself she was too late. Someone with really bad taste could have purchased the sculpture by now.

The Moonflower gallery was housed in a powder-pink building with a red clay–tiled roof. Andi spotted *The Golden Ballerina* immediately in a glass case in the center of the room. She got up so close her nose almost touched the glass. It still looked nothing like a ballerina. She completed a slow 360-degree circuit of the display case. There was no sign of any blood on the figurine. It didn't mean there wasn't any there, though.

A Black woman wearing fashionable khaki coveralls and a fabulous chunky necklace emerged from behind the counter and came over to stand next to Andi. She said, "It's a wonderful piece, isn't it? I can see you're really struck by it."

Andi wanted to say there was a good chance someone else had been struck by it. Struck so hard they were now dead. But she kept that thought to herself.

"It's certainly . . . impactful."

She pretended to browse some of the other artwork before leaving the gallery. She stood by the side of the highway, thinking. Traffic zoomed past, palm trees flapped, and the air smelled of warm exhaust fumes and brine. Adrenaline pumped through her veins. She should call Aribo. If *The Golden Ballerina* was the murder weapon, it would be the breakthrough in the case that he was looking for.

But Andi was torn.

It could mean clearing her name and removing the cloud of suspicion hanging over her.

But it would also mean helping to get justice for the man who had murdered her mother.

45

ANDI
AFTER

One week later.

Andi was in Marty Stein's backyard. He had requested the meeting to discuss "important business" relating to Petronia Property Group.

He lived in a plain but well-maintained bungalow on a quiet street in Woodland Hills, just off Topanga Canyon Boulevard. It was a simple, no-frills house, a bit like the man himself. His graying hair was neatly combed, and he wore a navy no-brand polo shirt with beige Bermuda shorts and once-white sneakers. She thought Krystal Taylor's assessment of him had been harsh. Not everybody was obsessed with material things.

They sat at a table under a covered patio. The backyard had a tidy lawn and flagstone paths and twinkle lights that would be pretty after dark, but thankfully, there was no pool. She'd been glad to mostly escape them while in New York, but it was something she'd had to learn to live with again in LA.

Stein poured them each a glass of cold lemonade and told her to help herself to a plate of cookies that smelled like they were straight out of the oven. Next to the lemonade jug was a copy of today's *Times* and a manila folder with no label.

Andi tried one of the cookies. It was good. She said, "When you suggested this meeting, I assumed it would be taking place at your office. But this is nice."

He grinned and pointed to a window. "That's my office right there. It's not the tidiest, and I thought the backyard would be more pleasant."

"You don't have storefront offices?" she asked, surprised. "I know Nolan Chapman had offices in Manhattan."

She'd looked Chapman up after spotting him that day in the diner. His building was only a few blocks from the brokerage she'd worked for back then.

Stein laughed. "I guess you could say I'm small time compared to Nolan. I mostly flip houses for a modest profit. The spare room more than meets my needs."

"How did you become involved with Chapman and Petronia Property Group?"

"Nolan and I were both in the construction game back in Florida many years ago, and our paths would occasionally cross. I moved out here to LA and got interested in flipping houses. Nolan did the same in Florida but with a lot more success than me. His business really took off when he relocated to New York. When he bought the lot at Malibu Beach Drive a few years back, he got in touch out of the blue. Asked if I wanted to be part of it. I said yes, and PPG was formed."

"So that's how you became business partners?"

"I was very much the minor partner. I put in a small investment, and Nolan paid me a salary to project-manage Malibu Beach Drive while he was in Manhattan. He was the money man and the one who was calling the shots."

He stopped talking and looked at her intently. "You know, it's good to finally meet you, Andi. I've heard so much about you."

She just nodded and drank some lemonade. Noticed for the first time the lemon, orange, and tangelo trees in the yard. "This is good," she said, and she meant it. "The cookies too."

Stein beamed. "Both homemade."

Andi wondered if there was a Mrs. Stein. She didn't think so. He wasn't wearing a wedding ring, and when she'd walked through the house to reach the backyard, there had been a distinct lack of family photographs. Nothing to suggest a wife and kids. No indication of a woman's influence anywhere in the sparsely furnished home.

"You wanted to talk to me about Petronia Property Group," she said. "Why? I already quit Saint Realty, so I won't be finding a buyer for Malibu Beach Drive. Assuming anyone would want to buy it now anyway. I'm not sure what any of it has to do with me anymore."

"It has a lot to do with you, Andi. PPG now belongs to you."

She almost choked on her lemonade. "What?"

Stein opened the folder. There were official-looking documents inside.

"It's true," he said. "Nolan left the company to you, which means you'll replace him as CEO. It also means you are effectively now the owner of Malibu Beach Drive. Or you will be once everything is signed. All the paperwork is right here." He gestured to the newspaper. "Now that the police have made an arrest, I don't see any reason why the handover shouldn't be quick and straightforward."

Andi's eyes fell on the *Times*. It was folded in half. The headline above the fold read: Ex-NFL Star's Wife Arrested for Murder of Millionaire Property Developer.

Even in her moment of infamy, Krystal was still relegated to the role of being the wife of someone more famous than she was.

Andi had shared her theory about *The Golden Ballerina* with Aribo. Forensic testing had since found minuscule traces of

Chapman's blood and skin on the base of the ornament. Krystal Taylor's prints were all over it. It was more than enough for the cops to obtain a search warrant for her property and car.

The Porsche had been spotlessly clean, and they'd discovered that Krystal had had it detailed the morning after Chapman's murder—when she'd claimed to be too ill to attend the brokers' open. The Taylors had also disposed of their washing machine, supposedly due to a fault. Aribo suspected the real reason was to prevent any trace of Chapman's blood being found lodged in the appliance from the clothing Krystal had washed.

Even so, the detective was confident they had enough evidence to secure a conviction.

Andi had spent several nights lying awake, her brain too busy with questions to sleep. Why did Krystal do it? Had Chapman turned violent and she'd retaliated? Had Andi done the right thing?

Even in death, she couldn't escape Nolan Chapman. And now this revelation about PPG. She was seriously pissed about it and told Stein as much.

"Maybe he wanted to make amends?" he said. "I don't know all the details, but I know he regretted you both not talking to each other."

"Trust me, you don't want to know the details. You don't want to know what kind of person he really was or the things that he did."

"Maybe he changed?"

"Men like him never change. What if I say no? What happens then? What if I don't want to be CEO of his company?"

"Petronia Property Group *is* Malibu Beach Drive. There are no other assets. The company would be dissolved, and the house would lie empty. With no proper maintenance, it would eventually fall into disrepair."

Andi was shocked. "But you're a director. Can't you just take it over?"

"It doesn't work like that, Andi. Nolan was very clear when PPG was formed—if he died, you would assume control of the company. I don't have any claim."

"And you were okay with that?"

Stein smiled wryly. "To be honest, I wasn't expecting him to die so soon."

"What about your investment? How much did you put into the company?"

"Quarter of a million."

"And how much of a return on that investment were you expecting to make?"

"One million dollars. That is, if the property sold for more than forty million. It didn't matter if it was a dollar more or ten million more. That was the deal."

"There were no other investors?"

"Nope," Stein said. "Malibu was Nolan's passion project, something he had been working toward for years. He put all the money in himself. My share was a token investment. Like I said, I was really brought on board to deal with the day-to-day stuff: dealing with contractors, overseeing the building work, and so on. Nolan offered me a way to make some extra cash, and I was grateful for the opportunity. I don't think he needed my money."

"So if I say no to PPG, you lose your investment and the house is left to rot?"

"Pretty much, but there are more important things in life than money. I'm not going to put any pressure on you, Andi. You have to do what you believe is the right thing."

But what *was* the right thing?

Andi's head was spinning with all this new information.

Stein went on. "You don't have to make a decision right now. This is just an informal chat. You can take the paperwork with you and go over it all with a lawyer."

She was quiet, thinking. Marty Stein, with his modest home and modest car in the driveway, had gotten involved with Nolan Chapman in good faith and didn't deserve to end up being the loser in all this.

"What are my options?" she asked finally. "I'm not going to live at Malibu Beach Drive myself, and I'm not going to lease it out. But I don't want you to lose your money, and I don't want a beautiful house to go to ruin."

"Then you do what Nolan was planning to do. You sell it. And, if you wish, you then dissolve PPG. Saint Realty still has the listing. Nothing has changed in that respect."

Everything had changed at Saint Realty, though.

They were down to one agent for the time being—Verona. Andi had met her for lunch a few days ago, and Verona had filled her in on all the developments.

Hunter had taken an extended leave to try to work on his marriage, but Verona didn't think it was looking good. He was renting an apartment in Beverly Hills, and his only contact with his wife was through their lawyers. Even so, Hunter was hopeful of a reconciliation. Andi hoped for Melissa's sake—and little Scout's too—that they could work something out.

Myles had left the hospital and gone straight into rehab. The night of his assault and robbery, he'd been trying to pawn his Rolex watch to pay off gambling debts. The police believed the pawn shop was involved in a scam where they'd tip off a local gang about customers with expensive items to pawn. The heavies and owner Bobby Gee would then split the proceeds of the robbery.

Myles had only confessed to his gambling addiction after his boyfriend had accused him of being in a seedy part of town to meet another man. The Lamborghini had been sold to clear the debt, and Myles's father was footing the bill for the five-star rehab facility.

Krystal wouldn't be selling any real estate for a very long time—which left Verona.

She'd had good news from her doctor. The lump in her breast *was* a benign cyst. She would continue to have regular checks, but her health was good. Andi was thrilled for her. She couldn't imagine the kind of stress Verona had been under. Andi wanted to repair their friendship, but it would take time. She was still hurt and a little shocked by some of the things Verona had done.

Even if she was content for Verona to find a buyer for Malibu Beach Drive, it would mean David Saint benefiting financially from the sale. Andi thought of his behavior the night he'd made a pass at her. How he had almost destroyed another young woman's life. How he had been a willing accomplice in Nolan Chapman's plan.

She said, "If I did take over PPG and put Malibu Beach Drive on the market, could I fire Saint Realty as the listing brokerage?"

Stein said, "Of course. You'd be in charge. You'd be able to hire and fire whomever you liked."

Andi could list the property herself—and it would be a hell of a way to kickstart her own brokerage—but it would be weeks before the business was fully up and running, and she wanted to be rid of any connection to Nolan Chapman as soon as possible.

"And any money I make from the sale of the house?" she asked.

"Same answer. Up to you. You can spend it any way you like."

"Meaning I could donate the whole lot to charity? Help out, for instance, victims of domestic abuse if I wanted?"

Stein nodded. He swallowed hard, like his throat was dry. Andi wondered if he knew about Chapman's violent past.

He said, "I'd say that sounds like a pretty good plan."

Andi wanted Marty Stein to have the money he was owed, and she wanted someone to be happy at Malibu Beach Drive, and she wanted some good to come out of this whole mess.

She thought she knew the right thing to do.

46

THE NIGHT OF THE MURDER

Marty Stein wiped his mouth with a napkin and asked for the check.

He'd been coming to the same restaurant every Thursday for years. The staff knew him by name, and they knew his order. Always the bruschetta to start, then the best lasagna outside Italy for the main, and a glass of red wine. Always a table for one. Marty figured it was better than being home alone with a TV dinner.

He'd had a few dates over the years, and some of them he'd even brought here, but never anything serious. His heart just wasn't in it. It'd been twenty years since his last proper relationship and since he'd last fallen hard for a woman. The staff knew Marty had been married once—that there was an ex-wife back in Florida—but he'd never offered up any details, and they'd never asked. They didn't know why his marriage had ended.

It was the same with his buddy, Bill, who lived next door. They met at least once a week to play bridge, enjoyed the occasional beer together, and attended each other's summer BBQs. Bill was on his own too, a widower rather than a divorcé, but like Marty, he never seemed keen to discuss affairs of the heart.

Marty paid by card and left a generous tip. He got in his car and prepared to make the short drive home. The clock on the dash told him it wasn't yet nine p.m. He knew that Malibu Beach Drive had been staged ahead of tomorrow's brokers' open, and at this time of night, he could be there in under thirty minutes. He could go and check it out. He was sure the decorator had done a good job because he hadn't heard from Chapman, who'd been planning on assessing the staging himself earlier this evening, and Marty definitely would have heard from him if he'd been unhappy.

Ultimately, it didn't really matter. Walker Young was going to buy the house, and Andi Hart was going to get the commission, and that's all there was to it. The brokers' open was nothing but a charade, but Nolan Chapman wouldn't want all those important people to think badly of his property.

He joined the 101 and headed south on Las Virgenes into Malibu and thought about Andi Hart.

Marty had been disappointed when she'd failed to show for the tour on Tuesday morning. He'd been looking forward to finally meeting her. The only time Stein had seen her was twenty years ago and that had been in a photograph. He'd resisted the urge to look her up these past few years that she'd been living in LA. He'd wanted to see what kind of woman she'd become, if she seemed happy. But it felt creepy. It didn't stop Nolan Chapman from doing just that, though, creeping around Laurel Canyon and the Strip in his rental, hiding behind its tinted windows.

Marty found a space in the parking lot of a strip mall not far from the beach. He would walk the rest of the way. It was something Marty had been doing these last few weeks. He'd gotten the idea from Chapman. It was only a ten-minute stroll, and he needed to lose a few pounds. Chapman always walked to the house from the hotel, which was more like thirty minutes, and said it was a great way to keep fit. Stein hated to admit it, but the guy did look good. The years had been kind to Chapman. Far kinder than they'd been to Marty Stein.

It was a beautiful night. Still some warmth in the air. Marty set off at a brisk pace, and it wasn't long before perspiration dampened his brow. Instead of walking along Malibu Beach Drive, he took the beach access at the foot of the street and jogged down the steps. Took off his sneakers and enjoyed the feel of the cool sand between his toes. Each stride worked the muscles in his thighs and hamstrings. The water was calm tonight, its sound soothing as it gently lapped the beach. He was tempted to roll up his jeans and go get his feet wet. Maybe on the way back to the car.

The floor-to-ceiling ocean-facing windows of the house glowed yellow up ahead, and Marty figured Chapman must still be there. He reached the staircase that led from the beach to the pool deck, which was also lit up but empty as far as he could tell. He climbed the steps, then sat down at the top, wiped the sand from his feet, and pulled on his sneakers. Got up and punched in the four-digit code: 0-2-1-5. He had set it himself. February 15. The date he'd kissed Patti Hart for the first time. The control panel flashed green, and he pushed open the gate to the deck.

Marty saw Chapman immediately.

He was lying on the ground by the side of the pool.

Marty's first thought was that he was passed out drunk. He knew Chapman was fond of his vodka martinis and had seen him sink a few in the hotel bar, but he'd never seen him blackout drunk before. This was a first.

As Marty got closer, he saw the blood.

Chapman wasn't moving. His face, usually so tan and healthy and handsome, was the same gray color as the concrete he lay on. His eyes were closed, and his lips were slightly parted. There really was an awful lot of blood, indicating he'd suffered serious head trauma. Had Chapman fallen, or had someone done this to him?

Marty knew he should check for a pulse, call 911, do something proactive.

But he didn't.

He crouched down for a better look. Chapman's arm was tucked underneath him, the fancy watch on his wrist just visible. The face was smashed. The tiny hands stuck forever at 8:41. Marty checked his own watch. It was 9:25. Then he heard a gurgling noise. There was a faint moan. One of his eyes half opened.

Chapman was still alive.

He was in bad shape, no doubt about it. But maybe, with proper and immediate medical assistance, he would survive.

There was another sound that might have been the word "help."

Marty had no desire to help Nolan Chapman.

He hadn't been able to save Patti, and he sure as hell wasn't going to save the man who'd killed her.

Marty had bought his first house to flip back in Kissimmee when he was still a construction worker. He'd saved some cash, got a dump real cheap, and used his own skills and contacts to make the place halfway decent. Then he'd hired Patti Hart to sell it for him.

The first time they met, he'd been totally bewitched by her. She was a beautiful woman, and it didn't take long to realize that she was a beautiful person too.

What started as a professional relationship soon turned into friendship. They'd go for coffee or lunch together, and they discovered they had a lot in common—including being lonely. Things hadn't been good between Marty and his wife, Nancy, for a long time, and they'd been sleeping in separate rooms for more than a year by then. He knew Patti was unhappy in her own marriage. The bruises that she tried to put down to "little accidents" told their own story.

Then one day, friendship blossomed into something more. They'd been sitting in his car, Otis Redding playing on the radio, waiting for a thunderstorm to pass, when Patti leaned over and kissed him. It was February 15. Marty felt like his life had finally begun. Within months, Patti's would be over.

Marty wanted out of his marriage with Nancy, and Patti wanted to leave her husband, Nolan Chapman. She'd finally told Marty about the arguments, the beatings, her fears that Chapman would turn his fists on their teenage daughter before too long. Marty knew the man was violent and dangerous and that Patti and Andrea would never feel safe while they were still in Florida.

So he'd taken a trip to Los Angeles and had put down a deposit on a house in Woodland Hills. Told Nancy he wanted a divorce and then made the move out west permanently. He had spent weeks turning the house in Woodland Hills into the perfect home.

Marty and Patti agreed on a date when she would join him in LA with Andrea. Patti admitted that Chapman was growing increasingly suspicious about an affair. Marty was worried he would figure out what was going on before they were able to leave.

On that last day, Patti had wanted to pack some things, clear her calendar for the week so she wouldn't be letting her clients down, and sit Andrea down for a talk after school. Marty just wanted the two of them on an airplane, stat. Forget about the luggage and the clients. Have the talk on the flight. They'd figure it all out once Patti and Andrea were safe, a long way from Florida and a long way from Nolan Chapman.

As he'd waited at LAX, Stein had been nervous. How would Andrea react? She'd never even met him. How would she feel about living with a complete stranger? It was going to be a huge shock and a big change. But he hoped she'd come to realize in time that he was a good man who worshipped her mother.

That it was possible to live in a house filled with love rather than fear.

Then Marty's nerves had turned to concern when the flight from Orlando landed and passengers streamed through arrivals but there was no sign of Patti and her daughter. His first thought was that Andrea had refused to get on the airplane. That she hadn't wanted to leave behind her friends, and her school, and the only life she'd known.

But Marty knew Patti would have called, wouldn't have left him waiting at the airport. His gut told him something was badly wrong. Standing there, surrounded by excited tourists, emotional homecomings, and tired businessmen, Marty Stein had never been so scared in all his life.

Later, when he'd learned of Patti's death, he'd known it was no accident. Patti Hart did not get smashed and fall into the pool on the same day she was supposed to be starting a new life on the other side of the country. Nolan Chapman had found out she was leaving him, and he had killed her.

For seventeen years, guilt and despair had eaten away at Marty. Then, three years ago, the past had come calling. Chapman wanted Marty to work with him on a major property project in Malibu. It had seemed like fate. An opportunity to get to know Chapman, get close to him, earn his trust. And maybe one day he might just let slip something about the day his wife had died. The tiniest detail after one too many vodka martinis that Marty could use to nail him and make him pay for what he did.

The sound came again now. The word clearer this time.

"Help."

Marty stood up. Then he stuck out a sneakered foot and kicked as hard as he could. Chapman rolled over the edge of the pool and went into the water with a splash. He landed facedown. Didn't move. Just floated. Marty watched until he was sure Chapman was never going to hurt anyone else ever again.

He turned off the lights and left the way he'd come by the beach access gate. This time, Marty did roll up his jeans and get his feet wet. He knew any chance of seeing $1 million from the sale of Malibu Beach Drive had likely just died along with Nolan Chapman. That Andi Hart would want nothing to do with this cold, beautiful house once she found out about her father's plan to engineer his way back into her life.

But it didn't matter.

Some things were more important than money.

EPILOGUE

Betsy Bowers gazed out the window as she finished her morning coffee. Ten stories below, traffic was steady on Wilshire. She could see workers drilling farther along the street, but she couldn't hear them. The triple-glazed floor-to-ceiling windows kept out the noise.

She set the empty mug on her desk and gave her reflection the once-over in the compact she kept in the drawer, then picked up the phone and called through to her assistant in the outer office.

"Sasha, send them in now."

Betsy took her place at the bespoke marble-and-bronze conference table as the door opened. The five agents in her employ filed into the room, led by Marcia Stringer. Betsy gestured for them each to take a seat facing her.

"Most of you have worked for me long enough to know that I relish a challenge, right?" she said.

The agents nodded in unison.

Betsy went on. "I signed off on a new listing agreement this morning, and it's going to be a hell of a challenge. But, if anyone can sell this property, it's the Bowers Group."

"Which property?" Marcia asked.

Betsy paused for dramatic effect. "Malibu Beach Drive."

The announcement was met with stunned silence and wide eyes.

Marcia was the first to speak. "You mean the Murder House?"

"Yes, Marcia, the Murder House. But we're not going to call it that anymore. Understood?"

One of the agents raised her hand. She was the newest member of the team, having joined just six months ago.

"I already told you, Jennifer—you don't have to raise your hand every time you want to ask a question. This isn't grade school. Now, what is it?"

"If the owner is dead, who's selling the house?"

"That information is on a need-to-know basis, and none of you need to know."

Marcia looked put out. "Are we at least allowed to know how much it's being listed for?"

"Sarcasm doesn't suit you, Marcia. The new owner and I have discussed the asking price, and we've decided to list at fifty million dollars, same as before."

"Do you think that's a good idea?" asked Jackson.

"Won't buyers be expecting a reduction?" agreed Kenny.

"Someone was *murdered* there!" Rachel said.

"Yes, thank you for pointing that out, Rachel. Marcia and I had a front-row seat, remember? We were the ones who found the body. And if I'm not squeamish about being the listing agent, no one should be squeamish about living there. We just have to make sure every trace of blood is gone and that someone checks the pool before our own brokers' open."

"I don't know . . . ," Jackson said.

Betsy said, "You don't know what, Jackson? How to sell houses? Malibu Beach Drive is still a superb property. Located on one of the best beaches in the world. State-of-the-art appliances. Porcelain and walnut and marble finishes. Incredible views. None of that has changed. I am going to sell this house, and the agent who brings me the buyer is going to earn one million dollars in commission."

That got them excited. Kenny and Jackson high-fived each other. Rachel and Jennifer both made little *O*s with their mouths. Even Marcia cracked a smile.

Betsy stood up and placed both hands on the marble tabletop and looked at each of the agents in turn. Then she said, "Now get out there and show me what you're willing to do for a million dollars."

ACKNOWLEDGMENTS

First and foremost, I want to thank my readers for picking up my books and giving them a chance. I am grateful every single day that I get to do my dream job, and that's all down to you. I very much hope you enjoyed reading *To Die For* as much as I enjoyed writing it. I had a lot of fun with this one.

A huge thanks to my brilliant agent, Phil Patterson, for all that you do and for always believing in me. And a big shout-out to the rest of the team at Marjacq for being amazing too.

To my wonderful editor Victoria Haslam—thank you for your enthusiasm and support. I love working with all the team at Thomas & Mercer and truly appreciate all the hard work you put into getting my books into the hands of readers. Thanks also to my developmental editor, Ian Pindar, for your excellent insight and feedback.

Big thanks to all the bloggers and reviewers who have taken the time to read and spread the word about my books, and to Sophie Goodfellow for the fantastic PR work. To my crime-writing pals—thanks for the friendship and fun. Special mention to Susi Holliday and Steph Broadribb for being fabulous cheerleaders and always saying nice things about my books!

To Die For is dedicated to my book buddy Danny Stewart—thanks for being such good company at all the crime festivals and book events over the years. Here's to many more to come. Thanks also to friends Lorraine and Darren Reis. Yet another book for the conservatory library!

Last but not least, a massive thanks to my family. Mum, Scott, Alison, Ben, Sam, and Cody—you always have faith in me when I don't have faith in myself. You mean the world to me. And to my dad, whom I miss every single day. I know you would be proud.

THE DARK ROOM BY LISA GRAY

IF YOU ENJOYED *TO DIE FOR*, WHY NOT TRY *THE DARK ROOM*, LISA'S REVENGEFUL, TAUT THRILLER?

Ex–crime reporter Leonard Blaylock spends his days on an unusual hobby, developing strangers' forgotten and discarded rolls of film. He loves the small mysteries the photographs reveal to him. Then Leonard finds something no one would ever expect, or want, to see captured on film—the murder of a young woman.

But that's impossible because the woman is already dead. Leonard was there when it happened five years earlier.

He has never been able to shake his guilt from that terrible night. It cost Leonard everything: his career, his fiancée, his future. But if the woman didn't really die, then what actually happened?

1

LEONARD

They say you never forget your first, and that was definitely true for Leonard Blaylock.

Angela had brassy blond hair, blue eyes, and a wide smile that showed off the gap between her two front teeth. She wasn't a knockout in anyone's book, but she knocked the breath clean out of Leonard the first time he laid eyes on her.

She was wearing a white dress that complemented her deep summer tan, and there was a burst of freckles on each shoulder where the skin had been burned by the sun. She was holding a glass of white wine, and she had a tattoo on the inside of her wrist that looked like a swallow.

Leonard liked to think that it represented her love of travel, that it showed she was a free spirit. But it was so faded and blurred by the passage of time that it could have been Elvis for all he knew. He guessed her to be in her midthirties.

Later, he'd taped her photograph to his bedroom wall, smack-dab in the middle, so he had a perfect view of her as he lay in bed. He'd lost count of the number of times he'd stared at that picture since, wondering what she'd been thinking at the exact moment the shutter went off. Was she happy? Or was the gap-toothed smile only on display long enough for the click of the button?

The camera never lied, but it rarely told the truth either.

He'd committed every line and every curve to memory, but in technical terms, it wasn't a very good shot. The composition was poor, the focus wasn't sharp enough, and the flash had bounced off a shiny surface in the background, resulting in a yellow blob directly above Angela's head. It looked like a halo.

Angel Angela.

That's why he'd given her the name.

Angela wasn't her real name, of course. Or maybe it was. Leonard had no way of knowing. She wasn't his first kiss or first lay or first love. She was a complete stranger. Just as the fifty-eight other people whose images were taped to his wall were complete strangers. But she was the first, and that made her special.

Leonard Blaylock wasn't a photographer. He never took any of the photos in his collection himself.

He was a memory collector, a rescuer of lost moments. At least, that's how he'd described the mystery-film enthusiasts—those who got a kick out of buying and developing other peoples' old, discarded, and forgotten camera film—in a newspaper feature he'd written a couple of years back.

A bunch of loons was how Leonard had initially thought of them when he'd first been commissioned to write the piece for a Sunday paper.

He couldn't, for the life of him, understand the appeal. He didn't have many friends left by then, not since the night his life had gone to shit, and they'd gradually melted away one by one. But he remembered all too well being subjected to their vacation photos or pictures of their kids back in the day. Smiling politely and pretending to be interested. That was bad enough. To actually seek out and then spend money on old rolls of film belonging to people you didn't even know? That was just crazy.

Even so, Leonard had decided to give it a go himself. It would add a nice, personal touch to the article. Provide an easy intro. Maybe even result in some decent images they could print along with the words.

So he'd logged on to eBay and made an offer on two used rolls of Kodak Gold 35 mm film from a seller in Knoxville, Tennessee. Twenty-five bucks plus another $5.25 for the shipping that he'd claim back on expenses from the newspaper on top of his fee. What did he have to lose?

A week later, he'd found a bubble envelope with a Tennessee postmark on it stuffed inside his mailbox, and Leonard realized he was intrigued by what he might discover. Maybe even a little excited. That was the start of it.

He should have called in a favor from one of the photographers at the *New York Reporter* and gotten them to develop the film for him. Leonard had spent twenty years at the paper, working his way up from intern to senior crime reporter. He had been the guy who broke the stories, the one who could always be relied upon for a front-page splash.

But that was then. Everything had changed thanks to the events of a single night. There was Leonard's life before, and there was Leonard's life after.

After, he was a freelancer, working for himself, finding excuses not to leave his apartment most days, barely scraping together enough cash to pay the rent. He'd quickly dismissed the idea of contacting any of his former coworkers. Decided he'd be better off going old school and having the photographs developed the old-fashioned way.

Rookie mistake.

That first time he'd had mystery film developed was two and a half years ago, but Leonard remembered the day like it was yesterday.

◆ ◆ ◆

The photo-printing place was a family-owned business that shared its premises with a dry cleaner's, which struck Leonard as an odd combination. Did their customers usually get a comforter or a suit cleaned while picking up the vacation pics, seeing as they were in there anyway? It was like those people who put slices of pineapple on their pizzas. They were both foodstuffs, but that didn't make it right. He dropped off the two film rolls and ordered the one-hour service. Then he went around the corner to a coffee shop where he was interviewing an actress from a daytime soap opera.

The interview dragged on forever. The only thing the actress loved more than herself was the opportunity to talk about herself. Her plumped-up lips moved and her hands gesticulated, and Leonard tried to nod in all the right places like he used to do with his buddies' boring photos. He couldn't focus on a single word she was saying. He didn't give a rat's ass about her exciting new storyline or that she would be appearing in an off-Broadway production later in the year. His head was full of what might be on those rolls of film.

Ninety minutes later—with two double-shot lattes churning in his gut—Leonard practically ran the three blocks to the store, pushing his way past passersby, nerves jangling from the caffeine and the anticipation. It was a pleasantly warm day, early summer, the temperature hovering around the low seventies. Blue skies and lots of flesh on show. By the time he reached the photo place, he was sweating like a criminal in a church.

Leonard finally understood, in that moment, the appeal of the mystery film. It was all about the gamble. The element of risk. The not knowing what the outcome would be but hoping for the best anyway. Like those people who religiously played the lottery twice a week, or the gamblers who kept the slot machines fed in the casinos, or the seniors who visited the bingo halls in Queens and Brooklyn on the weekend.

Anything could be on those rolls, and that was the thrill of it.

Leonard pushed open the door with eager anticipation, the electronic beep announcing his arrival as he stepped inside. He already had the ticket in his hand. Then he stopped dead, sneakers rooted to the carpet. He felt as if his heart had just stopped.

Anything could be on those rolls.

Why hadn't he thought of that before? Idiot. Half a dozen terrible possibilities crashed through his brain in quick succession, each one worse than the last. Nudie pics. Hardcore porn. Up-the-skirt shots. A long lens trained on a teenager's bedroom window. Oh, God. Something awful happening to little kids.

The woman behind the counter, who had been all smiles earlier, frowned at him. Her lips were a thin pink line of disapproval. He glanced around anxiously, expecting a burly security guard to appear at any second. Did photo-stores-slash-dry-cleaners have security guards? Did they need them? They did if perverts and weirdos wanted their sick photos developed there.

Maybe the counter assistant had called the cops already. Maybe they were on their way while Leonard stood there giving the statues in Central Park a run for their money. He considered turning around and getting the hell out of there, but he'd paid by credit card, hadn't he? It wouldn't take the NYPD's finest too long to track him down. What if he was arrested? What if they fingerprinted him? Once they had his prints, he was finished. Life over. They would find a match in their system, and they would know what he had done.

Then the woman asked, "Are you okay, hon?" And Leonard realized, with a flood of relief, that the frown and the grim expression were out of concern, rather than disgust.

He mumbled something about the warm weather making him feel woozy for a moment before thrusting the ticket at her. He shoved his quarry into his backpack, next to his notepad and voice recorder. One of the envelopes was depressingly thin, the other enticingly thick. As he made his way toward the nearest subway station, Leonard told himself he'd wait until he got back to the apartment before looking at the photographs. Just in case there was something bad on them.

The train car was stuffy and busy. The sweat from his back stuck his shirt to the plastic seat and made his skin itch. His beard was damp. As the train picked up speed, the distinct, dirty-warm smell of the subway became even more pungent in the humidity.

Leonard removed the envelopes from his bag, his fingers leaving damp marks on the glossy paper. He wouldn't look just yet. Best to wait. He tried to distract himself by reading the overhead ads for an energy drink and the perfect mattress and a new Don Winslow novel he'd already purchased. He idly wondered if he needed a new mattress. A handful of passengers disembarked at the next station. He heard the safety announcement and the doors sucking shut. The train was on the move again, accelerating fast through a tunnel, screeching and shaking. Leonard opened the fattest envelope.

The first three prints had been spoiled by the flash. The next was a photo of a tiled floor, the one after that a ceiling. Then two almost identical images of a glistening turquoise swimming pool, someone's foot resting on an outdoor chaise just in shot.

The eighth photo was the winning lottery ticket, the coins dropping into the slot machine's tray, a full row on the bingo card.

Blond hair, blue eyes, gap-toothed smile. White dress, white wine, swallow tattoo. Little yellow-blob halo.

Angel Angela.

Leonard stared at the photo for a long time. When he finally looked up, he realized he had missed his stop.

◆ ◆ ◆

Leonard never did give Angela to the newspaper. He'd known immediately he would be keeping her for himself.

The other envelope had contained a half dozen prints of someone's backyard. Downy woodpeckers and a small dog snoozing on a parched lawn. He'd scanned and emailed those along with his copy. Earned himself an extra fifty bucks for the photography.

Leonard had realized two things the day he first saw Angela. One: he was now completely hooked on the buzz of the mystery film. Two: he'd have to learn how to develop the film himself. The photo-store experience had been just a bit *too* adrenalized for his liking.

So, he'd turned his spare room into a dark room. Bought a red safelight, an enlarger, trays, printing easel, tongs, multigrade filters, resin-coated paper, developer, stop bath, and fixer. Watched a bunch of YouTube videos. Gradually added more images to his DIY gallery.

In the more than two years since Angela, his finds had ranged from complete garbage to pretty fascinating. The latter were the ones that made it onto the bedroom wall. There had never once been anything even close to illegal in what he'd picked up from eBay, estate sales, and flea markets.

Anything could be on those rolls.

Even so, Leonard knew he was wise to take precautions; that there was a chance he could come across a roll of film one day that contained something so damaging, so shocking and horrifying, that the police would be called, no doubt about it, if anyone other than Leonard was responsible for developing it.

Today was that day.

Leonard measured out the chemicals for each of the three trays, then placed a negative in the enlarger carrier and adjusted the height. He turned on the enlarger. Adjusted the aperture ring of the lens as the image was projected onto the baseboard. Even though he was looking at a negative, he could make out the shape of a woman lying on a bed. There was something dark on her clothing and the bedsheet.

Leonard's heart thudded hard. He licked dry lips. Wiped perspiration from his brow.

He went through the test-strip steps, then placed the exposed paper into the tray of developer. His hands trembled as he gently rocked the solution back and forth. Then, under the bordello glow of the safelight, the image gradually began to appear on the paper.

The woman's eyes were open but lifeless. It was clear that the stains on her clothing and the bedsheet were blood, even though the print was black and white. There was blood spatter on her face too. A knife was on the bed beside her. It had blood on it. There was a hell of a lot of blood in that room.

As he went to remove the print from the developer, Leonard's shaking hand knocked the flimsy plastic tray to the floor.

The woman was nothing like the fifty-nine portraits taped to his bedroom wall. For a start, she was dead. Not just dead. Murdered. She also wasn't a complete stranger. Leonard had known her. Had spent a night with her once, five years ago.

A different night from the one when this photograph of her murdered body was taken.

The night that ruined his life.

The night he thought he'd killed her.

ABOUT THE AUTHOR

Photo © 2022 Bob McDevitt

Lisa Gray is an Amazon #1, *Washington Post*, and *Wall Street Journal* bestselling author. She previously worked as the chief Scottish soccer writer at the Press Association and the books editor at the *Daily Record* Saturday magazine. She is also the author of *Thin Air, Bad Memory, Dark Highway, Lonely Hearts*, and *The Dark Room*. Lisa now writes full time. Learn more at www.lisagraywriter.com and connect with Lisa on social media @lisagraywriter

Follow the Author on Amazon

If you enjoyed this book, follow Lisa Gray on Amazon to be notified when the author releases a new book!

To do this, please follow these instructions:

Desktop:

1.Search for the author's name on Amazon or in the Amazon App.
2.Click on the author's name to arrive on their Amazon page.
3.Click the "Follow" button.

Mobile and tablet:

1.Search for the author's name on Amazon or in the Amazon App.
2.Click on one of the author's books.
3.Click on the author's name to arrive on their Amazon page.
4.Click the "Follow" button.

Kindle e-reader and Kindle app:

If you enjoyed this book on a Kindle e-reader or in the Kindle app, you will find the "Follow" button after the last page.

Made in the USA
Columbia, SC
21 September 2023